Reviewers Praise for
Every Crooked Nanny

"Julia Callahan Garrity is another of the feisty, irreverent, smart and smart-aleck, but insistent and clever female sleuths of the future."

—*Drood Reviews*

"A clever, colorful page turner, not to be missed."

—*Publishers Weekly* (starred review)

"A breezy debut mystery . . . The sleuthing chores are handled with crisp intelligence and earthy wit."

—*The New York Times Book Review*

"A peerless first novel that whets the reader's appetite for a long series."

—*The Toronto Star*

"*Every Crooked Nanny* is fresh, confident, intelligent, and amusing."

—Sue Grafton

BOOKS BY KATHY HOGAN TROCHECK

Every Crooked Nanny
To Live & Die in Dixie
Homemade Sin

Available from
HarperPaperbacks

HOMEMADE SIN

Kathy Hogan Trocheck

HarperPaperbacks
A Division of HarperCollins Publishers

This is a work of fiction. The characters, incidents, and dialogues are products of the author's imagination and are not to be construed as real. Any resemblance to actual events or persons, living or dead, is entirely coincidental.

HarperPaperbacks   *A Division of* HarperCollins*Publishers*
10 East 53rd Street, New York, N.Y. 10022

A hardcover edition of this book was published in 1994 by HarperCollins*Publishers*.

Cover illustration by Catherine Deeter

First HarperPaperbacks printing: June 1995

Printed in the United States of America

HarperPaperbacks and colophon are trademarks of HarperCollins*Publishers*

❖ 10 9 8 7 6 5 4 3 2 1

Dedicated with love and gratitude
to my spousal unit,
Tom Trocheck

Author's Note

Although some streets, locations, and neighborhoods referred to in this novel are authentic, I have occasionally rearranged Atlanta geography to suit my own purposes. *Homemade Sin* deals with themes of murder, family, and betrayal. Although certain real-life situations may have influenced the plot line, this is a work of fiction. The characters, incidents, and dialogue are the product of my imagination, and resemblance to actual events or persons, living or dead, is entirely coincidental.

Acknowledgments

The author wishes to thank family, friends, and neighbors who lightened the load during the writing process, and to express special gratitude to the following for their help in research. Any errors in fact or judgment are my own, not theirs.

Special agent Gregory Lockett, Atlanta office of the FBI; The National Insurance Crime Bureau; Beverly Thomas, vice president of public relations at Grady Memorial Hospital; Sergeant William Z. Miller of the DeKalb County Police Black Cat Unit; DeKalb County District Attorney J. Tom Morgan; Pam Frye, M.S.W.; Jane Cooper, M.S.W.; The Howard Schools and Kim S. Papastavridis, M.Ed.; Ann Dugan, lay administrator at St. Thomas More Church; Phyllis Akin, R.N., and the St. Joseph's Hospital Oncology Research Department; William T. Hankins III; Susan Hogan, R.N.; John Murphy; Mindy and David Secrest; Timothy J. Buckley; and Beth and Matt Lammers.

1

"NINE-LETTER HINT," I muttered, absent-mindedly winding a curl around my finger.

"Adumbrate," said a disembodied voice from behind the sports page.

I glared, but he didn't see me. Too busy reading about the ACC basketball tournament. Edna and I exchanged glances. My mother knows about my love/hate relationship with the Sunday crossword puzzle. I like to save them up and work them on Saturday mornings. I read the clues out loud. Helps me think. But I loathe it when someone tries to help me. And Lord help the person who tries to beat me to the puzzle. Edna knows better than to even talk to me while I'm working the crossword.

Reluctantly, I scribbled the letters in the box. Adumbrate worked, of course. Stupid word. Mac doesn't even bother with the *Atlanta Constitution*'s crossword puzzle. He usually picks up a Sunday *New York Times* at Oxford Books.

"Any coffee left?" said the voice again. With a small, martyred sigh I put down the paper and got up to refill both our cups.

I caught the telephone on the first ring.

"Callahan?" The voice on the other end was low, muffled.

"Yes," I said. "Who's this?"

The response was whispered.

"Speak up," I said. "I can't hear you."

"It's me, Neva Jean," she hissed. "I can't talk any louder. I'm at a pay phone."

I rolled my eyes heavenward. Edna saw me, got up, refilled the coffee cups herself and sat back down.

"Must be Neva Jean," she told Mac. "She's got that look." Mac lowered his paper and looked for himself. "Definitely Neva Jean," he said.

"Callahan," Neva Jean said. "You gotta help me. I'm in trouble. Big trouble."

This was not hot news. Neva Jean McComb is rarely not in some sort of mess. She's a hard worker, one of my best employees, and she usually means well, but Neva Jean is one of those souls who attract trouble like a black dress attracts lint.

"What's the deal?" I asked, leaning my back against the kitchen counter. "Where are you, anyway?"

"I'm at one of those fast-food emergency room places, over on Covington Highway," she said, raising her voice a little. "Swannelle's bad sick. Callahan, I might of sorta killed Swannelle."

"Might have?" I repeated. "Speak up, Neva Jean. Is he dead or isn't he?"

"I don't know," she wailed, up to top volume now. "He's been back in with the doctor for over an hour now. The nurse won't tell me nothing. For all I know Swannelle's dead and they've already called the cops to come get me."

"Calm down," I ordered. "Tell me what happened."

"It was that goddamned bass boat," she said, sobbing. "It never woulda happened if it weren't for that damn boat. I didn't mean to kill him, really. I was so mad I didn't know what I was doing. Is pissed off a defense for murder, Callahan?"

"What bass boat? Did you try to drown him or what?

Quit crying and quit talking in circles, damn it. Just tell me what's going on."

"Swannelle went to the boat show with Rooney. Rooney Deebs, that's his cousin. And when he came home last night he was towing a brand new candy-apple–red bass boat behind his truck."

Slowly, the motive for Neva Jean's attempted murder was becoming clear.

"He bought a bass boat? Aren't they pretty expensive?"

"Twenty-eight frigging thousand dollars," she said, gasping for breath in between sobs. "Our house didn't cost but eighteen thousand. And it's got plumbing. He put eight thousand down—all the money we had saved, and signed a note for the rest. Said he was gonna sell McComb Auto Body and him and Rooney was gonna go on the professional bass fishing tour together."

"So you had a fight."

"Not this time," Neva Jean said. "I was so mad, I thought I'd bust a gusset. I slammed the bedroom door and locked it. Then I took every piece of clothes he owns, and all his bowling and softball trophies, too, and pitched them all out the window. And you know it rained last night."

"So what did Swannelle do?" I was almost afraid to ask.

"Hollered at the locked door for a while. Stormed around, rippin' and rantin'. Then he got drunk. Knee-walking, commode-hugging drunk. Then he passed out on the living room sofa. I got up this morning. I saw the little prick, laying there, passed out on my good sofa, and when I looked out the front window and saw that twenty-eight-thousand-dollar bass boat, I got mad all over again. I picked up the nearest thing to hand, a can of Raid, and I emptied it on that bad boy."

"You sprayed Swannelle with a whole can of roach spray?" Poisoning was a new frontier for Neva Jean. The last time the two of them got into it, she'd taken a steak knife and cut off his ponytail while he was sleeping. She'd grazed him once with the pickup truck in the parking lot of Mama's Country Showcase out on Covington Highway another time. And then there was the memorable time he'd abandoned her in a Waffle House parking lot in Macon.

"It was more like half a can," she said, calmer now. "We've had a bad bug problem this year."

"What happened?"

She started sniffling again. "It was awful. He started coughing and choking. Grabbing at his neck like he couldn't breathe. Tried to sit up, but he fell back down again. His eyes were watering and his nose was running, he was drooling like a mad dog, and when I looked down I noticed he'd peed his pants, too. I never seen nothing like it in my life. He was dying, right there in front of me."

"You got him to an emergency room, right?" I said, encouragingly.

"Yeah," she said, pausing to blow her nose. "But he's been in there an awful long time. An hour at least. I just know something awful is happening. You reckon I killed him?"

She had me there. I'm a former cop and I've been dabbling in the private investigation business for a couple of years now, when I'm not running my cleaning business, but I'd never heard of death by Raid before. There's always that first time, though.

"Tell you what," I said, "give me your number there. I'll call Maureen and ask her. In the meantime, do you have a lawyer?"

"A lawyer?" she screamed. "What do I want with a lawyer? I didn't mean nothing by that roach spray, Callahan. I was just so mad I couldn't think straight."

"I know," I said. "And if ever there was a case for a justifiable homicide, you've got one. But if the worst happens, if somebody calls the cops, you really should have legal representation. You want me to call Katie Reilly?"

"That's the lawyer with the condo in Ansley Park?"

"Yeah," I said. "I think you clean her place alternate Thursdays."

"I reckon," she said, resignedly. "She keeps a real neat kitchen as I recall." Neva Jean gave me the emergency clinic phone number and then hung up.

"Did I hear right?" Edna asked, looking over the top of the bifocals that slide down to the end of her nose. "Did Neva Jean spray Swannelle with bug spray?"

"Half a can of Raid," I said, picking through the box of doughnuts Mac had brought. I found a cake, one with gooey chocolate frosting, and picked a piece of the frosting off with a fingernail. I'm trying to diet again. "They're at one of those doc-in-the-box emergency clinics. Neva Jean's convinced she's killed the one great love of her life."

"Are you really going to call Maureen?" Mac asked. He knows my sister and I are not on the best of terms. But she's a nurse at Grady Memorial Hospital's emergency room, and even if she is a bitch she knows emergency medicine.

My eyes met Edna's. "I thought maybe you'd call, Ma. It'd be quicker. Neva Jean really sounded scared."

"Gimme the phone," Edna said, slapping my hand away from the doughnuts. She dialed my sister's number and turned her back to me. After chatting for a moment or two she hung up.

"Maureen says Swannelle's probably sick as hell, but that Neva Jean probably couldn't kill the little pissant with Raid unless she managed to bash his head in with the can. She says they've probably got him hooked up to an IV with atropine; that's the antidote to roach poison. And your sister sends her love."

"I'll bet," I said. "Well, I guess I'll hold off calling Katie, since it looks like we've ruled out homicide."

Katie Reilly's an old family friend. She handles what little legal work I need, and in return we clean her condo every other week. I love cash-free transactions like that.

I called the emergency clinic back and asked for Neva Jean.

"Callahan," she said quickly, "he's all right. My lover man's gonna be fine. The nurse just came out and told me. Swannelle's gonna pull through."

"That's fine," I said. "Maureen says you can't kill a person with Raid. So I guess you don't need a lawyer unless you decide to divorce him."

"Don't even joke about that," she said, sniffing. "I'm just so thankful Swannelle's going to live. I'd never forgive myself if anything should happen to that man."

She started blubbering again, going on about how sweet and kind and good Swannelle McComb really was.

"Yeah, he's a saint, that Swannelle," I said, interrupting. "Listen, as long as he's okay, I really need to go now. I'll see you Monday, right?"

"Uh, well, the doctor says Swannelle's going to need some nursing, Callahan. Bed rest and fluids and like that. I thought I'd stay home and—"

"Put a six pack of Old Milwaukee on his side of the bed and leave the television on ESPN, Neva Jean. He'll be fine, but you'll be out of a job if your butt's not here at nine A.M. Monday."

"Aw, Callahan," she moaned. I cut her off and hung up. Edna and I run the House Mouse, which we think is the best damn cleaning business in Atlanta. Trying to keep Neva Jean and the other girls in line is a full-time job, but it beats the hell out of my last real job, which was as a detective for the Atlanta Police Department's property crimes unit. With the House Mouse I make my own hours (long) and my own rules (mostly flexible). We're making a decent profit now, and every once in a while I take on a private investigation gig, just to satisfy my own need to right wrongs and mind other people's business.

"What did Swannelle do to provoke Neva Jean this time?" Mac asked. While I was on the phone he'd swiped my crossword puzzle and was now busily filling in the blanks. With a pen.

"Messed with her crossword puzzle," I said, snatching the paper out of his mitts and glaring at him.

"Seriously," he said.

I sat back down at the table and sipped my coffee, which had gotten cool. "He came home with a brand new twenty-eight-thousand-dollar bass boat which he bought with the money Neva Jean's been saving up for a new kitchen," I said.

"Too bad she didn't spray him with something more lethal," Edna said, lighting up one of her maxi-length filter-tip cigarettes. "I'd have tried some of that Easy-Off Oven Cleaner if it'd been me. That stuff would knock a dog off a meat wagon."

"Jeez," Mac said, folding the sports page. "You're not serious, are you? You think it's all right to kill a man just for buying a bass boat?"

Edna leaned her head back and let twin streams of smoke drift toward the ceiling. "Aw, the oven cleaner's just a warning," she assured him. "A man like Swannelle McComb, a man like that, you've got to keep him in line all the time."

Mac reached across the table and grabbed my hand. "Tell me she's not for real. I can never tell when your mother is putting me on."

Edna had gone back to reading the wedding announcements in the newspaper's lifestyle section. "I'd say she's serious. So let that be a warning to you, Andrew McAuliffe. We Garrity women play for keeps."

"I'll remember," he promised.

The kitchen was quiet then. The kind of rare Saturday morning quiet that's filled with the sipping of good coffee, the turning of a newspaper page, the occasonal snicker at something in the funnies. The furnace clicked on. We were having an unusually wet and chilly March.

When the phone rang again the three of us jumped, simultaneously.

"Get that, Ma, will you? And if it's Neva Jean tell her she's got a full day Monday, and I'm not kidding, either."

Edna got up slowly, letting the phone ring twice more.

"Well hey, Jack," she said warmly. I looked up at the mention of my cousin Jack's name. But instead of grinning, as she usually did when her favorite nephew called, Edna's face had gone pale and her mouth was twisted with pain.

"Oh my God," she said, holding a hand to her mouth. "Are they sure? When? How did it happen? Sweet Jesus. What about the kids? Are the kids all right?"

She listened intently, her body tensed, the cigarette forgotten, dropped ashes down the front of her blouse. She brushed at them, then shut her eyes.

"I can't believe it," she was saying. "They're really sure? How's your mother? Is somebody with her? Yes. Yes. I'll come right away. Okay, love, see you soon. Thanks for calling."

"What?" I said, rushing to her side. "What's happened?" I think I knew before she told me.

"It's Patti," Edna said dully, massaging her temples with her fingertips. She pushed her glasses down and dabbed with a dish towel at red-rimmed eyes. "She's dead, Jules."

"When? How?"

Edna sank back down in her chair. "Yesterday. Jack didn't want to tell me everything on the phone, because Jean was sitting right there. The police are saying it was a carjacking. Dylan was in the car too, but he's been so upset they can't tell what he might have seen."

"Oh my God," I said.

Mac got up, got the coffeepot, and refilled our cups. "Is that Patti McNair, the cousin you told me about?"

I nodded, unable to speak. My throat had swollen

shut and my eyes burned with scalding tears. I buried my head in the crossword puzzle, watching while the ink blurred.

Patti. More a sister than a cousin, really. She was two years older than me. I'd welcomed her hand-me-down clothes, tagged after her as a kid. She'd treated me as an equal when my own sister Maureen had regarded me as a pariah. Patti had shown me how to be cool. How to shred the knees of my blue jeans, the way to light a cigarette, holding it just so between painted fingertips for the hippest effect. She'd been our family rebel, a vegetarian, a hippie; she'd even dabbled with Buddhism in a move calculated to drive my aunt Jean over the brink. She'd lived in a commune up in the North Georgia mountains after dropping out of Wake Forest University. She'd gotten married, barefoot, to Aunt Jean's everlasting horror, wearing a white Mexican peasant shift that barely hid her pregnancy.

The hippie days hadn't lasted, of course. Bruce, her husband, dropped back into law school, with Patti working as a secretary to put him through school. She'd gone back to college herself, too, and had earned a degree in psychology. Later, when Bruce's practice had taken off, she'd quit her job as a school counselor to stay home and be a full-time mom.

We saw each other irregularly now. At family things, holiday dinners, like that. Sometimes, on a whim, she'd call and we'd meet for lunch, drink bloody Marys and giggle again like teenagers.

"Dylan. Is that one of her kids?" Mac asked.

"Yeah," I whispered. "He's Patti's baby, must be eight or nine now, I guess. Her girls, Megan and Caitlin, are much older, sixteen and eighteen, I guess. Dylan has some kind of problem. Some speech and hearing thing. He's not retarded or anything like that, but he goes to a special school. Half the time nobody knows what the kid is saying."

When I looked up again, Edna was stacking the breakfast dishes and moving briskly toward the sink.

"I told Jack I'd come right over," she said. "Jean had that bypass surgery last fall, and the boys are worried about her. DeeDee has the kids at Jack's house."

"I'm coming with you," I said. Mac got up and shooed Edna away from the sink. "I'll take care of this," he said quietly. "You two get going. Call me if you need anything. Promise?"

I allowed myself a moment for a quick, tight hug. "Okay," I whispered. "I will."

2

THE QUIET IN THE CAR was deafening. It was thirty minutes to my aunt Jean's house out in suburban Marietta. Once I got on Interstate 75 I turned on the radio, jiggled the switch around. Country music. Acid rock. Moldy-oldies.

"That crap they call music gives me the whim-whams," Edna said. "Turn to WSB."

It was a Saturday morning sports call-in show and the host was droning on about The University of Georgia's football recruiting success. Only March and all this guy had to think about was the Bulldogs' chances come September. My hand snaked toward the dial again.

"Leave it," Edna snapped. "It's nearly ten, the news'll be on in a minute."

She dug around in her purse, got out paper and pen and started making a list.

Traffic on the interstate was light. I snuck a look at what she was doing.

"Groceries? Patti's dead and you're making a grocery list?"

She didn't look up. "I need you to stop at the Food Town on the way home. I'll put the ham on right away, and get started on some potato salad. Maureen can do the deviled eggs. Even she can't screw that up. I'll do that cherry Jell-O mold. Remind me to get some Cool-Whip. Maybe Agnes could do a chocolate cake for me. The women from Jean's church will bring stuff in . . . "

Unbidden, memories of Patti flitted through my mind. Patti, strutting down the shore at Panama City Beach in her first bikini, a trail of boys tagging at her heels. Patti, deliberately tossing her wildflower bouquet to me on a windy April day. Patti, beaming with pride, holding up her first child for me to inspect.

And then I saw Patti, slumped on the front seat of a car somewhere, her head shattered, blood and glass everywhere. And poor Dylan, cowering in the backseat, his mother dead in the front. I'd never worked homicide during my time on the Atlanta Police Department, but as a uniformed cop I'd seen more than enough crime scenes, seen what a close-range gunshot could do to the fragile human skull.

"Tell me exactly what Jack told you about Patti," I said, interrupting Edna's menu. I wanted to throw up just then at the mention of all that food, but I knew that was my mother's way of grieving. Up north, I guess, when somebody dies they worry about blue suits and shiny shoes. But where I come from you don't mourn without a ham and some deviled eggs.

My mother sighed, took off her glasses and wiped them on the hem of her blouse. "All he said was that they were stopped at a traffic light somewhere out on Bankhead Highway, near those public housing projects, I guess. Patti pulled to a stop and some black guy came out of nowhere, jerked the car door open, and when Patti screamed, he put a gun to her head and pulled the trigger. Her purse was gone when they found her. Jack said Bruce told him Patti had maybe eight bucks in her purse. Eight goddamn bucks. And he killed her for it."

"What about Dylan? What was he doing in the car?"

She put the glasses back on again. "Jesus, I was just repeating what Jack told me. He goes to that Miller-

Shipley School, maybe they have short days or something. All Jack said was that Dylan was so hysterical they couldn't get any sense out of him at all. I guess he was able to tell them that he was asleep in the backseat when it happened."

I glanced in my rearview mirror; an eighteen-wheeler was riding my butt, blinking its lights on and off to signal me to let him pass. I slowed down and the truck blew by me. "Asshole," I muttered.

"None of this makes any sense," I said. "First of all, what was Patti doing over in that part of town? Bankhead Highway's a long way from East Cobb. And why did Jack wait until this morning to call us if she was killed yesterday afternoon?"

"How the hell should I know what she was doing over there?" Edna said. "Maybe she was going somewhere and got lost. You know Patti had no sense of direction. Your Uncle Ray had to write her directions to get to the A&P and back. But Jack did say the police didn't contact Bruce until nearly midnight. Patti's purse was gone, so she didn't have any identification on her, and Dylan was totally incoherent, even more so than usual. Patti was driving some new car Bruce had bought her for an anniversary gift. A Lexus that he'd bought from one of his clients, so it was still registered to the client. The cops didn't reach the client until late last night, and then he told them he'd sold it to Bruce."

"Didn't Bruce wonder where Patti and Dylan were?" I asked.

"Jack said he was frantic. He drove every block of their subdivision, called every friend she ever had, cruised the mall parking lot for two hours. He even had somebody drive up to the house on Lake Lanier to see if they were up there."

"When did they tell Aunt Jean?"

"This morning," Edna said. "She knew Patti was missing, because Bruce had called to ask if she'd seen her.

But he didn't make a big deal of it, so I guess she wasn't too worried. Jack and DeeDee got there at eight and they told her. The girls were still up when the police got to the house last night, so they already knew."

"Jesus," I said. I'd been taking the Lord's name in vain a lot this morning. After the eighteen-wheeler incident, I'd absentmindedly slid into the far left lane. Now my exit loomed just ahead. I floored it and jerked the van through three lanes of traffic, sliding onto the Marietta Loop exit to the tune of a car-horn chorus.

Edna's face was white with fear. Her hands trembled as she reached for a cigarette. "You nearly got us killed."

I could feel my face set in stone, the anger at my cousin's death throbbed in my head. "Better in a traffic accident than to have your brains blown out for eight bucks," I said.

3

A RED PICKUP TRUCK, a green Honda Civic, and a dark blue Mazda Miata crowded the driveway of Aunt Jean's house. "Looks like all the chicks have come home to roost," Edna said. "DeeDee must still be over at Bruce's house. She just moved back from Miami last month. Still job hunting last I heard. I reckon the green car with the North Carolina tags is Michael's. He quit working for the county and moved to Charlotte, you know."

I didn't know that DeeDee had moved back or that Michael had moved away. Counting both sides of the family I must have a couple of dozen cousins, scattered all over Georgia and the South. I'd long ago quit trying to keep track of the whole clan.

"That's Jack's truck," she continued. "The Mazda must be Peggy's."

"I thought they were separated."

"They are," Edna sighed, "but Peggy treats Jean like her own mother, and vice versa. It's kind of weird if you ask me."

"Nobody did," I pointed out.

Edna glanced over at me, frowned, and bit her lip.

"What?"

"Nothing."

"Don't nothing me. Spit it out."

"All right," she said reluctantly. "I just wish you wouldn't go in that house and start asking questions. You know how you do. And everybody's upset right now. So nobody needs Miss Perry Mason doing twenty questions. You're not a cop anymore, remember?"

I felt my hands knotting and unknotting in my lap.

"Give me some credit here, Ma, would you?" I said bitterly. "Patti was like a sister to me. More than Maureen ever was, that's for sure. I'm as heartbroken as you are, but yeah, I've got questions. And I intend to ask them, too, but when I do I promise I'll be tactful and discreet. Okay? I don't want Aunt Jean having a heart attack any more than you do."

"Fine," Edna said, reaching around on the car seat for the suitcase-sized purse she carried. "I just needed to say that. Now let's go. And remember—discreet. You promised."

I scowled as I followed her up the sidewalk to the house. My aunt Jean's house is a two-story, gray cedar-siding job built to look like a primitive log cabin. Except there were dark brown and blue and green cedar-siding cabins of the same general description lining both sides of this street, and a satellite dish was planted in the front yard instead of a horse and buggy. Where a gut-busted washing machine or truck seat would have graced the porch of an authentic cabin, my aunt was displaying a wooden bucket planted with red and yellow pansies and a white concrete goose with a faded blue bow around its neck. I could still remember when this whole subdivision had sprouted all at one time like a particularly persistent rash, back in the seventies, in an abandoned cotton field. The developer had, in a fit of originality, named his creation "Green Acres." Aunt Jean lived on Kabin Kourt.

It felt weird to be going to the front door today. We Garritys have always been a back-door kind of bunch. My cousin Jack answered the door before we could ring the bell, simultaneously enveloping both of us in a rib-crushing bear hug.

The oldest of my aunt's four kids, Jack was the most like Edna's brother, my uncle Ray: tall and burly with a thick thatch of sandy-colored hair and good-natured blue-gray eyes brushed with no-color eyelashes. Jack still runs the construction business my uncle started after he got back from Korea in the 1950s.

"Hey, sweetie," a quavery voice said behind us.

Aunt Jean looked thinner and older than I remembered, and she seemed to have developed a widow's hump on her back just since the last Christmas family gathering. Her hair was cut in the same gray pixie she'd worn since I could remember, but her perpetual gardener's tan had faded and she wore a pink cotton housecoat and matching slippers.

"Oh, Jean," my mother said haltingly. "I'm so sorry."

The two women stood there, clinging to each other, wordless. Sniffing, Edna was the first to pull away. "I could use some coffee, hon. Is any made?"

I followed them into the kitchen. The small blue-and white-papered room was crowded with family and funeral offerings. My cousin Michael was on the phone, nodding, talking in a tone too low to be heard. Peggy, Jack's wife, or was it ex-wife, stood at the open refrigerator door holding a bowl of bean salad in one hand and a platter of fried chicken in the other. "Now where on earth am I going to put all this stuff?" she fussed.

I glanced around. Every surface in the kitchen was covered with food. The maple dinette table was wall-to-wall with cakes, pies, foil-wrapped casseroles and platters of sliced meats. Each stove burner sported a pan of soup or stew, and the counters held brown paper sacks of more groceries.

"Y'all had better be hungry," Peggy said, breaking an awkward silence. "'Cuz we got enough food here to feed the Russian army."

Michael hung up the phone then and after another round of hugging we managed to all squeeze around the dinette. He seated himself beside Aunt Jean, one arm flung protectively around her shoulders.

"You feelin' all right?" Edna wanted to know.

Jean nodded. "Numb. Just numb. I can't believe any of this is happening. Not to Patti. Not to my own child. It just doesn't make sense."

Michael edged closer to his mother. "A neighbor came over and took Mama's blood pressure just before you came. It's up just slightly, but that was her doctor I was talking to on the phone, and he says it's not too bad. She'll be fine."

Jean smiled weakly, her thin lips the same color as her skin. "It's a terrible thing that you have to lose somebody precious before your children can all come home at the same time, isn't it? I reckon the last time that happened was at their daddy's funeral. I'm so blessed to have my Jack and Michael and DeeDee."

"You and Ray raised a bunch of good ones, Jean," Edna said.

My aunt fiddled with the silver chain that held her eyeglasses. "I'm just thankful he's gone, Edna. Patti was Ray's pet. We all knew that. He loved that child like nothing else in this world." Tears rolled down her cheeks and made rose-colored splashes on the front of her robe.

"How's Dylan?" I asked. Edna shot me the look.

Peggy set mugs of hot coffee down in front of us, edging the cups in between the coconut custards and the sour cream pound cakes.

"He'll be all right," she said. "We were afraid he might have a concussion, but the doctors kept him in the emergency room for three hours and finally decided it's just a bad bruise. Nothing permanent."

"Is he able to say what happened?" I asked.

Peggy and Jack exchanged looks. Michael stared into his coffee mug, stirring the black brew with his index finger.

"We don't know yet," Aunt Jean said in a wobbly voice. "It'd be a blessing if he didn't see anything. Didn't remember at all. What could be more awful for a child than to see his own mother shot like that."

Michael covered her hand with his. "Don't talk about it right now, Mama. Please. We don't want you getting upset again."

"I don't believe I'll ever be not upset again," Jean said. "Let me talk about it, son. I want to."

He shrugged. "Whatever."

"Besides," my aunt continued, "Callahan feels as bad as we do. Don't you remember how close she and Patti always were? Frick and Frack your daddy used to call them."

"More like Mutt and Jeff," I said. "I can understand your not wanting Dylan to remember anything about what happened, Aunt Jean, but did anybody else see anything? Were there any witnesses at all?"

"The police won't tell us," Jack said, standing with his back to the kitchen doorway. "As far as we know, Dylan was the only one around. Poor kid."

I snuck a look at my mother. She shook her head. I shook mine back.

"Aunt Jean, just what kind of learning problem is it that Dylan has? Patti tried to explain it once, but I never quite understood."

"Oh, honey," Jean said sadly. "It's some term I don't understand either. Expressive language disorder. Patti called it a processing problem. She'd learned all about it, of course. Went to seminars and even joined a parents' support group. The way she explained it to me, Dylan's brain was sort of short-circuited. He's a right bright little fella, and he can hear and speak of course, but what he hears and says get all mixed up before it comes out. So sometimes he can't understand what people are saying to him and the things he says don't hardly make sense either. Patti and the girls could make him out pretty good, because they were so used to him, but I swear, half the time I don't know what he's trying to tell me, poor little thing."

We heard a clatter of feet and voices then and the back door opened, letting in a blast of cold, damp air.

Bruce McNair herded his two daughters into the kitchen and shut the door noisily. It had started raining, harder, and the three of them stood on the doormat, dripping wet like some storm-tossed shipwreck survivors.

Aunt Jean rushed to them, gathering them in her arms, urging them out of their shoes and their wet jackets. Caitlin and Megan looked utterly miserable. Caitlin's long red hair was bunched under a black baseball cap she wore with the bill backward, and she wore a baggy black sweatshirt reaching nearly to her jeans-clad knees. Megan's short, dark hair stuck to her head like so much limp seaweed. Her abundant eye makeup was smeared, and she wore a torn white T-shirt over what looked like green army fatigue pants and black lace-up boots. She stood, stony-faced, enduring her grandmother's embrace.

Bruce kicked off his moccasins and edged around the table, leaning down to kiss my cheek. The stubble of his beard was graying and he smelled like coffee and cigarette smoke. But even in the face of tragedy, Bruce McNair still reminded me of the same twenty-year-old scamp who'd stolen my favorite cousin away. He was wearing a red plaid flannel shirt over a dark blue T-shirt, and his khaki pants were wrinkled and faded, just a touch on the high-water side, probably the same pair he'd worn in college. He looked like one of those blue-collar beer commercial hunks, not the least bit like a successful attorney.

"Is he not the cutest damn thing you've ever seen?" Patti had whispered to me the first time she'd brought him home to the family. "We did the deed right out on the back porch glider after Mama and Daddy went to bed last night."

They'd played footsie under the dining room table, Bruce blushing bright pink while Patti had felt up his thigh all during dinner.

Bruce McNair had never quite renounced all his hippie ways. He still wore his straight brown hair just a shade on the shaggy side, still snuck off to see the Grateful Dead during their yearly visits to Atlanta.

"Thanks for coming," he said, squeezing my shoulders. "We've had a rough time of it."

Megan and Caitlin hadn't moved from their spot by the door. Finally Peggy took charge. "Come on now," she said, taking each by the arm. "Grandma's got all this food, and she wants ya'll to eat. Go sit down in the dining room and we'll fix you a plate."

Peggy ignored their pleas that they'd eaten already, weren't hungry, couldn't take a bite, and hustled them out of the room, followed by the rest of the family.

Bruce moved to the coffeepot, poured himself a cup, and sat down in the chair Michael had abandoned.

"Bad night," I said, searching for something clever, something comforting, to say.

"You'll never know," he said, inhaling the steam from the coffee. "I still can't believe any of this is real."

Behind him, Aunt Jean bustled around, gathering plates and silverware for Peggy to take into the dining room.

"Bruce, where's Dylan?" she asked, reaching into a cupboard for ice tea glasses.

"He's fine, Jean," he said. "Headache's a lot better. DeeDee took him to the video arcade over at the mall."

"The arcade?" Jean said sharply. "With his mama just dead and him right out of the hospital? Do you think that's the right thing to do, Bruce?"

Bruce sighed. He'd obviously expected this reaction. "The pediatrician recommended I talk to a psychologist and make an appointment for Dylan to start having counseling. Right away. Dr. Cook and I talked on the phone this morning and she said Dylan should be allowed to do something he enjoys. He loves those damn video games. Even the girls can't beat him at them. When DeeDee offered to take him, he perked right up."

"I guess you know best," Jean said, but her voice said she

wasn't so sure. She set a plate down in front of him, slices of ham, a chicken breast, a buttered biscuit, and sweet potato soufflé. "I want you to eat that," she said firmly.

While she ferried more food into the dining room, Bruce jumped up and emptied the plate into the trash, rearranging the discarded paper towels and coffee grounds to hide his crime.

"She means well," he said, sitting back down.

"Don't we all," I said ruefully. "Look. Edna warned me not to ask a lot of questions. She said I'd just get everybody upset. Damn it, Bruce, I've got to know. I can't help it. Will it piss you off if I ask what happened?"

He reached in his breast pocket, took out a package of Dentyne gum, and unwrapped it slowly, offering me a piece. "Patti'd been nagging at me to quit smoking for five years. Hadn't had a cigarette in three months. I guess if I can make it through this, I can do anything. No, I'm all right. Go ahead and ask what you need to know. But I really don't know much right now."

"Just tell me what happened. Edna got the barest details from Jack on the phone this morning."

Jean came back into the room then and grabbed up two pies. "Ya'll eat," she said, disappearing again.

"The details are pretty sketchy, Callahan. Patti was out running errands yesterday. She'd played her Friday tennis match over at those indoor courts at the Concourse, then she was going to have a conference with one of Dylan's teachers around two o'clock. She called me shortly before one, I guess, and we talked for just a minute. She'd won her match, but she was in a hurry to get home because the plumber was supposed to come and look at the downstairs bathroom. The toilet was dripping. That's the last time I talked to her. I tried calling her at home and on the car phone later in the day, but I couldn't get any answer. I didn't start to get worried until the girls got home around four-thirty and there was no sign of her or Dylan. The plumber had left a note saying he'd been there and gone since nobody was home. Patti was always on the run, but she tried to make it a point to be there when the kids got home from school. And she'd been trying to get that plumber for months."

"What was Dylan doing in the car?" I asked gently.

He looked up grimly. "He said he wasn't feeling well. Upset stomach or something. The school called Patti on her car phone, it turns out, and asked her to pick him up."

"She didn't mention it when she talked to you?" I asked.

"No," he said.

"Wait a minute. Isn't Miller-Shipley in Norcross? That's miles from where Edna said they found the car. Bankhead Highway, right?"

"It doesn't make sense to me either," Bruce admitted. "I can't imagine what Patti would have been doing over in that part of town."

"Maybe she was lost?" I suggested.

He smiled for the first time since we'd started talking. "Patti got lost going to the ladies room at the Burger King. You know how she was."

"Yeah," I said, "I know."

The reassuring sound of quiet conversation, of knives and forks clinking and ice cubes tinkling against glass, floated in from the dining room. It was impossible that we were all together, eating and talking in my aunt's house on this rainy March day, and that Patti was not here.

"Was Dylan able to tell the police anything at all?" I asked.

His face reddened. "You know Dylan has an, uh, learning thing, don't you? Patti, of course, made a big deal about it. Too big a deal, I've always thought. She enrolled him in Miller-Shipley. Damn place costs eleven thousand five hundred a year. Personally, I don't think Dylan's problem is all that severe. A speech impediment, yes, but in my opinion all this developmental disability stuff is a lot of crap. Anyway, Dylan told us he'd gone to sleep in the backseat of the car right after Patti picked him up. He says he only woke up when he heard Patti scream. When he sat up . . .

"God," Bruce said, swallowing hard. "Jesus God." He rubbed his temples with his fingertips, took a sip of coffee. "When Dylan sat up he saw a black guy. The guy jerked the car door open, put a gun to Patti's head, and fired. Like that. Point blank. When Dylan started screaming, the guy looked surprised. You know, that somebody was in the car. He reached over and grabbed Patti's purse, then reached over and popped Dylan on the head with the gun. That's all Dylan can tell us."

"Who called the cops?"

Bruce stared at me blankly. "What?"

"The cops?" I repeated. "Somebody must have reported it. Do you know who it was? Maybe there was another witness after all."

"I don't know," Bruce said slowly. "It never occurred to me to ask."

4

THERE WERE DOZENS more questions swirling around in my head. Had Dylan been able to describe his assailant? What did the murder weapon look like? Where exactly on Bankhead Highway had Patti been shot? What time had the cops found Dylan? And on and on.

But the doorbell kept buzzing. Neighbors and more family filtered in and out. Michael and Peggy took turns answering the phone, which never quit ringing.

At some point Megan and Caitlin joined us at the kitchen table. The four of us sat there, chatting quietly, sipping coffee, while activity ebbed and flowed around us.

"Bruce, girls," Aunt Jean announced. "Father Mart is here. Come out to the living room and talk to him, why don't you?"

Megan and Caitlin exchanged that patented exasperated look all teenage girls affect just as soon as they turn thirteen. Caitlin and Bruce stood up to go, but Megan didn't budge.

"Meg?" Bruce said tentatively. "Come on, honey, it's Father Mart."

"You go," she said stonily. "I've got a headache."

Aunt Jean opened her mouth to protest, but thought better of it. She patted Megan on the shoulder. "That's okay, honey," she said. "Do you want to go lie down on Gramma's bed?"

"I just want people to leave me alone," she said tearily.

"I'll get her some aspirin and sit with her, Aunt Jean," I said, trying to sound helpful.

Aunt Jean moved to the kitchen window and took a bottle of generic aspirin off the windowsill. She ran a glass of water from the tap and handed it to Megan.

"Father Mart is going to lead us in the rosary now," she said meaningfully.

It sounded like a command performance, so I trailed into the living room after the others.

I'm what you might call a back-slidden Catholic these days. My sister and brothers and I had a typical six-ties mackerel-snapper upbringing: parochial school, mass on Sundays, Mrs. Paul's fish sticks on Fridays. Once I left home, I drifted away from all that except for holidays, when I dragged myself to church to please my parents.

But after my dad died, and Edna feuded with our parish priest, we both defected for good. I haven't been back since Dad's funeral mass.

A Protestant would have found the living room scene distinctly weird. My aunt, cousins, even my mother for God's sake, were down on their knees on Aunt Jean's gray shag carpet, clicking their beads and murmuring Hail Marys.

Kneeling in their midst, eyes raised heavenward, was a thin, balding man in his late forties. He wore the collar, of course, but over it he'd tossed a worn gray tweed sport coat.

Bruce and Caitlin knelt too, at the edge of the cir-cle, beside Aunt Jean. My aunt looked at me, just once, her lips moving as she recited the prayer. Her eyes flicked meaningfully up, then down. I was the only one in the room still standing.

For a moment I had a crisis of conscience. I could

make my aunt happy and take one of the rosaries she'd placed in a basket on an end table. A few laps on the beads wouldn't hurt any, would they? Or I could stand my ground and refuse to give in to hypocrisy.

In the end I decided on a compromise. I sank into an armchair and sat on the edge, knees lowered but not nearly touching the ground.

As the prayers droned on I became fascinated with the priest, Father Mart. Like me, Patti had long ago abandoned the church. She'd had the kids baptized, of course, and she'd sent the girls to Catholic schools. But a couple of years ago she'd had a real renewal of the faith, or so she'd said. Since then she'd been a regular churchgoer, much to her mother's delight. Father Mart, Patti had told me, was a big part of her return to the church. "He's not like those dried-up old prunes we used to have, Callahan," she said. "He makes it real. You should come back to church with me and see for yourself."

I guess I was coming back today, if only for Patti's sake.

On closer examination, I realized Father Mart was probably younger than I'd first assumed. Old-fashioned wire-rimmed glasses and hair combed straight back from his forehead were probably deliberate attempts to instill confidence in a man still in his early to mid-thirties. His hair was nearly white-blond, instead of gray, and bright blue eyes blinked repeatedly behind those glasses. He had high cheekbones, a modified lantern jaw, and a deep voice that sounded too big for my aunt's living room.

Bruce's eyes were squeezed shut as he moved his lips to the prayers, but more than once I caught Caitlin staring at the priest, then down again at the jet beads she held limply in her right hand.

Finally the prayers came to an end. Father Mart stood, then helped my aunt and mother to their feet. They all stood around, shoulders touching shoulders, shaking the priest's hand and thanking him for his devotion.

Suddenly, the prospect of spending another second in the bosom of this grieving family was unbearable. In the kitchen, I grabbed our purses and jackets.

"We've really got to go now, Aunt Jean," I said, moving beside her and kissing her on the cheek. Edna came over, took her coat, and put it on.

"Visitation hour is at seven tonight at Patterson's," Jean said, dabbing again at her eyes. "I guess Jack told you services will be at Our Lady of Lourdes tomorrow at one?"

"A funeral on Sunday?" Edna said, sounding surprised. "How'd you pull that off?"

"Father Mart got Father Mulhern over at St. Thomas to cover for him tomorrow," Jean said.

"We'll see you tonight then," Edna said.

I waited until we'd gotten in the car and I was at the end of my aunt's street. "Not me, Ma. No way."

My mother dug around in her purse until she came up with a packet of tissues. She blew her nose, honking noisily.

"What?" she said. "Not me what?"

"Patterson's," I said simply. "You go. Make Kevin or Maureen go with you. I'm not getting within a mile of that place."

She knew better than to argue with me. "All right," she said. "You've put in your appearance, I suppose. I'll call Kevin when I get home. At least he won't go around asking pushy questions all night."

Now I understood. Edna likes to pick her fights. She'd capitulated on the funeral home issue, but now she wanted to stand her ground on something else.

"Look," I said. "Bruce said he didn't mind. He was upset, of course, but not at me or my questions. And you heard Aunt Jean, she said she wants to talk about it. She said that, didn't she?"

Edna pursed her lips. "Jean's half crazy with grief and shock. She doesn't know what she's saying. Jack and

Michael didn't appreciate your pushiness, I'll tell you that right now."

"Fuck Jack and Michael," I said vehemently. "They don't run my life. Patti's dead. Somebody killed her. That's a fact. And I have a right to try to find out who and why."

"That's the cops' job," Edna said. "Aren't you the one who's always telling me that a private investigator isn't supposed to meddle in a murder investigation? Aren't you?"

"This is different," I said, glancing in my rearview mirror before I merged back onto the interstate. "Patti was special, Ma. If this is really just a freak street thing, a carjacking gone bad, we'll have to accept that, I guess. But I want the cops handling this thing to know that Patti's family isn't going to shut up until they catch the fucking animal who did this and put him behind bars."

"Put him in the electric chair would be more like it," Edna said. "And what do you mean if it really was a carjacking? What's that supposed to mean?"

"Just what it sounds like," I said. "From what little Bruce told me, this is all too weird. I want to know how Patti got clear over to Bankhead Highway. There's nothing over there but that big old public housing project and strip shopping centers with liquor stores and thrift shops. What the hell was she doing over there? Patti was afraid to drive to our house, let alone down Bankhead. And I want to know who found the car. Who found Dylan? There might be witnesses. I need to know."

"You need to shut up and quit being such a hard-headed, selfish, insensitive shit," Edna said. "You act like you're the only one who loved Patti. We're all grieving. And right now Patti's kids and her husband and the rest of this family need to be left alone. The last thing we need is you poking around, reminding us of what happened."

"As if any of us could forget," I shot back. "Let's drop it, Mom. I'm going to do what I have to do. I'll try and stay out of the family's way, if I can. But I'm not gonna sit back and wait. So don't ask me to."

It was still raining lightly when I pulled into our driveway twenty minutes later. I left the motor running. "Go ahead in," I said. "I've got some stuff to do. I'll see you when you get back from Patterson's tonight."

She didn't look at me as she got out of the car, but she did slam the door. So I knew where I stood on the question of investigating Patti McNair's killing. Alone. All alone.

I backed the van up and headed back up toward Cobb County. It was years since I'd been in Marietta, the county seat. In Atlanta, folks are divided into two distinct camps, in-towners and suburbanites. Interstate 285 does a neat trick of delineating the borders, ringing the city as it does and hooking up along the way with Interstate 75-85, the north-south connectors, and Interstate 20, the east-west corridor. The Perimeter, as we all call 285, is the great dividing line.

I'd grown up just outside the line, in Sandy Springs, a bedroom community in Fulton County that had developed in the fifties and sixties. When we were kids you still went into Atlanta to shop at Rich's or J.P. Allen's, to watch a show at one of the big movie palaces like The Fox, or to eat at a really nice restaurant. Atlanta back then was a shining, exciting beacon for people all over the south.

In the late sixties, though, the malls beckoned. After desegregation, families fled the inner city and moved to the new all-white suburbs. Gradually, downtown Atlanta became a place to be feared. By the late eighties, all the big banks were abandoning their downtown office towers, the downtown Rich's closed its doors, and the only reason to come downtown was if you absolutely had to.

"I don't know when I've been downtown," my aunt Jean would say. "I'd be afraid to go down there now. Look at all that crime."

Our other family members had been shocked when I bought a little bungalow in Candler Park, an in-town neighborhood in the shadow of the city. And when Edna moved in, selling the brick ranch house in Sandy Springs, they'd been appalled.

"You'll both be raped in bed," my sister-in-law predicted. "Robbed and burglarized and who knows what."

But the only major crime wave we've experienced came last year when our house was deliberately torched. The perpetrator of said arson was not some nasty inner-city black gangster, but somebody who was trying to throw me off the track on a burglary-murder case I was working.

Insurance paid for the remodeling, and we got a new roof out of the deal, too.

As I headed back north I tried to think whether I still knew the names of any homicide detectives working for the Cobb County Police.

As a property crimes detective for the Atlanta Police I'd known some Cobb detectives years ago, but only as nodding acquaintances. The only real contact I had, Lamar Phillips, had been a homicide sergeant. But I'd read in the *Constitution* last year that he'd taken early retirement after a female officer had accused him of sexual harassment.

Too bad. Old Lamar had been a butt pincher all right, but if you bought him a beer and acted nice, he'd share what he knew.

Keeping one hand on the steering wheel I reached over with the other hand and flipped through a spiral-bound notebook I keep taped to the dashboard of the van. I found Bucky Deavers's number and dialed it on my car phone. I'd resisted buying one of these boogers for ages, but time and technology had finally caught up with me. If I don't keep in constant contact with the girls these days, I lose money. No more grungy gas station pay phones for Callahan Garrity.

Bucky's phone rang three, four, then five times. "Pick it up, Bucky," I mumbled.

When the phone did answer I was almost knocked from my seat by a sonic blast of rock music. "Deavers," a voice shouted breathlessly.

"Turn down the damned music," I bellowed.

"What?" he hollered back. "Wait a minute. Let me turn down the music."

There was another minute, valuable minutes on car phones, let me tell you, before the music was cut off and my old buddy was back on the line.

"You leading aerobics classes in your apartment these days, Deavers?"

"Callahan!" he yelled, laughing. "What's shakin'? I was just doing my new Stairmaster machine. It's boring as shit unless you got some tunes. So how are things? You ready to dump that old geezer for some young rock-hard talent?"

"Not likely," I said. "I need a favor, Bucky."

"What else is new?" he said. "No computer checks. I told you that after that last time. I ain't getting my ass in a sling again, even for you."

"Nothing like that," I assured him. "You know anybody working homicide in Cobb County these days?"

"Maybe," he said cautiously. "What have you got going up there?"

"My cousin was killed," I said. "Shot in the head over on Bankhead Highway."

"No shit," he said. "I'm sorry, babe. Was it another car-jacking? We've had three or four of those in Atlanta this winter. Another guy in the unit is working the cases, Jackie Wilkinson. You want me to have him give you a call?"

"Yeah," I said. "That'd be good. But in the meantime I want to see the incident report, talk to the first officers on the scene, like that. I need a friendly face. You know somebody?"

"Charlie Fouts is in homicide now," Bucky said. "I think he was on the DUI task force when you left Atlanta. Kind of a sawed-off little guy, with frizzy red hair, won all these awards for marksmanship?"

"Yeah," I said slowly. "I think I remember the guy. So he's with Cobb County now? Is he a good guy?"

"Helluva guy," Bucky said. "He's lived in Smyrna for years. Just went to work for Cobb year before last. Give him a try. Tell him Bucky says he owes me one. I got the guy a cream puff off-duty security job at a nightclub. Fifteen bucks an hour. He owes me a favor."

"So do I," I said fervently. "You going to the Yacht Club tonight?"

"I might if somebody else was buying," he said.

"I'm buying," I said. "See you around ten."

5

I CALLED AHEAD AND BY SHEER luck got Charlie Fouts just as he was getting ready to leave. After some initial reluctance he agreed to see me.

"I'm beat," he said tiredly. "Your cousin wasn't the only homicide last night. We got an eighteen-year-old girl over in Austell blew her common-law husband away with his own deer rifle early this morning, and a Jane Doe whose body was found in a motel room over on U.S. 41. I've been here since nine A.M. yesterday and I was hopin' to go home and log some rack time."

"This is really important," I pleaded. "Bucky says you're a good guy. How about proving it to me? It won't take more than thirty minutes, I promise."

There was a pause while he considered it.

"Please?" I was begging now and proud of it.

"You know where the Waffle House is on Delk Road?"

I glanced at the road marker up ahead. Delk Road was three exits up on the Interstate. "I know where it is."

"I'll see you there in ten minutes," Fouts said. "I'll bring whatever I can find, but I'm warning you, it won't be much."

"Anything at all will help," I said.

At the Waffle House I found a booth near the window, ordered coffee and a grilled cheese sandwich and watched the rain come down outside in dull gray sheets.

I'm one of those people who hate being stuck any-place without something to read, so I checked out the tabletop jukebox, more out of boredom than anything else.

Forget the road signs, I knew I was in Cobb County from the offerings on that Rockola. They had the entire Travis Tritt discography, Travis being a Marietta boy and all. Plus all the hat acts, Garth Brooks, Clint Black, and Randy Travis. They had country oldies, too. I nearly parted with a couple of quarters just to hear Faron Young sing "Hello Walls," but I knew better than to give in to the grief that nibbled around the corners of my mind. Better to focus on action than wallowing in sentiment I told myself.

The waitress brought my sandwich. It looked like they'd soaked the bread in grease for a couple of days, flipped it on the grill, and mashed it with a brick so that melted cheese ran out the sides and onto the sliced pick-les. Just the way I like it. After I'd taken a couple of nib-bles I glanced outside the plate-glass restaurant windows in time to see a dark blue Buick Regal pull to the curb and park in the slot nearest the door. A handicapped slot. Must be a cop.

Bucky's description was accurate. Charlie Fouts was no more than five seven, with a barrel-shaped body made more so by the bulky cable knit sweater and beat-up rain-coat he wore. He dashed for the door, then stood for a moment looking around. I raised a hand and waved.

He came over to the booth, shrugged out of the rain-coat and hung it on a hook. "Nice weather," he said by way of introduction.

The waitress was back in an instant, pouring him cof-fee and taking his order. She probably knew every cop on the Cobb County force by name and badge number.

"Mexican omelet, bacon, home fries, dry toast," he told her. "I know I didn't have breakfast or lunch yester-day, and I can't remember anything about dinner."

When the waitress had gone I reached across the table to shake his hand. "Callahan Garrity," I said. "Thanks for coming."

He looked surprised, but shook anyway. "It's okay," he said. "I understand you and Mrs. McNair were close, but don't you think it's a little unusual for a family member to conduct an investigation? Why don't you leave that up to us?"

"This isn't a formal investigation. I'm a former cop myself, as I told you, and I also do a little private investigation business. It's sort of a sideline. I'm licensed, by the way. It's just that this is all so bizarre. I have to know how it happened. Don't you find it bizarre?"

I searched his face for some answers. He had the fair complexion that seems to go with the redhead package. But there were layers of bags under his blue eyes and deep creases in his forehead. This guy lived his work.

"When is a homicide not bizarre?" he asked wearily. "What is it that you want to know about Patti McNair's?"

"I'd like to see whatever you've got," I said, trying to disguise my eagerness. "Her husband, Bruce, only gave me the sketchiest details this morning when I saw him."

"You saw McNair?"

"At my aunt's house. This morning. The whole family was there. Except for Dylan, of course. He was somewhere with DeeDee, Patti's younger sister."

"Rough for the kid," Fouts said, sipping his coffee. "What's with him anyway? Is he retarded or something?"

"Not at all," I said. "Dylan's really bright. He reads Stephen King. Nine years old and the kid's reading stuff I'm terrified of. I don't know much about it, but they tell me Dylan has some kind of language dysfunction. Could I see those reports now?"

Fouts set his mug down and flipped open the briefcase he'd put on the booth seat next to him. He handed me a slim folder full of photocopied papers. "You can read the stuff here, but I can't let you have the copies."

"All right if I take notes?"

"Yeah, I guess it wouldn't hurt anything," he decided.

While Fouts dug into his breakfast I read the incident report. It's a standard form completed by the first officer responding to a call. In the academy, they teach you to be concise and exact and to leave matters of opinion out of it.

The responding officer, a J. I. Johnson, wrote that he'd been dispatched to the 7000 block of Bankhead Highway at 3 P.M. Friday, March 19. I tried to envision where that might be. There was an Atlanta Housing Authority project, the whimsically named Garden Homes, I think it was called, somewhere along that stretch of road. I wondered if it was near where Patti's car had been found. A witness had seen someone stripping hubcaps off a new black Lexus stopped at an intersection there.

By the time Johnson arrived at the scene a crowd had gathered around the car. Someone in the crowd informed the officer that there were two bodies in the car.

The officer found a white female slumped over the steering wheel. No pulse. Large caliber gunshot wound to the forehead, over the right eyebrow. Massive head injuries where the bullet exited the head.

I swallowed the bile that rose in my throat. "Massive" was cop code for saying that the back of her head had been blown away. I blinked away the image of Patti's head, shattered like an overripe canteloupe.

A white male child, age unknown but approximately eight to ten years old, was stretched across the backseat of the vehicle. Boy's breathing was regular, but there was swelling over the cheek area and a laceration, apparently from a blow to the head. The child was actually conscious but frightened by the crowd around the car. He was unable to give a coherent statement at that time.

The Cobb Department of Family and Children's Services had been notified of the child's condition and a caseworker was being dispatched to Cobb General Hospital where the child was being taken by ambulance.

At three-thirty P.M. the Cobb Medical Examiner, Dr. Bert Josephson, had arrived on the scene and pronounced the victim dead, at which time the body was transported by Metro Ambulance to the Cobb County Medical Examiner's office.

I looked up from the report. Fouts was pushing bits of egg around on his plate with a piece of toast.

"Her purse and ID were not in the car?" I asked.

"Correct," he said. "We think they were stolen, hopefully by the murderer and not by some of the crowd hanging around the car."

"Okay. What about supplemental reports?"

He kept on chewing and shook his head no. "Nothing typed up yet. Our unit doesn't have clerical help on weekends. Budget cuts."

"Notes?" I asked hopefully.

He swallowed and took another sip of coffee. "Best I could do on such short notice was to dig around on a couple of desktops. Everybody else was long gone when you called. I scanned what I could find. What else do you need to know?"

"The incident report doesn't give the witness's name," I pointed out.

"Anonymous caller," Fouts said. "We did a door-to-door last night, came up with squat."

"Is that Garden Homes right there?"

"Yeah. You know what it's like in these projects."

I did know. Everybody wants to complain about crime in Atlanta's housing projects, but when it comes down to cooperating with the cops nobody ever sees or hears anything. It was downright amazing how many blind, deaf people these communities seemed to contain. And surprising how young the blindness set in, too.

"Have you heard the tape of the call reporting it?"

"I listened to it this morning," Fouts said. "Scratchy voice. A man's voice. Background traffic noises. The call came from a pay phone outside the Popeye's Fried Chicken there at Bankhead and Riggs Road."

"Do you have a transcript of the call yet?"

"Too early," he said. "But basically the caller said a nice new car was parked at a stop sign at that intersection there. The caller said he heard a gunshot, and when he looked, he saw the car parked there and a black woman stripping hubcaps off it."

"A black woman," I said, puzzled.

Fouts shrugged. "It's an equal opportunity world, Garrity. We've got woman lawyers, judges, astronauts, cabinet members, and car thieves."

"And murderers," I added.

"That too," he agreed.

"After they took Dylan to the hospital, did he make a statement?"

"Eventually. At first he was so hysterical we couldn't get anything out of him, even if the doctors had let us near him, which they wouldn't. They gave him some kind of shot and he slept for three or four hours, and when he woke up he insisted on trying to tell one of our people what had happened."

"Didn't he tell you his name and his mother's name and how to reach the family?"

"By the time the doctors and caseworkers let us question him, yeah, he told us his name. But by that time we'd already run the tag and VIN on the car, and we'd reached the guy who sold the car to Mr. McNair."

"What did Dylan say?"

Fouts frowned. "To tell you the truth, we're not a hundred percent sure we understood him, or vice versa. What we were able to piece together was that he fell asleep in the backseat of the car shortly after his mother picked him up at school. His mother tells him they've got to run an errand before they go home. Next thing he knows, he hears a voice, then his mother screaming, and a loud noise. Then somebody hits him on the head."

"Can he describe the assailant?" I'd unconsciously slipped back into cop talk.

"Scary black man," Fouts said.

"That's it?"

"Afraid so," he said. "We've asked Mr. McNair to let us have Dylan work with a sketch artist to see if we can come up with something more specific."

"What did he say?"

"He wants a shrink to talk to the kid first, to see if it'll traumatize the kid too much, but that doesn't happen until Monday."

"Shit," I muttered. The best chances of solving a homicide come in the first twenty-four hours after the crime. After that, details begin to blur, witnesses evaporate, and the trail grows cold. It was Saturday afternoon now, Patti was already twenty-four-hours' dead. I could sympathize with Bruce, he was truly worried about his child, but the police would have to have more to go on before they could start looking for Patti's killer.

"Anything found at the scene?" I asked.

"No shells if that's what you're wondering about. From the description the kid gives, and the head wound, we think it was a thirty-eight. So many people were standing around the car by the time our officer got there that the crime scene was nearly a total loss."

"And this rain doesn't help," I added. "So you've got a lot of nothing."

"Looks like it," Fouts agreed. "We're looking at those car-jackings Atlanta's had this year, seeing if this one fits the pattern. And we're working some other angles, too."

"Like?"

His lips smiled but his eyes didn't know it. "How close are you to the McNairs, exactly?"

"I told you, Patti and I were actually cousins, but

more like sisters growing up. We hadn't seen that much of each other lately though; her life is so different from mine, and she's busy with the kids and lives out in the suburbs. And she was afraid to drive to Atlanta; that's what makes it so weird that she'd be over on Bankhead Highway. But we usually talked on the phone at least every month or so, and we saw each other every couple of months."

"When was the last time?"

I'd thought about that while I was waiting for Fouts to arrive. We'd gone to the movies together sometime after Christmas, January or early February, I think. It was one of those sensitive women's movies. "Bruce wouldn't go see a Meryl Streep movie at gunpoint," she'd said. We'd watched the movie, then gone to a late dinner. Talked about her kids, my love life, the family. Like that.

"Late January or early February," I said.

"Did she mention any problems she was having?"

Instead of automatically running my mouth I decided to shut up for a minute and think. He motioned to the waitress for a refill on his coffee, then busied himself adding three packets of sugar and two of those little paper cups of creamer. No wonder he was nearly as wide as he was tall.

"If this is a carjacking why are you asking about Patti's personal life?" I asked.

"I thought you were a cop in a former life," he said. "We ask about everything in a homicide. You know that."

I didn't, but he didn't need to know that.

"I guess," I said slowly. "I know Patti had been upset about Dylan. His problem. She and Bruce couldn't agree on how severe it was, or what the best way was to handle it. She said Bruce thought she was over-reacting, being too protective of Dylan. And Bruce said something to me this morning about how expensive that school is."

"Were they having money problems?"

I nearly laughed. "He gave her that new Lexus for an

anniversary present. They live in a house in a subdivision out here where the new houses sell for four hundred and fifty thousand dollars. I know because there's a big sign at the entrance. They've got a house at the lake and a place down on St. Simon's Island. Bruce is a lawyer. I don't think lawyers have money problems these days."

"Did she mention any problems with the marriage?"

I had to think about that. Patti and Bruce had married so young, but they'd always seemed happy to me, even when she was putting him through school and they didn't have a pot to piss in. Edna was always throwing it up to me that I couldn't find a husband and Patti could. And a lawyer, too.

"She didn't say anything about marital problems to me," I said. "And I think she would have if it were true. Why? Has somebody else said there were problems?"

Fouts reached over and took the file folder and placed it in his briefcase, then snapped it shut.

"Were you aware that Mr. McNair never reported to the police that his wife and son were missing?"

"What?" I was stunned. "He told me he was wild with worry. He drove all over town, called all her friends, even had somebody drive up to the lake house to see if they were up there. I just assumed he had reported them missing. Did you ask him why he didn't?"

"He said he was embarrassed."

"Embarrassed?" I said. "What kind of shit is that? Are you sure you understood him correctly? Bruce has a weird sense of humor sometimes."

"I interviewed him last night, myself, at the hospital," Fouts said. "Mr. McNair told me he was reluctant to bring the police in because he thought Mrs. McNair had taken Dylan with her somewhere because they'd had an argument."

"Patti left Bruce?" I said incredulously. "I don't believe it. She adored the man. Did he say what they were arguing about, or why he thought she'd taken off?"

"Mr. McNair said they'd had disagreements about finances, and about the child's problem," Fouts said. His voice and manner were suddenly formal, as though he were reading something from a written statement. "Mr. McNair said his wife had done that once before, taken off without telling him where she was going. That time she went up to the lake house for the weekend, after they'd had a fight. But she called him on Sunday night to tell him where she was. He drove up there, they patched things up, and she came back home. This time he was angry at her for taking Dylan with her, so he got a friend to drive up there to see if she was there. The house doesn't have a phone."

Fouts looked at me, cocking his head to one side. "You had no idea there were any problems with the marriage?"

"Absolutely none," I insisted. "She never mentioned any of this to me. But even if there were problems, that wouldn't mean Bruce would be a suspect, would it?"

He lifted one hip off the seat and reached around in his back pocket for his billfold. Pale, stubby fingers extracted a five-dollar bill that he tucked under the sugar dispenser. He got up and reached for his briefcase.

"Why do I sound like Sergeant Joe Friday when I say this?" he asked. "Everybody's a suspect for now. See?" he said, displaying the first hint that he had a sense of humor. "I told you I sound like Joe Friday."

6

FOUTS WAS STILL STRUGGLING to get the seat belt ends to meet around his middle, so I had to tap on the window to get his attention.

He rolled the window down and I stuck my head in to get out of the rain.

"The car," I said. "Where did they take Patti's car?" Rain dripped down my neck.

"It's at the impound lot out on County Farm Road," he said. "You don't want to see it, trust me on this."

I yanked the hood of my jacket up over my head. "I don't want to, but I think I need to," I told him. "Can you arrange it for me? Please?"

He inhaled sharply and shoved the end of the belt into the buckle. "Can't do it today," he said. "The Saturday intake clerk is a by-the-book hard-ass. My guy won't be in until Monday. Call me then and I'll see what I can do."

Water slopped into my sneakers as I ran to the van. I got in quickly, started the engine, and turned up the heater as high as it could go. The one good thing about this van is the heater. The air conditioning doesn't work worth a damn, but in the winter, that baby will heat up. I pulled off my waterlogged socks and shoes and looked around in the back of the van for something else to put on my cold, wet feet. Like any Georgia cracker, I like barefoot best, but only when the weather is above seventy. I found a pair of thick-soled white clinic shoes, the kind Edna tries to make me wear when I fill in on housecleaning jobs. Didn't have any socks, but the nurse shoes would do.

I had a vague notion of how to get out to Bankhead Highway, so I got back onto 75 and then headed west on 285.

If you go past the Bankhead Highway exit off the interstate, which I recommend, the next exit takes you to Six Flags Over Georgia, the state's biggest amusement park. It ain't Disney World, but where else are you going to find a roller coaster named Scarlett O'Scara?

Should you desperately need to see Bankhead, some judicious door locking and window closing is called for. It had been years since I'd been out this way, but the scenery hadn't improved any.

Metal salvage yards, big-rig truck depots, and blocks of grimy warehouses line both sides of Bankhead, relieved only by the occasional kudzu-covered vacant lot. Every couple of miles there's a sad sack shopping center with a convenience store, laundromat, and cut-rate liquor store.

At one point an abbreviated bridge crossed over a thin, red-mud banked creek and a sign informed me that I was officially out of Fulton County and into Cobb.

Garden Homes was a mile or two inside the county line. Built in the fifties, the project consisted of rows of two-story mustard-colored brick buildings arranged in a series of *C*-shaped alignments, with concrete-slab court-yards in the hollow of each *C*. The truncated roads into the complex were lined with dilapidated cars and a huge rusting dumpster marked the end of each blighted block.

"Oh yeah," I muttered as I slowed down, trying to get a fix on where Patti's car had been found, "this is a garden all right. It's a friggin' paradise."

Just up ahead, on the right, there was a blinking yellow caution light and a fast food joint, a Popeye's Fried Chicken. The sign said this was Riggs Road. I swung right onto Riggs then made a quick left into the restaurant parking lot.

The rain had apparently dampened the neighborhood's enthusiasm for Cajun-style chicken that day. Except for three other cars, I had the parking lot to myself. I pulled into a parking space facing Riggs and Garden Homes and shut off the engine.

Without looking at the notes I'd taken of my conversation with Fouts I knew I was looking at the spot where Patti had been killed.

There was a stop sign at the corner of Riggs. Sodden paper cups and wrappers, half-eaten chicken bones, broken beer bottles, and scraps of yellow crime scene tape were strewn around on the road and the red-mud embankment. Crime in Garden Homes was apparently a popular spectator sport.

I zipped my jacket, got out of the van, and locked it.

Someone had once made an attempt to landscape the narrow strip of dirt between the parking lot and the street, but the grass was long gone and all that was left was red mud, gravel, and more broken glass.

I stepped gingerly on the slimy embankment, half walking and half sliding down the slope to the curb. With my hands thrust into my pockets, I walked up and down the stretch of pavement looking for some sign of what had happened here twenty-four hours before.

The trash was all there was. Cars whizzed by on Bankhead, throwing waves of rainwater in their wake. I kept my head down, trying to reenact Patti's last moments.

If she'd meant to come here at all, she'd come out here from the Interstate, of that I was certain. There was another way to come, from Marietta, out Austell Road to where it intersected with Bankhead. But Patti had a phobia about making left-hand turns on busy roads. She'd even quit going to her favorite hairdresser three years ago when he'd moved into a shop in the Merchant's Walk shopping center, a strip center in the busiest part of East

Cobb that she could only reach by making a series of lefts.

She must have come down Bankhead for a while, and once she'd seen the housing projects she'd made up her mind to turn around and go home. Maybe she'd turned into Popeye's to get something to eat; more likely she'd gone for directions. There was no other reason her car would have been on Riggs Road.

Rather than trying to climb the uphill slope, I walked the two hundred yards down Riggs to the restaurant driveway. I found a roll of damp, wadded-up dollar bills in my pocket. I peeled off a couple and walked inside the restaurant.

The place was empty. I blinked and looked around. Well, almost empty. A rail-thin black kid, maybe seventeen, sat at a booth near the door, his arms on the tabletop, his head resting on his arms. He was fast asleep.

"Excuse me," I said loudly. "Are you-all open? Is anybody working today?"

A voice came from behind the row of stainless-steel cooking vats in the open kitchen area. "KWAN-TAY! Get up. You got a customer."

Kwante stirred, raised his head, looked at me, then jumped to his feet.

"Sorry," he said, flashing a drowsy smile. He hurried behind the counter. "Can I take your order?"

I wasn't actually hungry after my little grilled cheese appetizer. "Uh, yeah, let me have a large iced tea, please."

Kwante looked annoyed. He'd had his nap interrupted for a lousy sixty-nine-cent drink. "That's all?"

I studied the menu mounted overhead. Nothing really appealed. "Oh, and uh, yeah, an order of fries too."

He turned and began drawing iced tea from a dispenser. A young woman in her late teens or early twenties strolled around from behind the cookers carrying a stack of cardboard boxes. She wore the same yellow and red-striped uniform shirt as Kwante, plus a ludicrous looking red beret with a yellow pom-pom on top. There was a badge over her left breast. "Margeneeda, Manager" it said.

She put the boxes on the counter and began filling a chrome dispenser with paper napkins.

"I heard there was a shooting here yesterday," I said, trying to break the ice.

Margeneeda looked up at me. The hair under the hat was short and processed and shiny, the color of cherry Kool-Aid. A hank of it flopped over one eye. A tasteful gold stud glowed on the right side of her nostril.

"We got shootin's all the time 'round here," she said.

"Not a white lady in a Lexus we don't," Kwante said. He was scooping french fries into a paper wrapper.

"I know that's right," Margeneeda said. "That was so sad, that little boy in the backseat. Them peoples thought he was dead, but he just be scared. Once the police came he be cryin'! I heard him cry from right here he be cryin' so loud."

"You were here when it happened?" I asked.

"Uh-huh," she said, preening just a little. "I'm day manager now. I was standing right where Kwante was, cooking some thighs and wings."

"She didn't see nuthin'," Kwante said. "Girl, you so bad." He put the fries in a bag and popped a plastic lid on my cup of iced tea. "A dollar forty-five," he said.

I gave him the two soggy ones, and he gave me the change.

"She didn't see nuthin' and I didn't see nuthin'," he informed me. "We had a mess of people in here yesterday. We heard a pop. Thought it was one of the MARTA buses backfiring out on Bankhead. Awhile later all these peoples were running out to the corner there." He motioned toward Riggs Road. "And then here come the police and the ambulance."

"But neither of you noticed the black car before then?" I asked.

Kwante shook his head no. "Naw-uh," Margeneeda

said. "I mighta seen it, but I didn't pay it no attention. You know?"

"How about that pay phone out there?" I asked. I had noticed it on my way into the restaurant. "Did you notice anybody using it just before the police came? Or did anybody ask to use your phone in here? A white lady with a little boy around nine years old?"

"Everybody asks to use it. This here's a business phone," Margeneeda said. "Can't nobody use it. And like Kwante said, we were busy yesterday. Church group from Mt. Zion A.M.E. come in on a bus and we did thirty-two box lunches."

"Was it just the two of you in here yesterday?" I asked. "Could somebody else have seen anything?"

"Nah-uh," Margeneeda repeated. "Lakeesha was sick yesterday. Sick today, too."

"Sick of working," Kwante put in slyly. They both laughed at this joke. I took my bag of french fries and my drink and went back out to the van.

I took a long sip of the tea and nearly spat it out. It was rancid. I touched one of the fries. Hard as nails. Probably left over from the day before. Kwante and Margeneeda wouldn't be named Popeye's Employee of the Month anytime soon.

As I got ready to pull out of the parking lot back onto Riggs Road I noticed a car pulling into the restaurant's drive-through window. "Save your money," I wanted to shout, but the car was too far away and I'd gotten wet enough already. "Let the buyer beware," I muttered. I locked the car doors as I turned left onto Bankhead.

7

WHEN I NOTICED THE RED Ford parked in the driveway at home I nearly backed out and turned tail.

I knew that "How 'Bout Them Dawgs" bumper sticker. It was my sister Maureen and her subhuman husband, Steve. Edna must have talked them into going with her to Patterson's for Patti's visitation hour.

It was just like those two to pull into what they knew was my parking slot in the driveway, forcing me to park on the street and make another dash through the rain.

The kitchen was warm and steamy; it smelled like baked ham and warm pound cake. Edna didn't bother to turn around when I banged the kitchen door shut behind me. She was standing at the sink, trying to coax a pink Jell-O salad out of its mold and onto a lettuce-lined platter.

"Take those wet shoes off before you track up my clean floor," she said sharply.

"Whose floor?" I asked, but I did as I was told. I opened the oven door and warmed my cold, wet backside in front of the heat that was supposed to be baking her squash casserole.

"Where's Fred and Ginger?" I asked, glancing around. Edna was alone in the kitchen.

"Shhh," she hissed. "They'll hear you. Steve's in the den asleep on the sofa. He worked a double shift last night. Your sister's in there too, watching something on TV."

"Probably roller derby," I said. "So what's the deal, couldn't you rope Kevin into going with you tonight?"

Edna turned to face me, wiping her hands on the dish towel that she'd tied around her waist. "He's meeting us there. Steve and Maureen are going to drive with me. You'll be the only one of our family not to show up."

"What about Brian?" I reminded her.

"If you live west of the Mississippi, you're automatically exempted from mandatory attendance at weddings, funerals, baptisms, and first communions." The voice came from the doorway. It was Maureen, my beloved sister.

I've been continuously pissed off at Maureen since kindergarten. She's always been shorter, thinner, and cuter than me. Also dumber and meaner. We don't have a whole lot in common, aside from the family bond, so I find it easier if I just avoid seeing her except for inescapable family events like this one.

Maureen was dressed in a long-sleeved, high-necked black dress with a small gold cameo pinned at the throat. Her light brown hair was frizzed in a halo around her head and she wore black three-inch spike heels, making her stand all of five foot two.

"The Sicilian widow look is you," I said, giving her a grudging compliment. "Don't I recognize that pin?"

She pulled the formfitting dress over her flat butt and did a little wriggle. "The black was so plain. Mom said you wouldn't mind if I borrowed Grandma's brooch. I'll give it back tonight, okay?"

Edna gave me the look. "Fine. No problem. Help yourself to anything at all. Need some underwear or panty hose as long as you're in the neighborhood?"

"Yours would be miles too big," she said. "Thanks anyway."

I had some choices here. I could slam her in the face

with Edna's still warm pound cake. I could reach over and rip my pin off her scrawny little neck. Or I could retreat to my bedroom and hide out until Maureen went away. I chose the bedroom and locked the door behind me.

After peeling off my soggy clothes I pulled on a pair of Mac's oversized gray fleece sweatpants and a raggedy old Atlanta Police sweatshirt, and stuck my feet into a pair of fleece-lined leather house shoes. It felt great to be dry and warm again.

While I was getting dressed I found a note from Mac on my pillow. "Callahan, I'm home if you need me. Mac."

I considered calling him but decided against it. It was a long ride through the rain from Alpharetta. And besides, I'd be going out after a while.

Instead I decided to get some work done on the computer. This year had been the year of technology for me and the House Mouse. I'd taken out a credit union loan and bought myself a crackerjack little personal computer. I've slowly been transferring all our clients into a database, along with employee files, payroll and tax information. All the girls except for Jackie were terrified of the computer. Baby and Sister, our two senior Mice, were particularly suspicious of the computer age.

"Computers is what do Social Security checks," Baby had pointed out. "Me and Sister know all we want to know about computers. Don't be puttin' nothin' in there 'bout us. We can't lose our Social check."

I settled into my chair, pulled it up to the mahogany worktable I'd picked up at an estate sale, and started to work. I guess I sort of lost myself in what I was doing, because when Edna knocked on the door it was almost seven o'clock.

Edna wore a dark blue suit and a prim little print blouse. Funeralizing clothes. She looked at my sweats and sniffed. "We're leaving for Patterson's now. I don't guess you've changed your mind about going?"

"Nope," I said. "I'll be at the funeral tomorrow."

"All right," she said in that martyred tone of hers. "I left you a plate of dinner in the kitchen. I'll be back around ten, I guess. We're going to take this food by Jean's after we leave Patterson's."

"I'll be gone when you get back," I said. "I've got to meet Bucky over at the Euclid Avenue Yacht Club. I shouldn't be too late, though."

She pursed her lips. "Bucky Deavers. Does that mean you're still intent on poking around in this thing and getting the family all upset?"

"I intend to find out everything I can about Patti's murder, yes," I said. "If that upsets somebody, I'm sorry, but I will not back off."

Edna's face clouded. Then she was poking me in the chest with her index finger.

"Stop this, you hear me? Stop it right now, Julia Callahan Garrity. Your aunt Jean is absolutely destroyed by all this. Bruce and the children are numb with grief. Poor Dylan, he'll probably be in therapy the rest of his life after what he saw yesterday. I won't have you doing this to my family. Do you hear me?"

I couldn't help but hear her. Hell, the crowd at Patterson's could probably hear her. Maureen came clicking hurriedly down the hall toward my bedroom. She stopped in the doorway. "What's wrong, Mama?" she asked, taking Edna's arm.

Edna wrenched it away from her. "Nothing. I can't talk any sense into this sister of yours. And I can't talk her into going with us. Let's go before we're late."

Maureen's eyes narrowed to thin little slits. "Nobody tells Miss Callahan Garrity anything. You oughta know that by now, Mama. Let's go. 'Bye," she said pointedly to me.

"'Bye," I said back.

After she'd left I wandered out to the kitchen. A plate sat on the counter, covered with a clean linen dish towel. I peeked under the covering. There were slices of ham, sweet potato casserole with pecan and brown sugar topping, crumb-topped squash casserole, butter beans swimming in bacon-scented juice, a couple of deviled eggs. She'd popped a tiny corn muffin on the side. Another plate held an inch-thick slab of coconut pound cake and a dollop of Jell-O salad. I sighed. No wonder I could never lose weight. I stood at the counter and picked at the food with my fingers. The Garrity weight-loss theory contends that if you don't use a fork the calories only count for half. I stared out the window at not much of nothing. Rain gurgled as it streamed from a broken downspout, and a moth fluttered around the back-porch light.

I thought of the back-porch light at Aunt Jean's house, and how, in high school, Patti would unscrew the bulb slightly so that her father wouldn't catch her necking out there after dates. Sometimes we'd double-date and spend the night at Patti's, sneaking out in the middle of the night to ride around the parking lot at McDonald's or to buy a pack of Virginia Slims at the 7-11.

Patti had been fearless back then—wild in the early seventies' kind of way, which mostly meant drinking beer or going out with boys whose futures included the county vo-tech rather than Georgia Tech or Emory or even Georgia. She'd spent most of her senior year of high school on restriction for various infractions of the rules.

I wondered when the wildness had worn off. When had a nervous suburban car-pool mom moved into the body of that reckless teenager?

After a few more nibbles I took the plate and dumped the food into the trash. Funeral food held no appeal.

The house seemed cold and empty. I wandered back to my bedroom and sat back down at the computer.

Almost without thinking I found myself opening a new file, naming it PMcNair. If I was going to dwell on Patti, I might as well make some use of the morbid depression I felt enveloping me.

Typing as quickly as I could, I wrote down everything I'd learned that day: Bruce's account of Patti's disappearance, the information I'd gotten from Charlie Fouts, what I'd learned at the crime scene, and the little Aunt Jean had been able to tell me.

Reading back over my notes, I saw the holes and inconsistencies again. What had Patti been doing in such an out-of-the-way place as Bankhead Highway? What had she and Bruce been fighting about? Had anyone seen anything at that intersection? A long bank of Garden Homes apartments overlooked that corner. Surely someone had been on their porch or looking out their kitchen window around that time.

Under the heading of "Things to do" I typed "Go door-to-door at Garden Homes." Then I added:

Talk to Patti's friends and neighbors. Best friend? (I couldn't remember the name of the woman who'd hosted the baby shower for Dylan. Maybe she'd be at the funeral tomorrow.)

See car at impound lot.

Talk to Megan and Caitlin and Dylan.

Talk to Fouts again.

It was all I could think of for the moment. I glanced at the clock radio on my bedside table. Nine-thirty. The Yacht Club was only a few minutes away, but the walls of the house were closing in on me by the second. Maybe Bucky would be early. Or I could always shoot the breeze with Tinkles, my favorite bartender-chef.

The rain had swept most of the punkers, bikers, freaks, geeks, and wannabees off the streets of Little Five Points. There was a slot right in front of the Yacht Club. It wasn't until I'd pulled in and parked that I realized I'd rushed out of the house without bothering to change. My feet were still encased in my house shoes.

The windows of the Yacht Club were fogged over, but it didn't look terribly crowded. What the hell, maybe I'd start a new fashion trend. My slippers looked a lot more comfortable than the black lace-up paratrooper boots I saw on the two young blonde chicks coming out of the bar.

I found a table in the front window, where Bucky would see me right off. I glanced around, looking for a familiar face. Tinkles was behind the bar, shooting the breeze with a hard-bitten redhead who wore an outsized nose ring and a black T-shirt proclaiming "Dyke Power."

When he looked up, I gave him the nod and he reached into the under-bar cooler, bringing out an icy bottle of Miller Genuine Draft Light, which was my current favorite beer du jour.

There were waitresses who were supposed to be taking orders, but it was a slow night, so the girl on my station was playing darts. Tinkles brought the beer over and sat down.

"Place is dead," I said, taking a long pull on the beer.

"I can stand it this once," he said. "Where's your squeeze tonight?"

"Home, I guess," I said. "You seen Bucky Deavers tonight? We're supposed to meet."

Tinkles looked around the room, swiveling so I could see the softball-sized bald spot that nestled in the gray-brown frizz of his hair. With his short, tubby build, round face, and beatific smile, Tinkles looks like a cartoon monk.

"Here he is now," he said, nodding toward the door, which was just opening.

Bucky Deavers has a thing about costumes. Every three months or so he gets into a new phase. The last time I'd seen him he was in his Harley-Davidson mood. Tonight he'd settled on a sort of Hoot Gibson motif. Tight black shirt with silver rope accents and pearl buttons. Tight white jeans. Ridiculous high-heeled cowboy boots in some strange leather I'd never seen before, and an at least twenty-gallon black cowboy hat with a feather cockade in the front.

The tall muscular black guy who trailed behind

Bucky wore wire-rimmed glasses, blue jeans, and a faded blue pullover sweater.

"Holy shit, Deavers," Tinkles called out. "You gettin' up a posse or something? What the hell kind of getup is that?"

Without looking in our direction, Bucky touched his companion's elbow lightly, guiding him toward our table.

"Tyler King, this is Callahan Garrity," Bucky said, squeezing himself into a chair. King shook my hand, smiled briefly, and sat down. Under the glasses the bridge of his nose was scarred where it had been broken more than once. When he smiled I saw a small chip out of one of the even white front teeth.

Tinkles was oblivious to the fact that he hadn't been introduced to our guest.

"Hey, Tyler King," he said, snapping his fingers. "I know you. Sweet Thing King. You played wide receiver for Tech, when? Lemme see, seventy-nine, wasn't it? What're you doing hanging around with a sorry sumbitch like Deavers here?"

King might have blushed a little. He definitely wasn't smiling anymore. "Nobody calls me Sweet Thing anymore," he said. "That was a media deal. Long time ago, you know? I'm in law enforcement now. Deavers here is a colleague, you might say."

Tinkles went back to the bar, poured a pitcher of beer and grabbed a bowl of chips, then came back to the table, sitting down between King and myself.

"Sweet Thing King," he kept saying. "Helluva ballplayer. Helluva pair of hands. I had season tickets that year. Saw every home game. You coulda gone pro, you know it? Sweet Thing King."

King squirmed every time Tinkles repeated his name. Finally I could take no more. "Look, Tinkles," I said kindly, "we need a little privacy now, if you don't mind. This is a business meeting, sort of."

He looked hurt, for just a minute. "Sure thing,

Callahan," he said. "You should have told me. I'm too busy to be messing around with you anyway." He took one last swipe at the table with his bar towel and wandered off, muttering to himself. "Sweet Thing King. I remember that N.C. State game."

When he was out of earshot, I turned to Tyler King. "Sorry about that. Tinkles means well. He's a major Tech fan. He'll probably go home now and look you up on his old game videos."

"It's all right," King said, flashing a smile that made his round, smooth cheeks look like twin russet apples. "I run into guys like that a lot now that I'm back in Atlanta."

"Back?" I said. "Aren't you with the Atlanta PD?"

"He's a fed, Callahan," Bucky said. "FBI."

I put my beer down on a waterlogged coaster. "I thought you said you were bringing some Atlanta detective who knows about all these carjackings. What gives?"

King wrapped long, surprisingly slender fingers around his glass. "Our office is working with Atlanta on the carjackings, and as of this morning, with Cobb County on your cousin's murder, too."

"The FBI?" I asked. "Since when?"

"Since Congress made carjacking a federal crime last fall," King said. "You remember that carjacking in Maryland, in ninety-two? Two guys forced their way into this lady's BMW while she was stopped at a stop sign. Her two-year-old daughter was in the back, and as one of the guys drove off, the lady's arm got caught in the seat belt. They put the kid out of the car after half a mile, but they dragged that poor lady another mile and a half before they ran up against a fence to try to dislodge her."

I did remember the case and winced at the details of the crime.

"I didn't realize carjackings had gotten all that bad," I said.

"Bad enough that the FBI's got a task force working on it," Bucky said. "Tyler's it for Atlanta."

"Got transferred from Scottdale four months ago," King said. "We had more than six hundred carjackings in Atlanta in ninety-two alone," he said. "But now, most of 'em don't wind up as homicides. Your cousin, unfortunately, was in the minority."

"What usually happens with a carjacking?" I wanted to know. "How do they go down?"

"All different ways," King said. "But there is a sort of pattern. Usually it's two to four guys, but not more than that 'cause they can't all fit in the car."

"And they pick luxury cars like Patti's Lexus?" I suggested.

"Not necessarily," King said. "See, carjacking's different than a regular car theft. Car thieves like Jettas and Lexuses because they're easy to get rid of. There's a ready market for them, or the parts. A carjacking though, these guys are usually planning on using the car to rob somebody else. They don't plan to keep the car for long because they know it'll be entered on the national computer, probably within an hour. These guys, they'll steal a car, ride around in it, maybe pull an armed robbery, maybe just go joyriding, get in a high-speed chase with the cops, then they drop the car or trash it on purpose."

"Yeah, but how does it go down?" I repeated. "Exactly."

He took a sip of beer and flicked a bit of foam from his upper lip.

"Like I said. Different ways. Sometimes they'll stake a car out in a parking lot, wait for the owner to show up and unlock it, disarm the car alarm if it looks like there is one. Then they'll jump him. Or somebody could be sitting at an intersection, the bad guys come up and stick a gun in the window and force the driver out. Looks like that could be what happened to your cousin."

"Only Patti never got a chance to get out," I said bitterly. "The animals blew her head away in front of her little boy."

"I know," King said soberly. "I'm sorry about that. I understand the boy was pretty torn up."

"Who's doing all these carjackings in Atlanta?" I asked.

King looked embarrassed. "Hate to say it. Mostly black males between the ages of twenty and thirty."

"Dylan told the cops it was a scary black man," I said. "Could it be gangs or something like that?"

"Not real gangs, not like in L.A. or Chicago," King said. "These guys in Atlanta may hang out together, but it ain't no real gang. You catch one guy, before you've read him his rights he's turning his buddies. Now a true gang, nobody sings. Nobody. These guys in Atlanta, they're just playin' at being bad."

I picked up a chip and nibbled the edge, slowly. "What kind of clearance rate do you have on carjackings? Do you ever catch these guys?"

"Well, it's hard to solve 'em unless the perps do something stupid," King said. "It's all a crime of opportunity, so you can't predict when or where it'll happen again. And it's hard to get a good description. Most people see their assailant for just a few seconds before they're forced out of their cars. They give it up and take off running. When they do get to a phone, half the time they have to go home and change their underdrawers and look up the tag number of their car because they don't know the license number offhand. All we get is a generic description of the perp."

"A young black guy wearing a warm-up jacket, carrying a big-ass gun," Bucky suggested.

"That's the dude," King agreed.

I picked at the paper label on the beer bottle, rolling the foil between my thumb and forefinger. "How closely does Patti's case resemble the others in Atlanta?"

King looked unhappy. "Too early to know. Charlie Fouts, one of the Cobb guys, faxed me some stuff this morning. In general, I'd say they look similar in some ways. But only one of the other cases ended in a homicide."

"Do you have a line on anybody in particular?"

King caught Bucky's eye. Bucky nodded. "There's some people been pulling home invasions this winter, Callahan. Real bad guys. They bust in the door of a house, storm the place, tie people up, knock 'em around. A couple of times women have been raped and sodomized. They clean the place out, threaten to kill everybody if anybody moves, then they leave. Sometimes they take cars with 'em. We think it could be some of the same people."

"Why?" I said. "The crimes don't sound too similar to me."

Bucky tried on an enigmatic smile. It didn't take. "Informants," he said.

"But nothing you care to share with an old and trusted colleague," I suggested.

"They're not my informants," Bucky said.

"They're mine," Tyler King said quickly. "And there's nothing to tell yet. We're working on it. We've got a lot to do yet. That's all I can tell you. How about you? You got anything we should know about Patricia McNair?"

I'd finished my beer and didn't feel like having another. Funeral tomorrow.

"Her husband didn't report her missing," I said. "Did you know that?"

King nodded. "Happens all the time. You used to be a cop. You know that. Or is there more to it than that?"

I wasn't sure. Suddenly it felt disloyal to be airing family laundry to this FBI man I'd just met. I dug in my pocket, came up with one of my House Mouse business cards, and handed it to him. "I'm going to the funeral tomorrow. Maybe I'll hear something. This is my home and office number. You got a number where you can be reached?"

He pulled a slim billfold from his hip pocket and fished out a card on thick vellum stock. Tyler King. Special Agent.

I looked at the card, then back at him. "Hey. How come they used to call you Sweet Thing?"

He scowled. "I was the eighth child, only boy. My grandmama, she used to make over what a sweet thing I was. Some wiseass sportswriter interviewed her after I signed with Tech in seventy-six. He put it in the paper, and everybody picked up on it after that. Don't nobody call me that anymore."

"Okay," I said, sorry to have asked. He stalked out of the Yacht Club as I was putting money on the table to pay our tab. That's when I noticed what a fine, tight behind Tyler King had. I'd be willing to bet there was at least one lady in Atlanta who still called him Sweet Thing. And I didn't think she was anybody's grandma.

8

BUCKY WATCHED ME watching Tyler King leave. "And you call me a lech," he said, wagging his finger in my face. "I thought you were living with that old dude, the guy who works for Fulton County."

I pushed his hand out of my face and poured us both another beer from the pitcher Tinkles had brought. "Just because I'm on a diet doesn't mean I can't go to the grocery store."

Bucky held up both hands in surrender. "All right, I stand corrected. You get what you needed from King?"

I sipped my beer and considered Bucky's face. A poker player he's not. He wore a goofy half-grin that told me he thought he knew something I didn't. Fortunately, one of Bucky's more endearing qualities is his tendency to run his mouth when he's got a snootful of beer. I had two twenties in my pocket and I intended to spend them both if that's what it took to get him to spill his guts.

"You were going to tell me about those other carjackings," I reminded him.

"Oh, yeah," he said, pawing through the crumbs at the bottom of the chip bowl. "I looked at the reports. They're all still considered active." He glanced longingly at the table next to ours, where a guy with a blue mohawk was digging into a cheeseburger.

"You hungry?" I asked. "Dinner's on me tonight."

Bucky half-stood from his chair, scanning the room until he spotted Tinkles. "Garçon," he yelled, snapping his fingers.

After a lengthy discussion, Tinkles agreed to fix Bucky a plate of his special chicken fajitas, with a side of guacamole salad. I poured Bucky another beer and got out my notebook. "Give," I said.

"Let's see," he said, taking a long gulp. "The first one happened in September, like the first Friday night of the month. This chick, she's like twenty-two, working her first job out of college, Daddy bought her a new red Blazer. She's been partying with friends at The Raccoon Lodge, you know the place, right there in Buckhead? She'd parked several blocks away behind The Buckhead Men's Shop; didn't want to pay for valet parking. She's unlocking the Blazer, gets in, and before she can shut the door a black guy opens the passenger side door, holds a shotgun to her head, and another guy appears at the door on the driver's side. She panics, screams, and the guy with the shotgun beats her on the head with it. They drag her out of the car, still screaming, beating and threatening to kill her. They hit her again, hard, straight in the face, and she passes out."

"Jesus H. Christ," I said. "The Buckhead Men's Shop? That's where we used to go to buy our uniforms for parochial school. Right in Buckhead? I can't believe it."

"She couldn't believe it either," Bucky said. "Lucky for her, some other guy from Jonesboro was also too cheap to pay for valet parking that night. He found her an hour later, in a pile of cardboard boxes near the store's dumpster. Her jaw and nose were broken, half her front teeth were knocked out, and she had a concussion. They took her car, her purse, and her jewelry."

An involuntary shiver ran down my spine. You never get used to hearing about violence so close to home, not even when it's been a part of your job for a long, long time.

"Three weeks later," Bucky said, "same thing, only this time at Underground Atlanta. A dentist, thirty-two, is parked in that lot over by the New Georgia Railroad. He's walking to his car, it's about two A.M., and he notices a black guy sitting in a car parked next to his Miata. The dentist is a white guy from Decatur, so he's nervous. He gets his keys out and he's gonna get in his car and leave as fast as he can. Before he gets the key in the lock, somebody grabs him from behind. The black dude jumps out of the other car and the dentist, he's scared shitless now, drops the keys and manages to wrestle away from the guy holding him. So he takes off running, and when he's like a hundred yards away, the guy in the car pulls out a shotgun, pumps once, fires and misses. The dentist pees in his pants but keeps running. When he gets back with the cops his car's gone, of course, and there's a big as hell hole in a Buick that could have been the dentist."

"Did the dentist realize how lucky he was?" I asked. "It sounds like these guys play for keeps."

"He knows," Bucky said soberly. "Especially after he read in the *Atlanta Constitution* about the black guy who got killed at the MARTA station."

"Was that the architect who was waiting to pick up his wife after work?" I asked. Like everybody in Atlanta, I'd read about that murder. It was particularly awful. This young guy had parked his new pickup truck in the "kiss-ride" space at the Eastlake MARTA station. He'd had his radio on and his windows open, and he was reading some work papers. Somebody put a gun to his ear and pulled the trigger. They dragged the body out of the car, dumped it, and took off. His wife got off the train just in time to see a crowd of people standing around her husband's body.

"I thought the cops made an arrest in that one," I said.

Tinkles brought a sizzling skillet full of chicken to the table just then and made a great show of arranging the salsa, chicken, guacamole, sour cream, and tortillas just so on the table.

Bucky stopped talking and began building a fajita of Olympian proportions. When he had it ready to eat, he took a bite and chewed slowly.

"They caught a fifteen-year-old kid joyriding the truck through the parking lot of a middle school near the train station," he said, pausing to dab his lips with a napkin. "Turns out the kid found the truck parked with the motor running in front of a liquor store, and he ripped it off a second time. The fifteen-year-old had nothing to do with the carjacking murder, though."

"How do you know?"

He laughed. "When the carjacking was going down, Billy the Kid was in juvie court explaining to the judge why he'd borrowed his mama's next-door neighbor's car."

I reached across the table, got a taco chip, and scooped up some of Bucky's guacamole with it.

"You're not telling me something," I pointed out.

He busied himself building another fajita. "King told you. It's an FBI deal now. Atlanta's working it, but because of the carjacking thing, they've got jurisdiction."

"I know all that," I said. "But you're working the home invasion and armed robbery angle, aren't you? Tell me about that." As an act of encouragement I poured him another beer.

"It's a joint effort," he said. "And it's not really my informant."

"I don't care if the informant is J. Edgar Hoover's dressmaker," I said. "My cousin Patti is dead. The FBI is interested, you're interested, the Cobb cops are interested, I'm interested. If you don't tell me something, I'll get it anyway, you know I will, Bucky. I'm not going to stop asking questions and I'm not going to go away. If it blows the FBI's case, tough shit."

Bucky chewed some more and sipped some more.

When he'd finished everything on his plate he wiped his forehead with the stack of paper napkins Tinkles had provided.

"You're a hardheaded bitch, Garrity," he said. "You know that? You're also not too shabby at what you do. If I tell you anything more, you've got to promise to stay out of the way. You've got to promise to tell me anything you hear, and you've got to promise to keep your mouth shut. Dig?"

"Dig," I promised.

"I'm gonna regret this," he muttered. "All right. Last spring we started hearing about a group of individuals operating out of Marietta. They call themselves The Wrecking Crew. And they are bad. Like King told you, they're not a real gang in the sense that they have gangs in Detroit or Chicago or L.A., but they're organized. And they were specializing in convenience store armed robberies. We had six or seven we figured they were good for just in the city. Cobb had four or five, and DeKalb and Fulton County each had a handful.

"We had nothing. Then they pull a job at a Circle K at West Paces Ferry and I-75. The clerk, a Georgia Tech student from Pakistan, hesitated before he handed over the money, and he got shot in the head for his troubles. This time, there was a screw-up. We got the guy on video. We popped him, and he's just a kid, seventeen. When we pointed out to him that he could go juvie or adult, and if he went adult he was facing the electric chair, he started telling us about The Wrecking Crew.

"He was scared shitless of talking, but he was just as scared of meeting Old Sparky down at Jackson. I went to see him in jail one night, we had a discussion. Like I said, this kid was not eager to chat. Period. But he finally mentioned a name, Maleek, and said Maleek didn't do no gas stations or convenience stores. Maleek was from Miami and he liked to do carjackings and house parties, that's what he called them, house parties."

"Maleek what?" I wanted to know.

"Kid said he didn't know last names. It was the first time he'd talked. I didn't want to push him too hard, so I told him I'd come back the next day, bring some candy bars and cigarettes."

A sense of dread washed over me. "What happened?"

Bucky had drunk a lot of beer, and up until now he'd been enjoying telling his epic and having me pry the details out of him. He wasn't enjoying it anymore. He pushed the beer mug away, still half full.

"Kid hung himself in his cell that night," Bucky said quietly. "Hell of a thing. We were prepared to try him as a juvenile because he was working with us so good. He got scared, I guess."

"Maleek," I said. "Did you ever get a whole name?"

"Maleek Tebbetts," Bucky said, drawing the name out. "Maleek Tebbetts."

9

MARCH IN ATLANTA is an iffy proposition. Lots of rain and a lingering chill that convinces you spring is but a dim figment of your imagination. Then one day you awaken to bright blue skies and the kind of sun kindergarteners draw. You kick off your shoes and walk barefoot through warm, damp soil, then bundle up all the winter woolens and haul them off to the dry cleaners. And the next day it snows three inches, followed by a week of January.

Sunday morning was one of those indecently fine March days. The sun streamed through my bedroom windows and I could hear surprised birds chirping at the feeder outside. I woke when I heard the back door slam shut. Edna must have decided to get a headstart on the funeralizing.

Let her. I took a long, hot shower and washed the last of the smoke from the Yacht Club out of my hair. Then I took a cup of coffee and the newspaper and sat on the front porch, letting the sun warm my shoulders.

I read slowly and deliberately, lingering over the national news and the latest White House follies. Somebody else's troubles held a certain appeal. But I was jolted back to reality when I turned to the local section of the paper. There was a big color photograph of Patti splashed across the top of the page. Patti in a Sunday school dress and a string of pearls. There was a headline screaming something about "Cobb Housewife Gunned Down in Tragic Carjacking."

I turned the paper facedown. I couldn't look at that stranger just now. Another cup of coffee helped. I read the business section, the travel section, sports, even the car ads and the Dow Jones listings. Then I folded each section and stacked it carefully on the steps. And turned back to the local section and forced myself to read about Patti McNair's violent death.

Words like "senseless," "puzzle," and "blood-spattered" seemed to leap from the page. Charlie Fouts was quoted as saying the police were looking at every possible angle. There were statistics about carjackings, a map that showed Bankhead Highway and Garden Homes, and a quote from Bruce offering a $20,000 reward for information leading to the arrest of Patti's killer. Tyler King contributed a non-quote, something about "questioning informants," and Patti's friends eulogized her as a happy, caring friend, mother, and neighbor.

I was still sitting on the porch, staring at the paper, when Mac drove up. He got out and gave me a quizzical look. He was dressed in a dark suit I hadn't seen before, and a starched white dress shirt and polished black lace-up shoes. He was a grown-up. By contrast, I was still in my robe, barefoot, my hair still damp from the shower.

He sat down beside me, kissed me lightly. "It's after noon," he pointed out. "Don't we need to leave soon?"

I sighed. "Better get it over with. Edna left hours ago. I'll be just a few minutes. You read the story in the newspaper?"

He nodded yes. "Get dressed. We'll talk on the way."

It didn't take long for me to decide what to wear. I have a long-sleeved royal blue knit dress I wear in the winter when occasions demand. A flowered silk scarf around the neck. Gold earrings and black low-heeled pumps.

"You look nice," Mac said when I was ready.

We didn't know what to say to each other. We'd been lovers for two years now. He'd seen me through my breast cancer scare, through radiation and my insistence on enrolling in an experimental drug trial. He'd been there after I'd nearly drowned in the river last year, and had let me move in after my house had nearly burned down, but I didn't know now if I was ready to share the naked grief I was feeling.

"You too," I said. He'd vacuumed the Blazer and gotten rid of most of the smell of Rufus, his black labrador retriever. I gave him directions to Our Lady of Lourdes, Patti's church in Marietta.

We rode in silence for quite a way. "You feel like talking yet?" he asked.

I tried to clear the lump in my throat. It felt like an unbaked biscuit. I told him what I'd learned the day before, about walking the place where Patti had been killed, talking to the Cobb police and to Bucky and the FBI agent with the cute butt. I left out the cute butt part.

"You covered a lot of ground yesterday," he said admiringly.

"And came up with a lot of nothing," I said.

"Oh, come on," he said. "It sounds like the police have some decent leads. This Maleek Tebbetts guy, for instance."

"You're right," I admitted. "I just find it so hard to believe that somebody like Patti could cross paths with a character like that, just because of some freaky coincidence, and end up dead."

"Callahan," he said patiently, "people get killed all the time because of freaky accidents. A drunk driver plows into a kid walking home from school. A deer hunter mistakes his best friend for a buck. It's horrible, but it happens. You of all people know that."

I drummed my fingers on the windowsill of the Blazer, enjoying the rhythmic tapping of my nails on the metal. "The problem is that you're talking logic. And I'm dealing with emotions here. Logic tells me there's no reason why someone I know and love can't be a homicide statistic. Emotionally, well, that's another story. I'm not ready to believe that a spirit like Patti's is snuffed out just because she met up with a murdering thug who had something to prove to his gang."

"That's you," Mac said. "It sounds to me like the rest of your family feels differently about this."

I glanced over at him. Mac can be amazingly perceptive, especially at the exact moment you're convinced he isn't paying attention.

"They're in shock," I said. "They're worried about Dylan. He's only nine, you know. I don't think it's occurred to Bruce or the others that he's probably the only witness to his mother's murder. Right now all they're concerned about is getting him to a shrink who'll help him start forgetting."

"You think that's what they really want?" Mac asked. He slowed the car down as we passed a large granite and timber *A*-frame building on the right.

"Turn into the parking lot just past the church," I told him. "Yeah, I know Aunt Jean doesn't want him to dwell on it. And my mother is furious at me for asking so many questions. She says nobody wants this thing to be drawn out."

"Nobody but you," Mac said.

"There's a parking space at the end of this row," I said, pointing to it. "We'll see. But if I am the only one who's willing to get to the bottom of this, that's all right, too. I'm not out to win the Garrity family popularity contest."

The church parking lot was full. It was ten after. I'd deliberately stalled getting ready to leave. We pushed open heavy doors with stained glass inserts depicting the Virgin Mary with hands outstretched to suffering sinners and slipped into the last pew.

A sea of dark suits and well-dressed suburbanites stretched in front of me, blocking most of my view. If I stood on tiptoe I could see a white-robed priest at the altar, swinging a brass incense burner on a chain. The church smelled of candle wax, perfume, and flowers. Stiff banks of gladiolas and spider chrysanthemums stretched across the front of the church. A blanket of pink carnations covered a gleaming cherry coffin. Pink carnations. The kind we wore to the eighth grade prom. I wanted to gag.

We stood, kneeled, and sat. I heard snatches of familiar phrases, mumbled old prayers without thought, making the sign of the cross automatically.

I recognized the priest's voice. Father Mart, the priest who'd said the rosary at Aunt Jean's. He'd just begun to instruct us on the inevitability of death and the certainty of Jesus's love when I felt the bitter coffee rise in my throat. I got up and fled.

Outside, I leaned against a pine tree and heaved. With the toe of my shoe I managed to cover the vomit with a layer of pine needles. I lurched over to another tree and put my head against the cool, grainy bark. The sharp tang of turpentine was an antidote to the suffocating sweetness of the church. I let an ant crawl over my hand, then I flicked it away.

Eventually, the heavy doors opened again, and people began to trickle out. Six men, including my cousins Jack and Michael, walked slowly out, the coffin on their shoulders. A black Patterson's hearse glided noiselessly to the curb, and an attendant got out and opened the back doors. I turned my back to avoid seeing more.

Unbidden, the words to a summer camp song came to mind: "If you should see a hearse go by, you will be the next to die."

"Are you okay?" There was a hand on my elbow. It was Mac.

"Fine. I tossed my cookies over by that tree though, so watch where you step."

His face showed concern. "Are you going to feel up to going to the cemetery? I can take you home instead."

"Better not," I said. "I'm already on Edna's shit list."

The cemetery was in what's left of the countryside in Cobb County. The old cotton fields had yielded to fancy import car lots, shopping centers and office parks. We followed the long procession of cars through a curving stone arch and finally parked, in ragged rows, on the shoulder of the narrow blacktop behind the Patterson's limousines.

The grass was light green and spongy beneath my shoes, and my pointy heels left a neat pattern of holes in the soil. They'd set up a large green tent over Patti's freshly dug grave and someone had carted along a dozen or so large flower arrangements from the church. People were making their way toward the tent. Up ahead I spotted Bruce, one arm around Caitlin on one side, the other around Megan on the other. A woman I didn't recognize at first trailed behind the others, holding a boy's hand. The boy's hair showed wet comb marks and he wore an ill-fitting new blue suit. The woman had short brown-blonde hair. She wore a chic dark red dress. She had Patti's slim hips and long legs. It was the kid sister.

"That's Dylan," I told Mac. "And I think the woman with him is DeeDee, Patti's younger sister. I haven't seen her in years, but Aunt Jean said she's moved back to Atlanta."

"Your aunt is going to need her now, with Patti gone," Mac said.

We kept on the grassy paths between the flat granite headstones and edged under the tent. I could see Bruce's shaggy brown head and the girls, and Aunt Jean, all of them standing close to the edge of the coffin.

Mercifully, Father Mart's voice was low now, and I couldn't make out anything he said. The old camp song came back to me. We'd shouted it from the back of a school bus that summer. Patti had been a junior counselor that year and I had my first bra.

"*They wrap you up in a big white sheet. Drop you down about fifty feet. The worms crawl in, the worms crawl out, the worms play pinochle on your snout. . . .*"

I squeezed my eyes shut, forced myself to think of something else, anything else, to shut out that song.

And found myself saying an act of contrition. "Oh, my God, I am heartily sorry for having offended thee. And I detest all my sins for thy just punishment. But most of all because they offend thee, my God, who art all good and deserving of all my love . . . "

I must have been whispering the words aloud, because Mac dug an elbow in my ribs and gave me a weird look.

"Old habits," I said. He took my hand and squeezed it. Here was warm flesh and blood. I squeezed back gratefully.

The droning prayers finally stopped. Bruce stepped forward, kneeled briefly, and dropped a flower into the open grave. Megan and Caitlin did the same, then stepped back. I could see Dylan, clinging to DeeDee, his shoulders shaking with sobs, his head buried in her arms.

"Let's go," I said. We walked quickly to the car. I was surprised to see a figure leaning against the hood of one of the Patterson's hearses, smoke rising above his head.

It was my cousin Michael. His face was pale and he gave me a quick, mocking smile. "You couldn't take it either?"

I shook my head no. "Michael, this is my friend Andrew McAuliffe. Mac, Michael is Patti's younger brother."

"Baby of the family," he said bitterly, tossing the cigarette to the ground.

"I'm sorry about your sister," Mac said, searching for the right words. "Everyone says she was very special."

"She was," Michael said. He ground the cigarette with the toe of his shoe, daintily, in an almost balletic pose. It struck me for the first time how different Michael

was from the rest of the family. He was fairer, slimmer.
As a child he'd been obsessed with his appearance, crying
if his mother made him wear a shirt he considered unsuit-
able, or a pair of jeans with patched knees. Michael, it
occurred to me, was almost certainly gay. I wondered if
the rest of his family knew.

"How's life in Charlotte?" I blurted out.

"Fabulous," he said. "I'm re-doing an old house in a
great neighborhood. High ceilings, wooden floors, three
fireplaces. I'm going broke of course, but I'm having a
great time."

"Patti always loved old houses," I remembered. "We
used to peek in the windows of those big old mausoleums
in Covington when we'd go visit your Great Aunt Alma. I
always thought she'd end up with a falling-down farm-
house out in the country."

"Yeah, well, Patti changed," Michael said.

"You noticed too?" I said eagerly. "My mother
thinks I exaggerate."

"It's not anything I could put my finger on," he said
apologetically. "And you know, Patti was ten years older
than me. When she left for college I was only eight, and
she never really lived at home after that."

"She'd changed a lot, and recently too," I insisted.
"When we were growing up, she was my hero. She'd try
anything. She was fearless. But lately she'd gotten so, I
don't know, timid, I guess is the word. And all wrapped
up in the church, which came as a shock to me."

Michael smirked. "Oh, yes, she'd gotten to be quite
the church lady from what I hear. This is awful, and I
shouldn't tell you, but DeeDee swears Patti was screwing
that priest. Father Mart."

My shocked expression seemed to amuse him.

"Oh for God's sake, Callahan, grow up. DeeDee
was probably kidding around. Patti would never have
been unfaithful to Bruce. Just forget I said that. I had a
Bloody Mary before church this morning, and I guess

it's gotten me a little tipsy. I've really got to keep my mouth shut."

"Michael," I said, trying to sound like the stern older cousin. "Were you kidding about that priest or not? This isn't funny, you know. Patti was murdered, and if she really was having an affair with someone, that's something the police need to know."

He started patting his pockets nervously, searching for another cigarette.

"I was joking, for Christ's sake," he said. "And if you mention a word of this to anyone, especially the police, I'll never speak to you again, Julia Callahan Garrity. And I mean it."

Mac tugged gently at my arm. "Let's go," he said under his breath. "Everybody's leaving."

He was right. People were trooping back through the grass, getting into their cars and pulling away.

"It was a joke," Michael repeated. "Look. Patti had bought into her life. And she loved the whole package. The tennis teams, country clubs, private schools for the kids. She loved her life just like it was. No way would she jeopardize that just for a roll in the hay with some washed-up priest.

"Uh-oh, here comes Mama. Are ya'll coming to the house?" He looked like he hoped we were leaving for another planet.

Mac looked at me for an answer. I could think of a dozen things I would rather have done that day. Root canals. Oven cleaning. Balancing my checkbook.

"Yeah," I said. "We'll be right along."

10

HALF AN HOUR," I told Mac. We were walking up the front steps of Aunt Jean's house. "We check in with the family, eat a slice of cake, and then we're out of here. I promise."

"Georgia Tech and Duke tip-off at three P.M.," Mac warned. "With you or without you I'm leaving here at two-fifteen Eastern Standard Time. Is that clear?"

It was perfectly clear. Nothing, not even my own funeral, would prevent Andrew McAuliffe from watching his beloved ACC basketball in March. So it was with some sense of urgency that we edged our way around the house, shaking hands, patting backs, and generally letting it be known that we were doing "the right thing."

Edna was presiding over the table in the dining room, slicing ham and dealing it onto a stack of glass plates. She leaned over and gave Mac a peck on the cheek when she saw him. Me she gave a curt nod of the head. I decided to play nice.

"Lovely service," I said.

"I didn't see you there," she said.

"We sat in the back," Mac said quickly. "My fault. I was late getting to your house."

That's what I like about Mac, he thinks quick on his feet.

"I'm out of coffee," I said, inching toward the kitchen. "Can I bring you a cup, Ma?"

"No thanks," she said coolly. "Jean and I drank a whole pot by ourselves this morning."

"I'll stay here and help your mother," Mac volunteered.

The kitchen was as crowded as the rest of the house. I wedged myself into a corner, sipping the coffee and surveying the room. Jack's ex-wife, Peggy, saw me there and waved from across the room, motioning me to join her and a tall thin blonde she was talking to.

"Callahan," she said, "this is Sherrill Mackey, Patti's best friend."

I'd met the gaunt woman in the hot pink linen suit somewhere before, at a dinner party at Patti's house a couple of years before. She'd been plumper then, with darker hair and a less pronounced sag to her jaw.

"We've met," Sherrill said. "For years Patti's told me stories about your exploits as kids."

Aunt Jean poked her head around the kitchen door. "Peggy," she said, "can you come help me out here?"

When Peggy was gone, Sherrill and I stood silent, at a loss for words.

"I can't believe any of this is real," Sherrill said finally. She had big hazel eyes and surprisingly dark lashes and eyebrows for a blonde. "Patti and I talked on the phone at least twice a day. Our kids lived at each other's houses. She was the first number on my speed dial. When I got divorced last year, Patti went to court with me and made me go out to lunch at the Ritz afterward. To celebrate, she said. God this is unreal."

She blinked back the tears, then said in a lower voice, "You're the cousin who's the private detective, right? What do you make of all this?"

I glanced around me. Caitlin and Megan were in the kitchen now, rinsing and stacking plates in the sink.

"Let's go outside for a minute," I said. "It's too crowded in here."

A few others stood around on the back deck, smoking cigarettes, drinking beer, and enjoying the rare afternoon sun. We stood with our backs to the railing, eyeing each other nervously.

"I can't believe it either," I said quietly. "It's hard for me to believe Patti's murder was just some freak street crime. Maybe it was, but I've got a lot of questions. Of course, nobody in the family wants to discuss it."

Sherrill nodded. "Denial. I went through it after my divorce. Is there anything I can tell you, anything that would help? The police asked me all kinds of questions."

I edged closer to avoid being overheard. "When did you last see or talk to her?"

She took a strand of hair and twisted it thoughtfully. "Wednesday, I think. Yeah, definitely. She took me to the dealership to pick up my car after it was serviced. And we were supposed to play doubles Friday, but she called that morning and told me she had to go pick up Dylan at school. I didn't talk to her long because I had to find a substitute to play her match."

"She didn't play? I thought Bruce said she did."

"Uh-uh," she said, shaking her head. "Maybe he just assumed she played."

"Are you saying Patti lied to Bruce?"

Her face reddened a little. "Well, not lied. But Patti didn't always tell Bruce exactly what was going on at home or with the kids. 'A need-to-know basis' she called it."

So much for my image of Patti as the perfect wife and mother. Michael had hinted that she was sleeping with her priest, and now Patti's best friend was insinuating that she kept secrets from her husband.

"So what was going on? Are you telling me there was something wrong with their marriage?"

Sherrill glanced around guiltily. "I feel weird telling you this. It doesn't seem loyal, you know?"

"I know. But it's not like this is just idle gossip. Patti's been murdered. There's a police investigation.

Sooner or later, if there were problems, it's going to come out."

She nibbled on a thumbnail. "Tell me if you see somebody coming, okay? Bruce is still a neighbor."

"What kind of problems were they having?"

"See, maybe it wasn't that big a deal. I don't want to give you the wrong impression—"

"Just tell me," I interrupted, losing patience with her hemming and hawing. "I promise not to jump to conclusions."

"Well, I know there were fights about money. After Dylan was born, Bruce didn't want Patti to go back to work. He was a lawyer, right? He didn't want people to think he couldn't support his family. If it was something that made him look successful, like the cars or the house or the club memberships, money was no object. But he nickel and dimed Patti all the time. She was on a strict household budget—so much for groceries, so much for clothes, like that. And she was always short at the end of the month."

"Did she ever mention whether Bruce was having problems with the law practice?"

"No," Sherrill said. "Patti said Bruce didn't talk much about work. But I just assumed something was up. Suddenly, money was really, really tight. A couple of months ago, we were shopping at the mall and Patti tried to charge a sweater at Rich's. The computers wouldn't let the charge go through. The salesgirl had to call the credit office, and Patti had to get on the phone; it was incredibly embarrassing. Her face was beet red. She put the sweater back and we left the store. I didn't ask what the problem was."

"The kids are in private school, aren't they? Isn't that pretty expensive?"

She rolled her eyes. "I'll say. The girls are at Marist, that's about nine thousand a year, apiece, and I don't even know how much Miller-Shipley is. But I do know Patti had to fight Bruce tooth and nail to get him to let Dylan go there."

"He told me himself that they disagreed about the school," I said. "Did Bruce call you Friday to ask where Patti was?"

"He came over," she whispered. "And as soon as I opened the door and saw him standing there, I knew Patti was in some kind of serious trouble."

"Why?"

"Bruce hasn't set foot in my house since my husband, Ben, left us last year," Sherrill said bitterly. "He told Patti that he didn't want to take sides after we split up. Of course, he plays racquetball with Ben nearly every week."

Sherrill Mackey was a gold mine, a walking, talking jackpot of information.

"Were their problems just about money?" I asked. "Do you think either one of them was, uh, fooling around?"

The sun was shining directly in our eyes now. She held a hand in front of her face to shade it. Just then, Mac's face appeared in the door to the kitchen. He held his wrist out and tapped his watch face. "Ten minutes," he mouthed. I could see Edna's face over his shoulder, watching me, wondering who I was talking to. I winked at her. She frowned and stalked off.

"Bruce I don't know about," Sherrill admitted. "He worked late a lot, or at least he told Patti he was working."

"And what about Patti?"

A smile. "God bless her if she was having a fling. Three or four times this year she called me, wanting me to cover for her."

"What?"

"Yes," she drawled. "Our little Patti. She said if Bruce called looking for her to say that she was at tennis practice, or had taken the kids to McDonalds or something like that. Luckily he never called. I'm a rotten liar."

"Do you have any idea where she really was?"

Sherrill nibbled at her nail again. "She wouldn't say.

And believe me, I bugged the daylights out of her trying to get her to confide in me. She just said she needed her private time."

"There you are," I heard a voice cry out. I turned around and saw DeeDee and Dylan stepping out onto the deck. Damn. I had a long list of things I wanted to ask Sherrill, and now I'd have to play nicey-nice with another of the cousins.

"I've been all over the house looking for you, Julia," she said. "Aunt Edna said you were out here." She gave me a big hug, or rather, she gave my midsection a hug. DeeDee was a good four inches shorter than me, and her hair tickled the bottom of my chin.

"So good to see you," she murmured. "Don't know what any one of us would do without family at a time like this."

"I know," I said, and for want of anything better to do, I patted her back. She was so petite she made me feel like a sheepdog next to a chihuahua.

DeeDee stepped back a little and pulled Dylan, who hung at her side, closer to me. "Can you believe how tall this boy has gotten, Julia?"

Dylan's pale cheeks blushed slightly and he hung his head.

"Hi, Dylan," I said softly. "How are you holding up?"

"Okay," he said, still not looking up.

I'd never heard Patti's son speak in anything but monosyllables. It looked like today would be no different.

DeeDee squeezed his shoulder affectionately. "Dylan, Cousin Julia is talking to you. It's polite to look a grown-up in the eye when they speak to you, remember?"

His eyes solemnly met mine. They were Patti's eyes, gray, with long, dark, curling lashes, and they were swimming in unspoken misery. He had a little freckle at the corner of his right eye in the same spot his mother had had a freckle.

"I. Am. Fine," he said, enunciating slowly, his tongue poking out of his mouth in concentration.

"I'm sorry about your mother," I told him. "She was one of my favorite people in the whole world. We're all going to miss her."

"Okay," he said.

DeeDee bit her lip. She gave Dylan another pat on the shoulder. "Why don't you go inside and ask Aunt Peggy to give you some dessert now? Can you do that?"

"Okay," he said. But he didn't move.

DeeDee knelt down so that her face was level with his. She put one hand on his shoulder and cupped his chin with the other so that he looked directly at her. "Go in the house," she said slowly. "Can you say that?"

He nodded. "In house."

"Good," she said. "Ask Aunt Peggy for some cake. Cake. Can you do that?"

His eyes showed confusion. "No coke. Dad said no."

DeeDee sighed and stood up, smoothing nonexistent wrinkles in her skirt. "When he's upset he has a harder time understanding. He's had a pretty rough couple of days."

Sherrill Mackey stepped closer and held out a hand to DeeDee, who'd overlooked her. "Hi. I'm Sherrill. Patti was my dearest friend. I'm so sorry for your loss."

Dylan looked up at Sherrill and favored her with a sunny smile. "Aunt Sher," he said.

DeeDee grasped Sherrill's hand in both of hers. "Oh, Patti told me how close you two were. And Mama said you've been an angel, helping with all the arrangements. I don't know how we can repay your kindness."

"It's nothing," Sherrill said. "We were neighbors. How about if I take Dylan inside for dessert? We're old pals, right, Dylan?"

He gave her another smile. "Aunt Sher."

Sherrill told me good-bye with the raise of an eyebrow that said "Call me." Then she guided Dylan into the house, leaving DeeDee and me alone.

"I don't know how that child keeps going," DeeDee

said. "He was up at five this morning. I heard noise coming from the den, and when I went in, he was sitting there playing Nintendo. At five A.M."

"You're staying at the house?" I asked. "I know that's a big help to Bruce and the kids."

"Somebody needed to be there," DeeDee said. "And Mama just doesn't have the strength. This whole thing has destroyed her."

"It's destroyed us all," I reminded her. "How are you holding up? Edna said you've been job hunting?"

She sighed and ran her fingers through her short hair. "I guess it's a blessing I've been so busy with the children. I've put the job hunting on hold for now. Bruce has a law practice he can't ignore and until he can get his affairs in order and hire a housekeeper, someone needs to be there for Dylan and the girls."

"Let us know if Edna and I can do anything," I said, feeling a wave of warmth toward her. "I could have one of the girls come over and clean if that would be a help."

"Oh, Julia," she said. "That would be great. I don't know how Patti kept up with everything. She's only been gone a couple of days and the house is a disaster."

"No problem," I said. "I'll have one of the girls over there tomorrow morning."

"There's something else you can do for us," she said, hesitating a little.

"What's that?"

"Quit going around asking all these questions," she said quickly. "I don't mean to be offensive, but somebody has to be the bad guy. Bruce is too sweet. He won't say anything."

I could feel my face getting hot. "Bruce told me he didn't mind talking about it," I said.

"That's just Bruce," DeeDee said. "He's terribly upset. We all are. Every time one of those detectives comes to the door, Dylan just gets hysterical. And the television news. My God. We hid the remote control. All he can watch is Disney or Nickelodeon. We just want this whole thing to be over. Let the police do their job, Julia. They can catch this animal without the family getting all involved, can't they?"

My petite, sweet cousin looked up at me innocently, obviously expecting me to agree with her reasoning.

"I'm sorry, DeeDee," I said. "The last thing I want is to cause Bruce or the children any more pain than they've already had. But there are too many unanswered questions. And I intend to get some answers."

Her eyes flashed and her chin jutted out in an unattractive way. The chihuahua had teeth. "I didn't think I could talk you out of it. But I'll tell you one thing, Julia Callahan Garrity. You are not to go near Dylan. Do you understand? He is in an incredibly fragile emotional state. We won't allow you to harass him with your questions. You stay away, you hear?"

I would have stood my ground and argued, but she whirled around and started to stomp away, running smack into Mac.

"You ready to roll?" he asked anxiously.

"More than ready," I said.

11

WINTER CAME BACK Monday morning. Rain pelted against my bedroom windowpane and I could hear the wind whistling through the leafless oak trees in the side yard.

I'd been awake since four A.M., knees drawn up to my chest, a trick I'd learned as a kid to combat tummy aches. This one wouldn't go away. I was dizzy and nauseous and unbearably hot, with my sweat-drenched nightgown clumped up uncomfortably around my waist.

With effort, I managed to kick the blankets away and turn to look at the clock for the hundredth time that morning.

It was after eight. I felt crappy. Like I was rode hard and put up wet, was how Edna would describe it. But duty called.

"Shit," I moaned, easing out of bed. I've never been a morning person, but since I opened the House Mouse and became my own boss, most mornings I look forward to getting to work.

Not today. As I stood under the shower I mentally reviewed the day's schedule with a growing sense of dread.

It was hopeless. Four new clients, plus our busy usual Monday schedule. Edna was pissed at me, Neva Jean's status was iffy, and I had apparently come down with some kind of stomach crud.

I toweled off, pulled on jeans and a sweatshirt . . . and got back into bed. That's where I was, rolled up in a ball, when I heard the bedroom door open.

"You sick?" Edna asked. I opened my eyes. "Stomach bug," I moaned.

"Well, your timing couldn't be worse," she said, moving to the side of the bed. A cool hand brushed my forehead. "Your skin feels a little clammy," she said grudgingly. "I'll call Mrs. Columbus and tell her we can't make it today. And I'll do the other new ones myself."

"Never mind," I said, sitting up. "I'll be okay. Just a little slow, that's all."

She looked at me doubtfully. "You sure? Your face is sort of gray. You look like shit."

"So I'll cancel my Star Search audition," I said gamely. "I'll be fine. Do we have any ginger ale in the house?"

"Might have a bottle left over from Christmas down in the cellar," Edna said. "I'll take a look."

For once, the smell of coffee perking in the kitchen failed to cheer. In fact, the odor sent me running for the kitchen sink.

I was splashing cold water on my face when Edna came up the basement steps with a liter bottle of Canada Dry. "You sure you're not pregnant?" she asked. "You sound a lot like I did when I was expecting your brother Kevin."

"Very funny, Mom," I said. "It's a bug. A virus of some kind. No big deal."

I got a glass out of the cupboard and poured the ginger ale over exactly one ice cube. Then I busied myself looking for a box of soda crackers, the age-old Garrity remedy for any illness of an intestinal variety.

The back door opened and Ruby came bustling in, followed by Jackie. "Nasty day out there," Ruby said cheerfully, unbuttoning her heavy wool coat and pulling off the scarf she'd tied over her hair. "How are ya'll this ugly old Monday morning?"

"Callahan here has some sort of stomach flu," Edna said. "So she's not moving too fast today."

Jackie took her coat and Ruby's and hung both of them on the coatrack in the corner.

"I read in the paper about your niece, Edna," she said softly. "I'm sorry, real sorry."

Edna sighed and patted Jackie on the shoulder. "Thanks, Jackie. This is one time I'm glad the weekend is over. I don't ever want to go through another one like that again."

From outside we heard a car pull up into the driveway, and the toot of a horn.

"That's Neva Jean," I said, peering out the window.

Swannelle's pickup truck, the one with the monster wheels and the ten acres of chrome, sat in the driveway with the motor running. The rain had slacked off some, and I could see Swannelle himself sitting in the passenger seat.

At least I assumed it was Swannelle. The passenger had what looked like heavy gauze bandages wrapped completely around his eyes, and some kind of rubber tubing running out of his nostrils. Swannelle's black John Deere tractor cap sat atop a familiar-looking set of jug ears.

Neva Jean slogged through the rain puddles, headed for the back door bundled up in Swannelle's red plaid hunting jacket and what looked like black rubber hip boots.

She threw the back door open with a flourish. "I'm here," she said dramatically. "Callahan, gimme the address of them new people. I got Swannelle out in the truck with the heater running. He says he breathes better if he sits upright."

Ruby went over to the door, stuck her head out, and got a good look at the suffering patient. "Oh my Lord," she said in her high-pitched voice. "Swannelle looks bad, Neva Jean. Real bad. What happened to him?"

"Aggravated assault with a can of aerosol roach spray," I said dryly. "How's he feeling, Neva Jean?"

"Not too good," she said, her voice thin and pitiful.

"I believe I'll go out and get a good look," I said, sounding brisker than I felt. "See if I can cheer him up a little."

"Oh now, Callahan," Neva Jean said quickly. "He's taking a little catnap right now. Poor baby was up all night coughin' and spittin' and gaspin' for air. I'll tell him you sent your regards."

But I pulled on my jacket and went outside, walking unsteadily toward the truck. Before I got within five feet of it I could hear country music pouring out of the rolled-up windows.

It sounded like George Jones doing a duet with a wounded bloodhound. Swannelle's head rocked back and forth vigorously to the beat, the bandages over his eyes making him oblivious to my presence.

"He stopped loving her today," Swannelle warbled.

I edged closer to the door to get a better look. The patient was dressed in faded blue flannel pajamas and a bathrobe from the Eisenhower administration. On closer inspection the bandages turned out to have been constructed of toilet paper and adhesive tape. There were thin plastic tubes running out of his nostrils all right, but the tubes ended at his waistline, connected to nothing. When the song ended, Swannelle reached in a Mrs. Winners bag at his side and pulled out a cat's-head sized sausage and biscuit sandwich. He took a bite that very nearly demolished it.

"How ya' doin', Swannelle?" I said, yanking the truck door open.

He exploded into a spasm of heart-rending coughs and sputters, at the same time whisking the remains of the biscuit out of sight.

"Poor," he wheezed, "right poor. Is that you, Miss Edna? I can't see too good with these here bandages. Doc said I got vertical spigotosis of the aurora borealis. Might be a thirty or forty percent loss of vision. That Neva Jean, she's an angel, ain't she? Taking care of me in my hour of need?"

"Yeah. She's a regular Florence Nightingale," I said, reaching over and yanking the toilet paper off his head. The toilet paper came off, but the adhesive paper needed another healthy rip.

"Ow," Swannelle yelled, rubbing at the reddened skin around his eyes. "Oh, it's you, Callahan. How come you're yanking at my bandages like that?"

"I got a vision problem of my own," I said, suppressing a laugh at the ridiculous sight of a grown man with tufts of toilet paper fluttering from his forehead and aquarium tubing running out of his nose. "I can't see why I shouldn't fire Neva Jean for trying to pull a stunt like this when she knows how busy we are today."

"Aw, now, Callahan," he sputtered, but I slammed the truck door shut and marched back into the house.

The kitchen curtain flapped where Neva Jean had been peeking out at us, but when I walked in she was seated at the table, innocently sipping from a can of Mountain Dew.

"Nice try, Neva Jean," I said, leaning back against the kitchen counter. My stomach lurched, but I swallowed hard.

"You think that little charade with Swannelle dressed in his jammies and a roll of toilet paper is supposed to make me feel guilty for making you come to work today?"

Neva Jean looked only slightly ashamed of herself. "He really is sick, Callahan," she insisted. "Honest."

"Fine," I said, closing my eyes to make the room stop tilting. "Take him home or take him to the doctor. Edna, cut Neva Jean a check for her last week of work. Ruby, didn't you tell us there's a woman at your church looking for a cleaning job? Give her a call and tell her we've got an opening."

"Wait," Neva Jean yelped. "I'll work, Callahan. Don't fire me, honey. You know I need this job."

I opened my eyes. Big alligator tears made pink streaks through Neva Jean's heavily rouged cheeks.

Edna got up from the table and gave her a quick hug. "Never mind, Neva Jean. She can't fire you without my say-so, and I don't say so." She glared across the room at me, daring me to contradict her.

"Callahan here don't know the meaning of family loyalty," Edna said. "She can't understand how it hurts to see somebody you love suffering."

Neva Jean sniffed loudly and rubbed at her eyes.

"You take Swannelle home now," Edna continued. "Put him to bed. Then you go over to the Columbuses, 644 Treetop Way, over near Chastain Park. It'll only take a couple of hours. I'll do the Bonfilis myself."

She gave me a defiant toss of the head. "Is that all right with you, Miss Banana Republic Dictator?"

My stomach churned again and suddenly I felt I was smothering in the heat of the kitchen.

"Do whatever you want," I said weakly. "I'm going back to bed."

12

THE LAST TIME I REMEMBER staying in bed for two whole days in a row was when I came down with the Asian flu in 1986. By Tuesday morning I'd stopped vomiting, but I still felt queasy and physically and emotionally drained.

Around noon, Edna came into the bedroom dressed in a pink House Mouse smock. I'd heard her leave earlier in the morning, presumably to clean one of the houses I was supposed to have been handling.

"Are you feeling any better at all?" she asked, not bothering to hide her impatience with me.

I was halfheartedly watching one of those television talk shows with Jennie or Vickie or somebody like that. Today's topic was infertility. I'm not married and don't especially want children, but listening to the guest couples describe their desperate quest for a baby made me feel overwhelmingly sad. Before I knew it, my eyes were brimming with tears.

Edna felt my forehead again. "Well, if you're so sick you're crying, maybe you need to see a doctor," she said.

I brushed her hand away. "It's not that," I said, choking back the tears. "It's this damn television program."

Before I could explain, the phone rang. It had been

ringing steadily all morning, but I'd been letting the answering machine pick up.

Now I jerked the receiver off the hook. "House Mouse."

It was Stuart Kappler, my oncologist. I had a tiny malignant lump removed from my right breast a couple of years ago. Six months ago, I talked him into enrolling me in an experimental trial for an anti-cancer drug called Tamoxifen. I take two little pills every morning, but I have no idea whether I'm taking Tamoxifen or a placebo. Stuart had called last Friday, and again Monday, but I hadn't had time to return his calls.

"Callahan," he said evenly. "Did you get the message I called? You're not avoiding me, are you?"

"Hi, Stuart," I said. A small chill ran down my spine. And Edna's face registered alarm. There's a history of breast cancer in her family—she had a mastectomy years ago—and she hates the idea of this drug trial. She sat on the side of my bed so she could monitor the conversation.

"I'm sorry I didn't call back," I said. "Work's been crazy, and then I've felt sort of crappy the last couple of days. Was there some problem with the latest blood work or something?"

With the drug trial, I go back to St. Joseph's Hospital every six months now for blood work, a breast exam, and a mammogram. Plus they make you fill out a detailed questionnaire about all your symptoms and your sex life. It's not as bad as having breast cancer, but it's also not my favorite way to spend a day.

"Crappy how?" Stuart asked.

"Oh, nausea, vomiting, fever. Probably a stomach flu. I'm feeling better today, though. Just tired."

"You know all of those things could be side effects of the Tamoxifen, don't you?"

"To tell the truth, it hadn't occurred to me that it might be the Tamoxifen," I said.

"Any other symptoms?" Kappler asked. "Dizziness, depression?"

"Yes and yes," I said. "But I chalked the depression up to the fact that a close family member died this past weekend."

"Could be the drug or the family situation," Stuart agreed. "But look. I've been looking at your last blood work, and your bilirubin level is up slightly. It's nothing to get real alarmed about, but I do want you to come in and let us run it again."

"What's a bilirubin level?" I asked. The last thing I felt like doing today was trekking forty minutes to St. Joseph's to get poked with more needles.

"It's your liver enzymes," Kappler said. "A reading of one point two or less is normal. Yours is up to one point four. It's only slightly elevated, but that could mean that the Tamoxifen is irritating your liver."

"If I'm taking the Tamoxifen and not a sugar pill," I pointed out.

"You know I don't have any idea which it is," Kappler said. "The only folks who do know are the computer programmers at the national headquarters of the cancer study. So what about it? Can you come out today for that blood work?"

"Today?" I said, annoyed. "Can't it wait until next week or something?"

"I've been calling you for three days," Kappler said. "We need to find out if your bilirubin level is still up. If it is, we'll take you off the medication for a month to see if your liver function is back down. And if you're still having nausea, I can give you some Compazine, which should make you feel better."

"Why don't I just stop taking the pills for a while?" I suggested. "You can call in a prescription for the Compazine, can't you?"

"I'd rather see you today," Kappler said. "Why are you being so stubborn about this?"

"I'm not," I said stubbornly. "I just have a lot of work to catch up with today. If I have to go all the way out to Sandy

Springs and back, that shoots the rest of my day. What about it—can I just quit taking the pills and see you next month?"

"It would be better my way," he said reluctantly. "What drugstore should I call this in to?"

Before we hung up I ageed to have another round of blood work in April, and that I'd call if I noticed any other symptoms.

"Geez," I said, getting up to switch off the television. "Kappler's as much an old lady as you are, Edna."

"What did he say?" she said, her face pinched with concern.

"It's nothing," I assured her. "My whatzit level is up a smidge. Something to do with the liver. I'm going to stop taking the pills for a month, he'll run the tests again, and I'll start back again. The good news is that this nausea and stuff is a side effect of Tamoxifen. Which must mean that I'm taking the real McCoy and not a placebo."

"Hooray," she said sarcastically. We both knew she was worried about the other side effects, the more serious ones like killer blood clots and uterine cancer. Every time she sees a newspaper or magazine story about the dangers of Tamoxifen, I find it clipped out and stuck under my morning cereal bowl.

"You know how I feel about this," I warned her. "Kappler and Rich Drescher both think the Tamoxifen trial is a good idea. My mammograms and breast exams have been spotless for the past year. Now will you get out of here so I can get dressed?"

She got up and smoothed the bedcovers into place. "I thought you were sick."

"I was," I said, running my fingers through sleep-matted hair. "Kappler's getting me some pills for the nausea. I'm going to go pick them up at Plaza Drugs, then I've got some errands to run. Is that okay with you?"

"Do any of those errands have to do with messing around in the police investigation of your cousin's murder?" she asked.

I went into the closet to find some clean clothes to put on. "None of your business," I said, pulling a pair of khaki slacks off a hanger. I stuck my head out of the closet door. "But for your information, Aunt Jean won't even know I'm talking to the people I'm talking to, so you won't have to worry about it."

I could have saved my breath, though. The room was empty.

I bought a can of Diet Coke at Plaza Drugs and washed down the nausea pills with it.

Outside in the van I dialed Sherrill Mackey's number. I didn't dare do it from the house with Edna watching my every move.

"Mackey house," a childish voice said.

"Can I speak to your mama?" I asked.

The phone dropped to the floor with a clatter. The Mackeys must have had tile floors. "Mo-om, phone for you."

"I've got it," Sherrill said. "Hang up now."

"Sherrill? It's Callahan Garrity. Patti McNair's cousin."

"Oh yeah," Sherrill said. "I don't have much time. I've got to leave in five minutes to pick up my daughter at preschool. What else can I tell you?"

"What else do you know about Patti and Bruce's marriage?"

"Well." She thought for a moment. "You knew Bruce left his old law practice, didn't you?"

"No," I said. "When did this happen?"

"At the beginning of last year, I think," she said. "Patti had a fit when Bruce told her what he'd done. He didn't even discuss it with her. Just one day announced that he and Beverly Updegraff had decided to dissolve the partnership."

I'd met Beverly Updegraff at parties at Patti's house. Found her warm and intelligent, but a real street fighter who'd gone to night law school while working days as a legal secretary. That's where she and Bruce had met, as I recalled. She'd worked as a secretary for his first law firm.

"Patti never said a word about it," I said.

"It was just another example of Bruce leading a completely separate life," Sherrill said. "He'd go off on a two- or three-day business trip and not tell Patti he was planning to go until the day he left. I wanted her to hire a private detective, have him followed. After what I went through with my ex, I told Patti, you can't trust the bastards."

"And what did she say?" I asked. In the old days, I would have expected that Patti might have confided this kind of stuff to me. But the old days were gone.

"She said I was being over-dramatic," Sherrill said. "If it weren't so awful, I'd say it was ironic, wouldn't you?"

13

WEDNESDAY MORNING, I noticed that Edna had taken my bottle of little blue pills off the kitchen table. I was feeling good enough to sip at a cup of coffee. Which was when I remembered about my promise to DeeDee about cleaning Bruce's house.

"No way," Neva Jean said, slamming her Mountain Dew bottle down on the table for emphasis. She dabbed at the spilled green soda with a paper towel, but her face stayed defiant. "I have got to take Swannelle back to the doctor at eleven to be hooked up to this big breathing machine they got there. There is no way I can get all the way out to Marietta to your cousin's, then back home in time to pick Swannelle up. You'll just have to get somebody else."

I looked across the table at Edna, who was running a pencil down the day's House Mouse bookings. It was only seven A.M., but a chastened Neva Jean had gotten to work early, and it was conceivable that she could finish her first job before she had to take Swannelle for his bug-spray cure.

"Ruby's got the Finkelsteins at eight, the Boltons at noon, and the Thrashers at three-thirty," Edna said, frowning.

"What about Jackie?"

"No good. She's loaded down too. And David is scheduled to do the Allens' house. He's not strong enough to do more."

"David's sick again?" Neva Jean asked quickly.

David DeSantis is our one and only male House Mouse. He used to work at the beauty salon run by Edna's buddy Frank, but a year ago, when the HIV test came back positive and his hairdressing clients turned negative, he came to work for us. When he's feeling well, he cleans a few houses, and he's always in demand. Who else would clean a client's house, reorganize her wardrobe, and leave fresh flowers behind?

"His T-cells are wacky," Edna said. "But they've got him on a new drug regimen, and the doctor said he just needs to take it easy for a week or so."

Neva Jean took a long swig of her drink. "Looks like that leaves you, Callahan."

"I'd love to," I said, "but Miss Bossypants DeeDee made it clear Sunday that she doesn't want me anywhere near the kids. As if I were going to interrogate them or something."

"Callahan's got everybody in the family turned every which way," Edna told Neva Jean. "I told her to leave it go, but she won't listen."

"Well then, Ma," I said, "I guess that just leaves you, doesn't it? Unless we want to send Baby and Sister."

Edna pointed with her lit cigarette at the open page of the book. I brushed away the glowing ashes. "Look right there. See where it says 'Edna' and there's a line drawn from nine 'til three? That means I've got appointments of my own all day. Got to take the Electrolux out to the factory service center to look at that switch. Then I've got a condo in midtown to clean, and at two P.M. I meet with a new client in Decatur who wants us to do their house and the mother-in-law's apartment, too."

"All right, all right," I said. "Call Baby and Sister and

tell them I'll pick them up in fifteen minutes. I'll take them over to Bruce's and get them started. If DeeDee objects to my being there, tough shit. She can clean the place her own self."

"That'll be the day," Edna muttered.

I went to the closet, put on a clean smock over my turtleneck sweater and jeans, and grabbed two more smocks for my assistants.

I got to the Easterbrooks's senior citizen high-rise a few minutes early, so I parked at the curb to wait. Just enough time to get in a little work.

Liz Whitesell's number was in my address book. I dialed the number on my car phone. Busy. I hung up and glanced up and down the street for any sign of the sisters. Then I dialed again.

She answered on the third ring, "Liz Whitesell." Crisp and efficient. Liz had been like that since we'd played together on a summer league girl's softball team twenty years ago.

"Whitesell," I said, "you still playing reporter on that pathetic Papist tool of a newspaper?"

Liz is a reporter for the *Atlanta Catholic*, a monthly archdiocesan newspaper. She was taken aback for only a minute. "Garrity, you sniveling liberal twit," she said. "When are you going to get a real job?"

We chatted for a moment about our mutual love lives, work, etc.

"What's up?" she asked finally. "I know you, Callahan, you don't make social calls."

"I'm looking for some info on a priest," I admitted. "Do you know Martin Covington?"

"Our Lady of Lourdes," she said promptly. "Why?"

"No special reason," I said. Liz can smell a story a mile off. I didn't need her sniffing around this one.

"Spit it out, Callahan," she warned.

I sighed loudly for her benefit, and craned my neck for any sight of the sisters.

"My mother is thinking of returning to the church," I said. "And my aunt Jean has been telling her how wonderful Father Mart out at Our Lady of Lourdes is."

There was a long period of silence. "No sale, Garrity. Try again."

"Really," I said, trying to sound sincere.

"I'll bet," Liz said. "But I don't have time to wrangle the truth out of you right now. You do know that there's talk Covington might be in line for a promotion, don't you?"

"I didn't know that," I said. "What, to a bigger church?"

She laughed. "No, you idiot. We're talking monsignor. Martin Covington's name is on a very short list of people being considered for monsignor."

"Yeah?" I asked, my curiosity piqued. "How come?"

"He's got all the right stuff," Liz said. "He's politically correct, he's in tight with the archbishop, he got good press for that inner city mission he started, and Our Lady of Lourdes is big and rich thanks to Father Mart."

"He sounds like a saint," I groused. "You mean nobody has any dirt on the guy?"

She sucked her breath in. "You are after something, Garrity. Let's just say nobody's worried about Father Mart playing ring around the rosary with the altar boys."

I looked at the clock on the dashboard. The sisters were running late now, which would mess up the schedule I'd made for myself today.

"What's that supposed to mean, Liz?"

"God, you're dense," she said. "Don't you read the newspapers? It means he's not a pedophile. He doesn't like little boys. That alone is a giant plus these days."

"Oh yeah," I said, distracted. Where the hell were Baby and Sister?

"A very big oh yeah, as far as the church is concerned," she said.

"Does that mean that he likes women?"

"I didn't say that," she said quickly.

"But you're not denying it. So what do you know?"

"Well, his last assignment before he came to Our Lady of Lourdes was in Baltimore. Another big, rich, suburban church. I heard Father Mart was a spiritual advisor for the wife of a really wealthy old guy there." She said spiritual advisor like it might have quote marks around it. "This guy invented something to do with VCRs. He was loaded. He died and he left everything to the wife, Father Mart's close friend. Three months later the wife gives her big mansion and all the land around it to the church, and she splits for Fort Lauderdale."

"So he does like the ladies," I insisted.

"Let's just say he has a way. And nobody minds it when it means the church ends up with a nice bequest."

"That's all you know?" In a way I was disappointed. I was hoping, I guess, to hear that Patti's priest friend was an infamous womanizer.

There was tapping at the window. I turned to see a pair of tiny antique black women tugging at the front and back doors of the van.

"Thanks, Liz," I said, reaching over to unlock the doors. "I'll call you soon."

"No, I'll call you," she said. "I want to know the real reason you're interested in Martin Covington."

I hung up the phone and hopped out of the van to let the sisters in.

"Callahan," cried Baby, holding onto my arm as I boosted her up to the front seat, "how did you know me and Sister was needin' to work this week?"

Even dressed in two of her cotton housedresses with a thick wool coat, wool stockings, and her heavy lace-up black oxfords, Baby might have weighed eighty pounds. I put my lips close to her ear. Baby's eyesight is almost as good as mine, but she's very nearly deaf. The scent of her baby powder tickled my nose. "Miss Baby, you know we can't run House Mouse without you."

"Dat's what I tol' her," Sister piped up. "I tol' her

Callahan be needin' us this week and not to worry 'bout gettin' grocery money. The Lord provides. Yes he does."

As she talked, I was gently guiding Sister to the threshold of the van's back door. When she was seated I leaned in and buckled her seat belt.

The coat she wore this morning looked familiar. It was a green and brown camouflage jacket so big it hung down past her knees, which were covered with a faded pair of blue jeans. "I like that jacket, Miss Sister," I said. "But I'm surprised Mac gave it away. It was his favorite."

"She took it right out of the closet at your house," Baby tattled. "I told her you gon' put her in jail for stealin', didn't I?"

"And who spent all the grocery money buying Georgia Lotto tickets?" Sister demanded. "Tell Callahan which old fool thinks she gon' be a millionaire from buyin' a one-dollar ticket?"

The two of them fussed back and forth like that most of the way out to Marietta. Sunday's sunny weather was nothing but a memory today. It was cold and gray and blustery, and gusts of wind blew the van around the interstate like an autumn leaf.

When I turned into the Stately Oaks subdivision where the McNairs live, the sisters stopped feuding. "Look like this be where the millionaires live," said an awed Baby. The lots were small, but the houses were gigantic, faux French chateaux, faux Spanish colonial, and faux Greek Revival. Each sat on a miniature sweep of manicured lawn, impossibly green in late winter.

"Look here, Sister," Baby shouted. She forgets her sister is nearly blind, not deaf. "Callahan's cousin is rich. We'll get lost in these big old castles."

"Bruce's house is big," I admitted, "but I'll help you girls clean. The main thing is to get the laundry done, and the kitchen and bathrooms scrubbed. I'll see if Caitlin and Megan won't help. In the meantime, if you two were to do a little snooping when DeeDee isn't looking, there might be a bonus in your paycheck this week."

"What's that 'bout bein' stupid?" Sister said.

"No, fool," Baby said. "She talkin' 'bout snoopin'. Callahan wants us look for clues, 'cause her cousin got killed. She gone give us a big raise can we find some clues, ain't that right, Callahan?"

Megan was still rubbing sleep out of her eyes when she opened the front door. She was barefoot, wearing an oversized T-shirt of her father's for a nightgown.

"Callahan," she said sleepily, "Dad's not here. He took Dylan to the doctor."

I gave her a quick hug. "That's okay, hon. We're here to clean, not socialize. See, I brought help."

In the kitchen, Caitlin sat at the dinette eating a bowl of cereal. "Aunt DeeDee's still asleep," she said. "Want me to wake her up?"

I shook my head in the negative. As promised, the place was a mess. Dirty dishes were piled in the sink and on the countertop, and every cupboard door was ajar. From where I stood I could see into the laundry room, which was heaped knee-high with dirty clothes.

"Let her sleep," I said. Then, with my hands on my hips, "Aren't you girls supposed to be back in school today?"

Caitlin reached for the Rice Krispy box and poured more into the bowl, slopping stray krispies onto the tabletop. "Uh-uh. The principal called and left a message on the answering machine. We can stay out till tomorrow if we want." Both girls grinned at this reprieve from school.

"All right," I said, snapping my fingers. "Let's get busy then. Sister, Caitlin will show you how to work the washer and dryer, and then she's going to help you with the laundry. Right, Caitlin?"

Caitlin pulled a small face, nodding without enthusiasm.

"Miss Baby," I said, raising my voice, "I'll go get the vacuum and supplies out of the van. Then you can start upstairs and work your way down. Megan will be your assistant."

"That's good," Baby said placidly.

In an hour's time, I'd whipped through the kitchen and all three bathrooms. Then it was time to survey the bedrooms. On the second floor, the door to Caitlin's room, where the girls said DeeDee was staying, was firmly closed.

Which was fine with me. I had no time for confrontations today. I moved on to the master bedroom, where Baby was stripping the king-sized bed. I stepped into the room and stopped suddenly, overwhelmed by Patti's presence. The room smelled of her perfume, Miss Dior. It was painted her favorite shade of peach and the dressing table looked like she'd just gotten up from it. It was a jumble of silver-framed family pictures, jewelry, makeup, and little crayon- and construction-paper school projects Dylan had made for her.

A pair of silly elephant-head slippers poked out from under her side of the bed. A silky peach robe was flung carelessly on a hook on the open closet door.

I closed my eyes and sank down on the bed. She was here, but not here. When I opened my eyes again, DeeDee was standing in the doorway. It was her turn for hands on hips.

"What's going on here?" she snapped. "What are you doing in here, going through my sister's things?"

I stood up and gathered the bedclothes in my arms. "I told you I'd send someone to clean. Remember?"

The defiant jut of her chin softened. "Oh yeah. God. I'm sorry, Julia. Bruce and I stayed up late last night, talking about Patti and the old days. I overslept, and then when I heard all the commotion of the vacuums, I guess I got out of bed on the wrong side. I'm no good mornings until I've had my coffee. Forgive me?"

"Never mind," I shrugged.

Baby, sensing that the situation had been settled, bustled around the room, dusting, picking up scattered items of clothing and books and papers.

"This is Miss Baby, one of our House Mouse girls," I said, loud enough that Baby could hear. "Miss Baby, this is my cousin DeeDee, Aunt Jean's younger daughter."

Baby smiled and nodded and kept working, humming to herself, something that sounded like "He's Got the Whole World in His Hands."

"Miss Sister is downstairs doing laundry," I told DeeDee. "I've pressed Caitlin and Megan into service, too. Most of the heavy stuff is done. I'm going to shove off, get some errands done, and I'll swing back by to pick up the girls around two P.M."

"Great," DeeDee said, unsuccessfully trying to stifle a yawn. "This is wonderful of you, Callahan, just wonderful."

I glanced around the room. The smell of Baby's lemon-scented furniture polish had overpowered the Miss Dior. Baby had tucked the bits of clothing and shoes away in the closet. Patti seemed to disappear, too.

"We can't spare the girls on a regular basis, unless Bruce wants to do a contract," I warned. "Bruce is going to have to get the kids to pitch in and help until he hires someone permanently."

She made a little face. "Those girls, even Dylan, they're horribly spoiled. Patti never made them lift a finger around here. She did it all herself."

"I know," I said.

She straightened her shoulders and cinched the belt of her cream-colored bathrobe. "But all that's going to change," she said firmly. "Bruce and I have discussed it. He's in complete agreement. The kids will go on allowance, and they'll have to do all their chores around this house before they get a single penny of spending money."

"Of course," I said. It occurred to me that DeeDee had never had to do much in the way of manual labor in her lifetime either. And she was nearly thirty. But I kept that to myself.

14

SINCE I WAS IN THE neighborhood, I told myself, I called Charlie Fouts. He agreed, reluctantly, to meet me at the police impound lot.

The lot was part of Cobb County's huge vehicle shop. School buses, seemingly hundreds of them, were lined up in vast rows in one quadrant of the lot, while another was given over to heavy equipment: bulldozers, front-end loaders, and garbage trucks. There was even a rust-covered snowplow.

I found Fouts's unmarked car parked beside a large metal quonset hut at the edge of the lot. He was talking on his car phone when I pulled up next to him, but he hung up quickly.

He slid out of the driver's side. Today Fouts wore his business look, a light-blue sport coat worn over a plaid knit vest and navy slacks. "Car's in here," he said, apparently deciding to dispense with the hi-how-are-you formalities. He walked quickly inside the hut with me following along behind.

Patti's black Lexus was a classy-looking machine, oddly incongruous next to the dilapidated wrecks that filled the quonset hut.

I peeked in the driver's-side window, steeling myself

for what I expected to see. But the front seat was gone, leaving only the clean black carpet and the metal brackets where the seat had been bolted onto the chassis.

"The seat's at the crime lab," Fouts explained. "Blood and tissue samples, bullet evidence, that kind of thing."

The black leather dashboard and interior upholstery were smudged with a thin waxy-looking substance. I sniffed. It smelled like airplane glue.

"New fingerprint stuff," Fouts said. "Super sensitive. You spray it on instead of dusting."

I nodded knowingly. I'd read about the new solution in one of the law enforcement magazines I still subscribe to.

"Find anything useful?"

He shrugged. "Lots of prints. Who knows if there's anything useful? Mr. McNair said both girls sometimes used the car, and you know how teenagers pile kids in a vehicle. The outside of the car was smudged with at least a dozen prints, probably from the crowd that had gathered before our people got there."

I looked in the car again. It had been swept clean. The backseat was empty. There was nothing to see.

The cradle that should have held the car phone was empty. "Bagged up with the rest of the stuff we found," Fouts said, noticing where I was looking.

"Was there anything valuable left behind?" I asked. "I'd have thought a carjacker would strip the car."

"If he had time," Fouts said. "Her purse was gone, with credit cards, and probably seventy, eighty dollars in cash, and her checkbook, stuff like that."

"What about her jewelry?" I said. "She had at least a two-carat diamond engagement ring, and the last time we had lunch, she was wearing one of those expensive diamond tennis bracelets."

"The diamond ring and wedding band were on the body," Fouts said. I winced at his reference to "the body." "Mr. McNair said the tennis bracelet is gone. He couldn't remember whether she was wearing it that morning when he last saw her."

I stepped away from the car and circled it once more. The tires were mud-spattered, and it reminded me of that muddy, trash-littered street and parking lot on Bankhead Highway. The driver's-side tires were missing their hub-caps.

Fouts motioned toward the tires. "By the time our officers got to the scene, at least ten minutes had passed. Like I said, a crowd had gathered. People like that, in that neighborhood, they might take advantage of a situation. Take what they could. White lady's dead, she ain't gonna mind, right?"

"I guess," I said. "How about letting me see the inventory of what was found in the car?"

He pressed his lips together disapprovingly. "Don't have it."

"But you could get it," I suggested.

"The major wouldn't like it," he said.

"The major doesn't have to know."

He shook his head stubbornly. "Sorry. The answer's no."

"Is the FBI calling the shots now?" I asked.

His eyes narrowed. "What do you know about the FBI, Garrity?"

I smiled serenely. "I know they're working the case with you. I met Tyler King, the agent in charge, Saturday night. We had a beer together. Nice guy. He used to play football at Tech, you know."

He took his sunglasses out of his coat pocket, buffed them on the front of his shirt and put them on, then started walking toward the door.

"Nice try, Garrity," he said over his shoulder. "Maybe you did meet King. But he didn't tell you diddly. I know the guy. He's not the type to go shooting off his mouth around town."

Fouts's cockiness was giving me a royal pain.

"Maleek Tebbetts," I said casually.

He turned around, quickly, planting both feet wide apart. "What?"

"Maleek Tebbetts. The Wrecking Crew." I let the words spill out slowly, enjoying the effect.

"I don't know where you got that name," Fouts said finally. "But King didn't give it to you. Guy's ass is water-tight. If I were you, I wouldn't go throwing Tebbetts's name around so loud."

I had to nearly run to catch up with him. He was getting in his car.

"Maleek Tebbetts is a suspect, isn't he?" I asked, grabbing the edge of the car door to keep him from shutting it.

"Maybe," Fouts said evenly. He pulled the door shut and gave me a good-bye wave.

The van was stone cold. I let the engine idle and hugged myself for warmth while I went over my options. I could go back to Bruce's house, try to talk to the girls. But if DeeDee was on guard, it'd be useless to try. Besides, Dylan was the one I really needed to talk to. Maybe he knew what his mother was doing on Bankhead Highway last Friday. DeeDee had made it clear she didn't intend to let Dylan near me. I wondered if the "doctor" he was seeing this morning was a psychologist. Poor kid. He was going to need some major head shrinking to be able to deal with what he'd witnessed last week.

A shiver went down my spine. Someone walking on my grave, Edna would say. She believes in signs, my mother. If your nose itches, somebody's talking about you. If your hand itches, you'll come into money. If it's your foot that needs scratching, you'll take a long journey. I pulled my pea coat closer, buttoning the top button.

The dashboard clock said I had another hour or so before I had to pick up Baby and Sister. Maybe it was time to have a chat with Martin Covington.

The elderly woman who answered the phone at Our Lady of Lourdes rectory was uncertain where Father might be. "Let me check his study," she said. I could hear metal-tapped shoes clicking down a hallway. She must have been a nun. Nobody but nuns wears those taps on their shoes anymore. She was back a couple of minutes later.

"Father is over at the teen club this afternoon," she said. "Do you know where that is?"

I didn't, so she told me. The Youth in Action club was only about six or seven miles from my cousin's house in Stately Oaks, and the nearby church, but if you looked at socioeconomic strata, the Kenneyville Court housing project was located on another planet.

Austell Road, which leads to the project, isn't exactly Easy Street. By the time you get near Kenneyville, you start seeing the seedy apartment complexes, the kind where curb space is taken up by the ragtag belongings of tenants who've been evicted by the sheriff's deputies. The Kenney sock factory, which for decades had provided the economic focus of the neighborhood, was a low-slung cement block affair surrounded by a high cyclone fence. The parking lot beside it held a hundred or so cars and trucks, the day shift in full swing.

The streets behind the factory were narrow and in need of repair, with tiny little clapboard mill houses crowded up against each other. At the intersection of Factory and Second Street, I saw a faded sign with an arrow pointing to Kenneyville Court, off to the left.

At the end of the dead-end street a wooden plank sign announced that I'd found Kenneyville Court, except that half the letters on the sign were missing, and some-one had spray-painted undying love for Lil'Bit over what letters were left.

Kenneyville Court consisted of a couple of dozen flat-roofed two-story town houses covered with faded green asbestos shingles. As public housing goes in Atlanta, it wasn't too awful, a run-down relic of a time forty years before when nobody expected people to make a career of poverty.

I cruised the short streets slowly, looking for the teen club. It was at the back of the project, a large square building that had the look of a community hall or a school.

A new sign hung over the front door: Youth in Action Teen Club. A small playground lay to the left of the building. A young black girl, maybe fourteen or fifteen, with a wool hat pulled over her hair, pushed a toddler swathed in a dirty red snowsuit on a swing set. A basketball court was empty, the backboard hung with a naked, rusting hoop.

I pushed open the heavy metal door. The smell of old sweat assaulted my nose. Shouts echoed from somewhere nearby. Through the postage-stamp window in the inner door, I could see that the inside of the building had been gutted and a combination gym/cafeteria/assembly hall now occupied what had once surely been classroom space.

A dozen or so teenagers ran up and down the floor, their rubber-soled shoes squeaking against the polished wood. Good-natured shouts—"My man," "Shoot, shoot," "He's open."

In a corner of the gym a group of little girls stood in staggered rows, hands on hips, clapping and stomping rhythmically.

"Uh-huh, yeah. I say yeah. Kenneyville got the plan. Kenneyville, you the man. Uh-huh. Say yeah." In unison, the girls squealed and jumped in the air.

A section of bleachers had been pulled out of the walls, and I spotted Martin Covington, hunched forward, watching the action.

I crossed the gym floor, narrowly avoiding a collision with two kids in a point-on-point battle. I climbed the bleachers and sat down beside Covington. He was dressed in navy slacks, with a long-sleeved black shirt and the clerical collar.

He didn't look surprised to see me, but held out a hand in greeting. "Callahan, isn't it?"

I shook. His hand was warm, his grip strong.

"Patti told me a lot about you," he said, his blue eyes fixed on my face. "You're the detective, right?"

I nodded, shoved my hands in my coat pockets. The high-ceilinged room was chilly. "She told me a little about you," I said. "She tried to get me to come back to church."

He nodded. "Maybe when you're ready. Finding your faith again could help you accept her death, you know."

"No," I said, "I doubt it. That's why I'm here, actually. I can't accept that Patti's killing was a random act."

"Why not?" he asked. His face was fine boned and the flesh clung to the high cheekbones and forehead, the narrow nose and pointed chin. "Because she was rich, white, somebody you loved? Do you think poor black people are the only ones who deserve to become crime statistics?"

He gestured toward the kids playing basketball. "Should one of them have been killed instead of Patti McNair? You think their mothers love them less than your family loved Patti?"

I took a deep breath. "Not at all. I'm sorry anybody has to die. Sorry it seems to be open season on young black men in Atlanta. But I'm a detective. I know how and why crime happens. And Patti's murder doesn't fit. It doesn't work, Father."

He took his glasses off and wiped his eyes. "What did you want to see me about? Obviously not to discuss social action or theology."

"I want your help," I said simply. "You were close to Patti. I've talked to her best friend, Sherrill. She's says Patti's marriage was troubled. Did Patti talk to you about that?"

"We talked about it quite a lot," Covington said. "She and Bruce came to me for counseling. That's not a secret. The children even came along for family sessions on at least one occasion. They were married young, and people change over the years. Bruce was busy with his career, Patti felt abandoned sometimes. It's not an unusual occurrence."

"Were they headed for divorce?"

He jerked his head violently. "Not at all. Patti was seeing me right up until her death. I'm certain she and Bruce were reconciled. She wanted the marriage to work, wanted it for the children."

"There were money problems," I said. "Did you know about that?"

He smiled sadly. "Patti had gotten accustomed to a certain standard of living. From what Bruce told me, after he left the old law firm and started this new one, their financial picture changed. Patti thought Bruce's insistence on budgeting was an attempt to control and belittle her. She really understood very little about finances."

"Who is Bruce's new partner, do you know?"

"I don't," he said. "Just that Patti resented all the time Bruce was spending building his new practice."

Which reminded me. "Her friend Sherrill thinks Patti might have been having an affair with someone. What do you think?"

"Good God," he exploded. "That's impossible. And it's just the kind of malicious gossip that tears at the fabric of our families. I hope this woman isn't spreading her filth where Bruce or the children could hear of it."

His face had paled; he was clearly shocked.

"Sherrill says Patti asked her to cover for her with Bruce on three or four occasions this last year. If she wasn't having an affair, why did she need to lie to her husband?"

He rubbed at his face with both hands. "I told her to talk to her family about it," he said, his voice muffled. "She was convinced they wouldn't understand."

"Understand what?"

He sat up straight. "Patti would go on retreat, out to

the monastery at Conyers, once a month. For prayer and meditation. She was exploring her own spirituality, but she told me Bruce was uncomfortable with that. I suppose that's why she kept it from him. It had nothing to do, I promise you, with anything like an affair."

I considered what he'd just told me. Rolled it around in my brain for a while. I watched the kids below shucking and jiving on the courts. They'd stripped off shirts and sweaters and their bodies gleamed with sweat, their shouts echoed in my ears.

"You have any problems with gangs in Kenneyville?" I asked.

The abrupt change of subject took him aback.

"Some. Most of these kids come from single-parent homes. They're looking for an authority, something to look up to, to be a part of. That's one reason the church took on this mission—to show these kids someone cares about them. Keep them busy, give them an alternative to the streets."

I thought about the streets I'd just driven through. Knots of sullen youths stood in the shadows, drinking from paper sacks or talking quietly. Hangin' in the 'hood. In the eyes of a former cop, trouble waiting to happen.

"Ever hear of a gang called The Wrecking Crew?" I asked.

"No," he said quickly. "We've got a community policing program here. There's a group that calls themselves The Aces, another called The Lords. They do punk stuff, threaten each other, minor acts of vandalism. Once in a while somebody beats up somebody else. It's nowhere near as bad as they have in the projects in Atlanta."

"Okay," I said, getting up to leave. "You know, one of my cousins told me Sunday he thought you were having an affair with Patti. Funny, huh? A future monsignor risking his career on an affair with a married parishioner?"

Covington wasn't laughing. Not at all. "I'd invite your cousin to take a look at my schedule at my rectory," he said calmly. "I counsel dozens of couples. Speak with unhappy women several times a day. If I were having an affair with every troubled person I see, I wouldn't have the strength to work, let alone run a parish the size of Our Lady of Lourdes. I was Patti's friend and spiritual advisor. That's all. To suggest anything else is blasphemy. You can tell your cousin that for me."

15

HE WAS DRESSED IN a black Atlanta Falcons
sweatshirt, black jeans, socks and no shoes. His
hair was tousled and he had the look of a child
roused from sleep.

"Hi, Dylan," I said softly. "I'm here to pick up Miss
Baby and Miss Sister. Is your aunt DeeDee here?"

"Okay," he said, and turning his back to me he trotted back into the house leaving the front door open.

I closed the door behind me. The house was quiet. I
found Dylan in the den, stretched out on his stomach on
the sofa, totally absorbed in a cartoon show I'd never seen.

"What's this?" I asked, sitting on the floor.

"Bevis and Butthead," he said, not bothering to look up.

"Butthead?" I said. "They let a children's cartoon program be called Butthead? And your folks let you watch it?"

"Mom never let him watch it," Caitlin said, walking
into the room from the kitchen holding a bag of potato
chips and a can of Coke. "But these days he gets to do
anything he wants, don't you, Mr. Shrinkhead?" She took
the remote and flipped to one of those twenty-four-hour
comedy channels.

Dylan raised his head from the sofa cushion and
stuck his tongue out at his sister.

I tried to hide a smile, but I doubt I was successful. "So

where is everybody?" I said breezily, looking around the room. I could tell Baby and Sister had been hard at work. All the games and books on the den's bookshelves had been neatly arranged, the carpet was vacuumed, and the late afternoon sun shone weakly through shiny windows.

"One of those ladies of yours, I can't tell them apart, is in the laundry room folding clothes," Caitlin said. "I think the other one is watching television in Mom and Dad's room; she's got the door shut, but the sound is turned up really loud."

"That's Baby," I said, glancing at my watch. "It's four o'clock, she must be watching the end of 'General Hospital.' Where's your sister and DeeDee?"

"At the store," she said, holding out the chip bag. "Want some?"

What I wanted was a sandwich and something to drink. I hadn't realized how late the day had gotten. "No thanks," I said. Before I could ask any more questions, the phone rang and she leapt out of the recliner she'd been sitting in and ran for the kitchen.

Now it was just me and Dylan. A commercial for a chiropractic clinic came on the television, and he sat up and stared at me.

Just the opportunity I'd been waiting for. "How are you, Dylan?" I asked. "Does your head still hurt?"

He shook his head no.

"I guess you're missing your mom, huh? I miss her a lot too. She was my best friend."

He nodded and picked at a small hole in his sock.

I glanced toward the kitchen and could see Caitlin seated Indian style on the floor, cradling the telephone under her chin and yakking away happily.

She'd be busy a while, I decided. "You know, Dylan," I said, "the police are trying to find out who hurt your mama. And I'm trying to find out, too. I'm a detective, just like some of the detectives you see on television. Did you know that?"

"Detective?"

"Somebody who finds out stuff," I explained. "I want to find out who hurt your mama. Did you see that person? The person who hit you?"

He nodded yes, and his eyes got very still.

"Can you tell me about him? Can you tell the police? So the man won't hurt anymore?"

Just then, the number for accident victims to call the chiropractic clinic flashed on the screen, and moments later a redhead carrying an accordion was onstage, cracking jokes about her boyfriend's impotence. Dylan's head swiveled back toward the box like a flower to the sun.

"Dylan?" I asked.

"She screamed and screamed," he whispered. "Scared. Hit me. People. Black peoples. Looked at me. I went to the place."

"The hospital?" I prompted.

He nodded.

I sighed. This was rougher going than I'd anticipated. "Did you talk to the doctor today? Did you talk about what you saw the day your mama was hurt?"

The redhead finished her act and flipped her skirt up to show her panties. This was comedy? A young black comic in a brown leather jacket came onstage.

"Dylan?"

He frowned. "We read a book. Me and Cookie."

"Cookie?"

Now I was confused. "Is Cookie one of your friends? From school, maybe?"

He shook his head no.

Caitlin came back into the den then, holding a gizmo the size of a transistor radio. She sat down and started playing it. I craned my neck to get a better look. It was a GameBoy, one of those little hand-held computer games.

Dylan lunged at her, snatching it away. "My GameBoy," he said, throwing himself back on the couch.

Caitlin straddled him on the couch and tried to

wrench the game away from him, but her brother turned over on his stomach, holding the game under him and away from her grasp.

"Give it back, brat," she shrieked.

They wrestled like that while I watched ineffectively. "Hey, guys," I said finally. "Why don't you play it together?"

She gave me a look that said drop dead. "Only one person at a time can play. Shrinkhead here thinks he owns it, but Dad bought it for all of us."

"So take turns," I said, reaching over and trying to pry her off her brother. "And I don't think it's nice to call him that, Caitlin."

"Callahan?" Sister stood in the doorway, her purse in her hand. "We ready to go home now. I reckon Baby's story is over by now."

I got up, relieved. All this sibling bickering was more than I could handle.

Dylan sat up on the couch, clutching the GameBoy in his hand and leaned way over to the right because I was blocking his view of the television. He started screaming at the top of his lungs. "Mama. Mama. No. Nooo."

That's when Caitlin closed in and grabbed the game back. "Got it," she crowed. But Dylan reached out and slapped her hard, on the arm.

"Ow," she cried. "See what a brat he is? Mom spoiled him just because he doesn't talk right." She reached over and thumped him on the top of the head with her closed fist. "How do you like that, Shrinkhead?"

He must not have liked it much because he howled in protest, rolling himself into a ball and screaming as though he'd been doused with boiling oil. "Mama, Mama, Mama," each call for his mother ending in an ever-higher crescendo.

Which is when DeeDee rushed into the house, followed by Megan. She ran to the sobbing child and gathered him into her arms.

"Mama, Mama," he sobbed. She smoothed his hair with her hands, bending down to try to hush his heart-shattering cries. "Shush, darlin', DeeDee's here."

She looked up at me, enraged. "You sneaky bitch," she hissed. "You wormed your way in here, acting like you were doing a favor. I should have known better. You've been pestering Dylan, haven't you? Asking him questions, getting him all upset."

"No," I protested. "He and Caitlin were fighting, he got mad because . . . "

She struggled to her feet, still holding Dylan, whose long legs dangled like some ridiculous oversized rag doll. "You need to leave now, Callahan. And forget about doing us any more favors. When Bruce hears about this he's going to be furious."

I gathered my stuff with as much dignity as I could and turned to Baby and Sister, who were standing watching in the doorway, mops, pails, and cleaning caddies in hand. As I was leaving I felt like a kid caught stealing quarters from his dad's pants' pockets.

The girls were quiet until we'd loaded everything in the van and were on our way home. Baby surreptitiously tucked a bit of snuff between her gum and her upper lip. "That lil' ol' gal is too big for her britches, you ask me," she said. "She got no call talkin' to Callahan like that."

"She done left her bed for me to make up," Sister chimed in. "And her a grown-up lady woman."

The two of them got into a discussion then of other grown women they'd known who refused to make up their beds, a sure sign of a slattern in their opinions. My mind drifted off and away, back to what Dylan had said about the man who'd shot Patti. Just what had he been trying to tell me?

"Mr. Bruce now, ooh, I feel sorry for that man," Sister said. "He bring that little boy in the house, and he be real quiet. He kiss him and hold him before he go off to work. And that Dylan's a cute little boy; too big to be crying, too little to understand about Mama being dead. I fixed him a big old bowl of vegetable soup for lunch. And he 'bout ate up a whole pan of my cornbread."

Baby leaned forward in the backseat and hollered for her sister's benefit. "Yeah, he cute. He come in and watched while I cleaned the bedrooms. He say he got hit on the head and that's why he go to the doctor today. 'Cause some skinny black man in a truck shoot his mama and hurt him too."

"What?" I asked, nearly rear-ending a car in front of me. "You talked to Dylan about his mother, Baby? Are you sure you heard him right?"

"He sittin' right next to me, on the bed there," Baby insisted.

"That old fool can't hear nuthin'," Sister said. "Now me, I hear a mouse fart two houses down in the middle of a 'lectrical storm." She laughed at her own joke. "Hee. Hee. Yes I can."

"Sister," I said, "did you hear Dylan tell Baby anything about the man who killed his mother? Think now. This is important."

Sister thought about that. "No, ma'am. We talk about how his mama fixed him chicken noodle soup. That's his favorite. But wasn't no chicken in the house, so I just got a little bit of stew meat—"

"He said the man was skinny and he drove a truck," I yelled. "Is that right, Miss Baby?"

"I told it exactly like he told me," Baby said indignantly. "Guess I can hear that much."

But I wondered. Between Dylan's language disorder and Baby's hearing loss, who knew exactly what the teller was saying to the tellee?

When we got to the senior citizen high-rise, I double-parked at the curb, next to a mail truck, and got out of the van to help the girls out.

Before Sister got out, she shrugged herself out of the

purloined hunting jacket and handed it to me ruefully. "Bible says 'thou shalt not steal,'" she said.

"Sure do," Baby said gleefully. "'If you break my commandments I will punish you with terrible woes, with wasting and fever to dim the eyes and sap the life.' That's Leviticus. You cut out that stealin', maybe you could see better, Miss Thing."

I took the jacket and felt a wad of papers in the right-hand pocket. "What's this?" I said, drawing out a bunch of envelopes and advertising circulars.

Sister squinted through her thick coke-bottle glasses. "Well now," she said slyly. "The mailman come while I was shaking out a rug on the front steps, and he hand it to me, and I must have forgot all about it. That there's Mr. Bruce's mail. You reckon there be somethin' extra in our check this week, sugar?"

The letters tingled nicely in my hands. I didn't remember any commandments that said anything about reading thy neighbor's mail. "Reckon there will be, Miss Sister," I said.

16

WHEN I GOT HOME, Edna was still gone, but she'd been back at some point in the day because I found a whole stack of messages she'd pulled from the answering machine.

I leafed through them absentmindedly while I spread the McNairs' mail out on the kitchen table. Call Dr. Kappler. Later, I promised myself. Call this client and that client. There was a message from Linda Nickells, a girlfriend of mine who's also an Atlanta cop, and another from Mac. I stuck the messages from Linda and Mac in my pocket and swept the others into the trash.

Then I turned back to my mail, or rather, Patti and Bruce's mail. They got a lot of it, advertising circulars from Rich's, Macy's, and The Parisian. A church bulletin, a legal newsletter for Bruce, a couple of home-and-hearth–type magazines for Patti, and a Lands End catalog. There was what looked like a form letter from the Heart Fund to Patti, a Visa bill, and a letter to Bruce from Southern Life Fidelity. All the good stuff was securely sealed.

I decided to sacrifice the Heart Fund letter for research purposes. I turned it over, tried sliding a metal letter opener under the flap. No good, the paper tore slightly. Envelope glue was a lot stronger now than it was in the days when I surreptitiously opened my sister's love letters from her boyfriend away at college. Those babies were so steamy they practically opened themselves. A few seconds with the teakettle and I knew every thought poor horny Wendell was having.

What I needed, I decided, was some high-tech chemical capable of dissolving the envelope glue. I looked under the kitchen sink. Formula 409? Fantastick? Windex? None of them looked promising. I went to the bathroom and found a bottle of nail polish remover and some Q-tips in the medicine cabinet.

I swabbed the remover on the envelope flap with the Q-tip and with the letter opener tried to nudge the flap open but it barely budged and it made the paper wrinkle in a funny way.

Maybe the old teakettle method was best after all. I was filling ours when I remembered the microwave: the working woman's friend. I ran a damp dish towel over the envelope back, popped it in the oven and nuked it for twenty seconds, which is how long I usually use it to soften butter for my morning toast.

Et voilà! With only a minor bit of resistance, the Heart Fund envelope popped open. I ran the dishcloth over the other two letters and gave them the same treatment. Then I tore up the junk mail and buried it and the magazines in the bottom of the kitchen trashcan.

I gathered the good stuff and took it to my bedroom for closer examination. I didn't want any witnesses to my latest act of mail fraud.

The McNairs' Visa statement showed a current balance of only about $360—not bad for a family I'd heard was having financial difficulties. But the previous month's balance told a different story. In January, they owed a whopping $6,682.43. Somehow, in the last month they'd managed to pay the bill off.

The card receipts themselves gave a mini financial history. A $60 charge for athletic shoes, a couple of gas purchases from a Shell station near the house, and a $16 purchase from the Book-of-the-Month Club. Like me, Bruce and Patti seemed to use their credit cards mostly for entertaining and eating out. I found a $36 receipt for a dinner at Red Lobster marked February 14, Valentine's Day, their anniversary. What a cheapskate, I thought. There was a $132 dinner at Bones, though, a pricey Buckhead steak house, and a $14 charge from a place called The Texas Tearoom. Bruce had signed the receipt, but the idea of the former Deadhead at a country music joint like The Tearoom made me laugh.

I jotted down the dates, places, and amounts for all the charge slips and carefully reassembled the bill to its original state, re-sticking the envelope with a dot of glue.

The letter from Southern Life Fidelity was an eye-opener. Bruce must have faxed in his claim for Patti's death benefits. And why not? Her policy was worth $1.2 million.

Although the letter stated that Georgia law required them to settle the claim within no more than fifteen working days, the letter stated the company's intent to seek "additional information concerning the policyholder's death before paying out accidental death benefits."

Whoa. I read the letter over again to make sure I understood just what all the legalese meant. What it implied, I thought, was that the insurance company also found something fishy about Patti's death.

"About darned time," I muttered under my breath as I resealed the letter. $1.2 million was a heavy chunk of change to carry on someone like Patti, who wasn't contributing a dime, as far as I knew, to the family income.

I was scrawling "Delivered Wrong Address" across the envelopes when I heard Edna come in the back door. I tucked the mail in my purse and scooted over to my computer terminal, pulling up the month's billing records.

I heard her drop her keys and purse on the kitchen counter with a loud clatter. Then I heard her come stomping down the hall toward my room. I could sense storm clouds gathering.

"You had to do it, didn't you?" she said, standing in my open doorway, hands on her hips. "You had to bully poor motherless Dylan into talking about Patti, didn't you?"

Her lips were pressed together, white with rage. I didn't stand a chance.

"DeeDee called Jean, and Jean called me in tears to tell me what you've been up to," she said. "I cannot believe you, Julia, I cannot believe my own child would do something so callous, and so spiteful, especially after everyone in this family has made it perfectly clear that they want this left up to the police. Don't you understand how hurt we all are? Don't you?"

Tears welled in her eyes. I started to try to defend myself. "Mom, I only—"

"No," she cried, putting her hands to her ears. "I do not want to hear a single word you have to say. And neither does anyone else in this family. DeeDee and Bruce are so angry at your meddling that they're talking about getting a court order to keep you away from Dylan. He was so hysterical when you left that they had to take him back for a session with Dr. Cook, and then give him a sedative. I wouldn't blame them if they sicced the cops on you. If I could turn you over my knee and whale the tar out of you, I'd do it, but you're too big, dammit." She turned on her heel and stalked off down the hallway.

"Shit," I said. I'd stepped in it this time. I'd hoped not to antagonize Bruce if I could help it, and now he and DeeDee were more determined than ever to keep the kid away from me.

I scrolled down the list of billings, my mind not really on what I was doing. It was after six, too late to try to find out anything about Bruce's insurance claim. And Mac would already have left his office. I dialed Linda Nickells's home phone number.

My friendship with Linda was a fairly recent one. We'd met when she worked a homicide case I was involved with the previous year. She'd moved in with her homicide captain, C. W. Hunsecker, who was an old buddy of mine. When they became romantically involved, Linda asked for and got a transfer out of homicide to the vice squad. These days she works weird shifts, which means we mostly keep in touch by phone.

"Nickells," she said crisply.

"Boy, once a cop, always a cop," I said. "Don't you ever go off duty, Linda?"

"Hey, girlfriend," she said warmly. "Feels like I spend all my time at the office. Guess I forget how to act when I get home."

"What's going on?"

Hunsecker, she said, was out of town, attending a white-collar crime training session at the FBI Academy at Quantico, Virginia. "He's been gone two days and I miss the old coot somethin' awful," she admitted. "I'm going stark raving sitting here at home. You wanna get together for a drink or something tonight?"

"Yeah," I said, my mind racing. "That'd be good. Maybe you can help me with something in the meantime."

"Like what?" she said warily. "It's not a homicide, I hope. You know how C. W. is."

"Carjacking," I said quickly. "It happened in Cobb County, so I wouldn't be stepping on C. W.'s toes."

"Uh-huh," she said, unconvinced. "Tell me more."

"The FBI is working on it with Cobb, and I heard a rumor that they think a gang might be involved. Hell, I didn't even know we had gangs in Atlanta."

"Yeah, well, they're here," Linda said. "And they're bad. Which bunch you wanna know about?"

"The Wrecking Crew. I'm particularly interested in a guy named Maleek Tebbetts. He's sort of their chief. Anything you could find would be great."

"Tebbetts," she said. "Spell that."

I did.

"What are you doing messing around with a carjacking in Cobb County for, Callahan?"

"Long story. The victim was a good friend, my cousin, actually. Some son of a bitch blew her away right in front of her nine-year-old son."

"Yeah, I read about that. Bankhead Highway, right? Didn't know she was related to you. I'm sorry."

"Can you help me any?"

"I'm not promising anything," she said. "I'll make some calls. Where do you want to meet and what time?"

A thought occurred to me. "You know a place called The Texas Tearoom?"

She laughed. "The redneck joint out on Covington Highway? We did an undercover drug buy in the parking lot there a couple of months ago. You going country all of a sudden?"

"Nah," I said. "The place just came to mind. Meet you there around nine, nine-thirty?"

"That'll be fine," Linda said. "Guess I better get my shit-kicker boots out, huh?"

"You could be the first black cowgirl those dudes ever saw," I told her. "This could be fun."

"Fun my ass," she said. "I'll see you there."

I heard heavy footsteps in the hall again, then looked up to see Mac leaning in the doorway, his tie undone and a bemused expression on his face.

"Hey," I said, getting up to give him a kiss. "I didn't hear you come in. What are you doing in this neck of the woods this time of day?"

He flopped down on my bed, kicked off his loafers and unbuttoned his top shirt button. "I had a late meeting at the Fulton County courthouse and rather than try to fight traffic on Georgia 400 I thought I'd stop off here and have dinner with you."

"Great," I said, flopping down beside him. "Do you want to eat here?"

"Are you cooking?" he asked. "Edna is in the kitchen right now eating a plate of warmed-up leftovers. She looked kind of pissed when I came in."

I took a pillow and popped it under my head. "Oh yes. She's pissed all right. And that's putting it mildly."

He grabbed the other pillow and put it under his head. "About your looking into Patti's murder?"

"How'd you guess?"

He took my hand and kissed it, then got up. "Men's intuition. Okay, where do you want to go?"

"Somewhere quick and cheap," I said, getting up to look at myself in the mirror. I ran my fingers through my dark curly hair, picked up a tube of mascara and gave my eyelashes a quick coating, followed by a slash of lipstick.

I was wearing black stirrup pants and a long pullover black knit sweater, which would do fine for what I had planned.

"Makeup for me," Mac said, peering over my shoulder. "I'm flattered."

"For you and for later," I said, picking up my purse. "I'm meeting Linda Nickells at The Texas Tearoom at nine-thirty. So we'll need to take two cars."

"Sure will," Mac said. "The Tearoom is a little too low-rent for my tastes. How come you and Linda are going there?"

"Tell you later," I promised.

We ended up having dinner at a place called The Avondale Pizza Cafe. In the seventies the place was a hippy hangout called The Mellow Mushroom, a funky little screen-door kind of place where the help always looked slightly stoned. A few years ago somebody else bought the place, slicked it up, added a line of imported beer and fancy cheesecakes. Now it seems to appeal to the yuppie family set from Avondale and Decatur. The bathrooms are cleaner, but I kind of miss the old 'Shroom.

We ordered The Avondale Avalanche and a pitcher

of beer and watched the television mounted near the ceiling while we waited for our food.

Channel eleven was running a special series, "Women in Jeopardy," pointing to a spate of violent crimes against women, including the brutal carjacking murder of Cobb County housewife Patti McNair. The mid-thirties–looking newscaster had a Donna Reed PTA–mom sincerity and an annoying Midwestern accent. Her solution to crimes against women? "Learn self-defense. Keep your car doors locked. Get a can of mace. Consider purchasing a car phone for emergencies."

While I was still raving at Donna Reed, the waitress arrived at the table with a pizza that looked like the cook had dumped everything in the kitchen on it.

"Shit," I sputtered, picking an artichoke heart off the pizza with my fingertips. "None of that stuff would have saved Patti's life. When that animal pulled out his gun, it was all over. I tell you, Mac, since all this started I've seriously considered starting to keep my gun in the van."

His eyebrows shot up. "You're serious? You? Miss Gun Control Freak of the World? With a gun in the glove box?"

I pulled a slice of pizza off the pie and nibbled at the loose strands of mozzarella that stretched between the slice and the mother pie.

"This thing is getting to me," I admitted. "Edna is absolutely furious with me. I haven't seen her this mad since the day Kevin called home to say he'd dropped out of college and gotten married to his pregnant seventeen-year-old girlfriend. Everybody else is pissed too. I thought DeeDee would scratch my eyes out today when she came in the house and saw Dylan crying. And it wasn't even all my fault."

He reached across the table with a napkin and dabbed at a spot of food on my chin. "If it's upsetting you and everybody else, why not leave it alone? Just walk away. You can't right every wrong, you know. Let the cops handle it. You told me the FBI was involved. These guys are experts. And you're not, not at this kind of thing."

"I know," I sighed. "But I can't help it. This is like a scab I've just got to pick. I keep thinking of Patti. How much she'd changed and how little I find I really knew about her. It's like I'm trying to find out who she was so I can find out why she died. And I just, I know this sounds conceited, but I just can't believe the cops can get to the bottom of it the way I could."

"What is it you think happened?" he asked.

"I'm not sure," I said. "Little crumbs of information keep falling out on the table. Like today, Dylan may have told Sister something really important about the killer, that he drove a truck. I wonder if he told the cops that. I bet not. And then I find out that Bruce had over a million dollars' worth of insurance on Patti."

"So?" he said, sprinkling parmesan cheese on his pizza. "Lots of people have life insurance. It's dirt cheap these days, you know. Besides, I thought you liked Bruce. You're starting to really suspect him, aren't you?"

"God, I don't know. I don't want to. I've known the guy for like twenty years. He helped draw up the House Mouse incorporation papers. He closed the loan on my house and didn't charge me anything."

Mac pointed to the last slice of pizza on the plate. "Are you going to eat that?"

I waved it away. The queasiness had disappeared, but I didn't want to push my luck. "Eat it. I'm full."

He picked up the slice and started chewing at the pointed end. "He's a nice guy. That's what you're telling me."

"Was," I corrected. "People change. He'd left his old law practice to start a new firm. He and Patti were having real money problems. And I think the marriage was in trouble. He'd even started going to country and western bars, for God's sake. This from a guy who thought Frank Zappa played bubble-gum music. I do think he was under a lot of pressure. And Patti had changed, too."

"Lots of people are under pressure and they don't kill their wives," he reminded me. "Besides, didn't I hear on the news that the cops think gang activity may be connected to all this?"

I took a napkin and dabbed at my face and sweater with it. Eating pizza is usually a total-body immersion experience for me. There was a speck of pepperoni clinging stubbornly to my sleeve, and a smear of tomato sauce over my right breast.

"That's what I'm hoping to check out tonight when I see Linda," I said. "In a way, if it was a gang, it would be a relief. Then it would mean she wasn't killed by somebody she knew. That's what I'm hoping for. But I've gotta know, Mac, I just gotta."

17

I KNEW I MUST BE getting close to The Texas Tearoom after I passed the forty-foot-high bow-legged cowboy in front of a western-wear store called Cowpuncher's Palace.

The Texas Tearoom would have been hard to miss anyway, a huge red barn with movable neon crossed branding irons mounted on the roof. The stadium-sized parking lot was only about a third full; traffic ran to pickup trucks and big American gas guzzlers.

The woman at the door, an anemic-looking brunette with hair teased into a perfect jet-black snowball, barely looked at me. "Ladies' night tonight, no cover," she said, not bothering to stifle a yawn.

Inside, The Tearoom looked like somebody from New Jersey's idea of the Old West. Neon cactus clusters glowed from walls covered in a dusty brown shag carpet, and hay bales, old nail barrels, rusted farm implements, and a broken-down buckboard had been dragged in to contribute to the rustic look. There was a mechanical bull mounted in the middle of a pit surrounded by nasty-looking stained mattresses, but nobody was riding tonight.

There were three bars dotted around the cavernous room, with a big wooden dance floor in the middle.

Only one bar was in operation tonight. A couple of

hundred people might have been there, a good crowd for a smaller joint, but small potatoes for a place this size.

A raised platform at the edge of the dance floor held equipment for a band, but they must have been on break, because the sound system had Willie Nelson warning mamas not to let their babies grow up to be cowboys.

I took a seat at the bar and waited for the bartender to finish his conversation with the waitress.

"Jack and water," I said when the bartender turned to me. The waitress glared at me. Tips must be pretty crappy on ladies' night.

He brought me my drink and I sipped it slowly, scanning the room for Linda. On the dance floor, a dozen or so women were performing some intricately choreographed dance, all of them with their thumbs hooked in jeans pockets, high-heeled cowboy boots kicking, sliding and thumping in time to the music. The men in the room, outnumbered and out-gunned, stood around in clusters at the edge of the floor, eyeing the women like prize heifers at auction.

"Don't girls dance with boys anymore?" I asked the bartender.

He grinned. With his red polo shirt, khaki slacks, and neatly trimmed hair, he looked as out of place among the pearl button and big belt buckle crowd as I did. "They do when there's enough to go around. Wednesday nights is hen night here. Everybody dances, with or without a man."

"Has that dance got a name?" I asked.

He squinted and looked. "Looks like the Electric Glide to me. You want to learn how, Rochelle, the girl in black there, she gives free instructions."

I followed where he was pointing. At the head of the line a lithe blonde aerobics instructor wearing a black cowboy hat, black halter top, black fringed boots, and the shortest, tightest, black cut-off jeans I'd ever seen was walking a short, balding dentist type through the moves of the dance. He wore a frozen smile and stared intently at his white patent-leather loafers, willing them to do his bidding.

"No thanks," I said. "Last line dance I tried to learn was the Hully-Gully. These days I like to have a partner when I dance."

"Know what you mean," he said. He walked away to fill the waitress's order while I sat and sipped.

He was back a few minutes later. "So if you don't Texas two-step, what are you doing someplace like this?" he asked, resting his arms on the bar.

"I've driven by this place a hundred times and wondered what it was like inside, so I decided to find out," I said. "Plus I just found out a friend of mine comes in here sometimes. He's not exactly the country western type either. Bruce McNair, you know him?"

He squeezed his eyes shut and thought. "Is that the lawyer guy, kinda shaggy hair going gray, maybe forty or so?"

"Yeah," I said, surprised. "Does he come here often?"

"Oh yeah," the bartender said. "He's a friend of the owner, Mr. Stovall. He comes in with him and some other guy. Your friend drinks Tecate with lime, right?"

"I guess."

"Haven't seen him in here lately, though, not since Mr. Stovall opened the new club."

"New club?"

"Yeah. The Laffactory. It's a comedy club out on Johnson Ferry Road, right next to the Ramada Inn there. Our other club, Boot Hill, is across the street. So Mr. Stovall only comes around here on Friday nights, to check how we're doing."

"And how are you doing?" I asked.

He shrugged. "Okay. Wednesdays are usually like this. Kinda slow, but it's a way to pay the light bill. The waitresses bitch about getting stiffed by the women, but Mr. Stovall says it's a clientele builder."

"So when are you busy?"

"Weekends," he said. "Friday night, that's when we have our Buns and Boots contest."

I eyed the crowd on the dance floor again. "Is that what it sounds like?"

"You bet," he said enthusiastically. "Man, they eat it up. Fridays, we got all three bars going, the place is wall-to-wall. Unbelievable tips. We give away a couple of thousand dollars' worth of prizes. Trips to Daytona, free dinners . . . "

"Mud flaps. Tire gauges. Cans of hairspray," I added.

"What?"

"Never mind."

"You ought to come back this Friday," he said. "We got Wynonna Judd's second cousin, Sonya Stuckey, this week. You close your eyes, you'd swear to God she was Wynonna."

Just then, Linda sauntered up. She was wearing a short, tight black skirt, an oversized black leather jacket over a white shirt, and a metal-studded leather baseball cap pulled down over her short-cropped hair. Nickells always looks like Nickells. The child has style.

We ordered her a wine cooler and me another Jack and water and found a table overlooking the dance floor.

The house band, Streets of Cheyenne, started to warm up.

"Not bad," Linda said, as they swung into "Here's a Quarter, Call Someone Who Cares." "Kind of a cross between a bargain basement Alabama and Sons of the Pioneers."

I eyed her suspiciously. "What's a black chick from Chicago know about hillbilly music?" I asked.

She winked. "Don't tell C. W., but when I can't sleep at night, I get up and watch The Nashville Network on cable. It's like looking at a parallel universe, you know? They got some good music on there. You ever hear Sweethearts of the Rodeo?"

"Probably not," I admitted. "So how is old Carver Washington?"

We spent the next thirty minutes hashing out our personal problems. C. W., it seems, had gotten his divorce from Vonette finalized and wanted to get married and have a baby. Linda wanted a baby like a cat wants a bubblebath. I told her about how Mac and I were struggling with our own relationship. We both want to live together, but with my business, and Edna, and his goofy black Lab Rufus, it seemed unlikely to happen anytime soon.

The waitress came by to check on our drinks. I ordered a Diet Coke, Linda asked for club soda with lime. The waitress rolled her eyes in disgust.

When she was gone, Linda dug in her purse and pulled out a small spiral-bound notebook.

"Maleek Tebbetts," she said.

"I'm listening."

She glanced down at her notes. "The boy is bad, Callahan. Twenty-four. Born in Belle Glade, Florida. Got a sheet as long as your arm. Started with shoplifting at eleven, burglary at thirteen, on to auto theft, aggravated assault, armed robbery, sale and possession. He was released from Lake Butler two years ago September, moved up here, and was staying with a sister out at Garden Homes."

"Garden Homes," I said, interrupting her. "That's right near where Patti was killed."

"Yeah, well, he didn't stay there long," Linda said. "I talked to a friend of mine at the housing authority. She said they kicked the sister out because Maleek started a one-man crime wave there. Turned the apartment into a crack house. He's been gone from there since April of ninety-three."

"So where's he living now?" I asked. The waitress came back with our drinks and slapped them down on the table, sloshing coke, soda, and ice all over the tabletop. "Sorry," she said, flicking a bar towel across the mess.

Linda took two singles out of her purse and let them flutter down into the puddle. "Me too," she said.

"He doesn't live anywhere that anybody knows of," Linda said after our waitress stormed off. "Like they say on the streets, he stays with a couple of different girls that we know of, got about half a dozen little babies scattered around."

"Share the wealth," I said, sitting back in my chair. "Do you know anything about any of the girlfriends?"

Her eyes glanced down at the neatly written notes. "Here's one. Nichelle Lattimore. She's sixteen, lives in Grady Homes with her grandmother. Has a ten-month-old son by our friend Maleek. She went up behind another girl, fifteen years old, who she suspected of sleeping with Maleek, went up behind her in the hallway at school after lunch and stuck a sharpened nail file between the girl's shoulders. Blade went in a couple of inches, too."

I winced. "Yikes."

"Yeah," Linda said. "She's playing for keeps. Maleek got right ill about Nichelle sticking his new lady. He slapped her around pretty good. Fractured her arm, dislocated her shoulder, knocked out a couple of teeth." Linda shook her head. "The grandmother swore out a warrant against Maleek. All the cops have to do is find him."

Things were happening out on the dance floor. "Everybody up for the Tush Push," the band's lead singer announced. People swarmed from their chairs.

"Tush push?" Linda asked. "And ya'll complain about suggestive lyrics in rap music?"

The Tush Push looked to be like a square dance with some extra bump and grind action thrown in. We both watched, fascinated, as close to a hundred people kicked and wriggled and shimmied across the floor.

A thought occurred to me. "You reckon Nichelle's still mad at Maleek?"

"Wouldn't you be?"

"Maybe she'd like to talk to a sympathetic listener," I suggested.

"Maybe she'd cut you like she did that fifteen-year-old," Linda pointed out.

Getting sliced with a manicure implement didn't appeal to me right then. "Has she gone to court yet?"

She shook her head no. "She's out on bond."

"Maybe a kindly, understanding female vice cop could convince her to talk about Maleek if the charges against her were dropped," I said.

Linda laughed. "You think we haven't thought of that? The grandmother won't let us in the apartment. She's scared witless of Maleek. Smart old lady."

"But you'd still like to talk to her, wouldn't you?"

"They'd like ice water in hell, too," she said. "Every cop in Atlanta would like to put his hands on Tebbetts. Word is he's got his crew bringing cocaine up from Miami. And he's making the money for the buys with all these armed robberies and home invasions."

I sensed someone standing behind me. It was our friendly waitress, waiting for another lucrative drink order. "Anything else?"

We both said no at the same time. "Come back when you can stay longer," she snarled and left.

Linda laughed in disbelief. "Tell the truth now, Callahan. What are we doing in this dive?"

"I wanted to see what the place looked like," I said. "I, uh, found a credit card receipt signed by my cousin's husband, Bruce. It caught my interest because Bruce is definitely not a bolo tie kind of guy."

"Well?" she said expectantly.

I scooted my chair around so I could see the bar. "The bartender says Bruce is good friends with the owner, a Mr. Stovall. Ever hear of him?"

Linda craned her neck to see what I was looking at. "Grady Stovall. Yeah, I've heard of him. He's owned nightclubs around Atlanta for years. No police record, or the county would pull his liquor licenses."

"What about that drug buy you mentioned? Did Stovall have anything to do with that?"

"Not that we know of. I wasn't on that one. But I heard about it because the bad guys tried to rip off our guys. Just as the deal was going down a carload of guys pulls up and opens fire on our guys. Luckily, they were both wearing bullet-proof vests. One guy, J. T. Shoemaker, got nicked in the calf, the other guy, Dave Alexander, had his ear creased."

"Jesus," I said, glancing around. "Place looks pretty harmless tonight."

"Yeah," she said, watching one cowboy two-step by in a pair of painted-on jeans. "It ain't like these guys could conceal a weapon in these tight-butt britches. I bet if you took a sperm count in here you wouldn't get out of the single digits."

18

S O MAYBE I DID oversleep. All I know is, by the
time I got up and dressed Thursday, my life was in a
shambles.

When I stumbled into the kitchen, Ruby, Jackie, and
Neva Jean were all sitting around the kitchen table, reading my newspaper and drinking my coffee on my company time.

"What's this?" I asked, not bothering to stifle a yawn.
"Why aren't y'all working? It's," I glanced at the kitchen
clock, "nine A.M. Jesus, nine already? Where's Edna?"

"She's gone," Neva Jean announced. "When
Swannelle dropped me off at eight she was just backing
down the driveway."

"Gone where?" I asked, opening the refrigerator
door and scanning the shelves for something to eat. The
news was not good. We were out of milk. Out of eggs, out
of juice, out of butter. I closed the refrigerator and flipped
open the bread box on the counter. Out of bread too. I
stood at the pantry door. The only cereal I saw was a half-
full box of Lucky Charms left over from the last time one
of my nephews had spent the night. I took the box, sat
down at the table and scooped up a handful. Stale. Why
was I not surprised?

"Edna said she was going to stay with your aunt Jean

for a few days on account of she almost had another heart attack because the police come back and been asking a lot of questions about your cousin Patti," Neva Jean said. "You gonna eat all that cereal yourself? I didn't have no breakfast this morning cause Swannelle had another of his coughing fits and we had to run out to the drugstore . . . "

"Help yourself," I said, shoving the box across the table toward her.

Ruby and Jackie put down their newspaper sections and looked at me expectantly.

"Me and Ruby are supposed to work together today, Edna said yesterday," Jackie said. "New clients."

"So?" I wondered if there was any coffee left in the pot. I got up and poured myself the last half cup.

"So, we need to know the people's names and where they live at and what all they want done," Jackie said.

"Edna didn't tell you yesterday?"

"No'm," Ruby said sadly. "She wrote it down in the book. I saw her do that after she talked to the people. Put it right in the book."

I went to the shelf above the microwave where Edna keeps all our important stuff: the company checkbook, the appointment book, our insurance policies, and the current issue of *TV Guide*. No appointment book. A quick check of every other nook and hidey-hole in the kitchen also failed to turn it up.

I sank down into one of the creaking oak chairs and tried to think. Where would Edna have put the appointment book?

Neva Jean had the Lucky Charms box in her lap now and was munching away happily. "Vif fuff ith wood," she said through a mouthful of yellow moons and green clovers.

"Neva Jean," I said sternly. "What are you doin' sitting around here with Ruby and Jackie? I know for a fact you do the Mealors every Thursday morning."

She shook her head violently, sending small puffs of colored cereal crumbs floating through the air. After more chewing and an exaggerated swallow, she took a swig of coffee.

"Mrs. Mealor called and had Edna switch her with some friends of hers, the Deardorffs, I think the name was."

"Then why aren't you at the Deardorffs drinking their coffee?"

"Because I don't know where they live or what time or what they want or nothing."

"Don't tell me," I said. "Edna wrote it down in the book."

"That's right," she sang.

It seemed we were right back where we started. "All right," I sighed. "I'll call Edna at my aunt's and see if we can straighten this mess out."

My cousin Jack's ex-wife, Peggy, answered the phone at Aunt Jean's.

"Oh. Hello, Julia," she said frostily. When you're on the ex-in-law's shit list, you know you're in trouble.

"Your mother is helping Jean get dressed," Peggy said. "I'll tell her you're on the phone."

While I waited for Edna, I renewed my search for the book, opening cupboards and drawers and searching the shelves. I found two pairs of sunglasses and about three hundred expired grocery coupons, but no appointment book. The girls sat and read and tried to pretend they weren't interested in knowing what was going on between me and Edna.

"Yes?" she said when she came on the line.

"Mom," I said, "you might have told me you were going to Aunt Jean's."

"You were asleep," she said. "So now you know. What's the problem?"

I looked at all my Mice sitting around my table. "I've got Neva Jean, Jackie, and Ruby sitting here twiddling their thumbs because they don't know where they're working today and I can't find the book. Do you know where it is?"

"I've got it," she said. "I have a bunch of calls to make today, to line up next week's schedule."

"Well that's just great," I exploded. "You take off without having the courtesy to tell me you're leaving, and then you leave everything here in a big mess. Just how did you expect me to run the business while you're out there holding Aunt Jean's hand?"

"Don't you talk to me in that tone of voice," Edna warned. "You've done enough talking this week, I'd say. Enough to give your aunt an angina attack and to send your cousin's child to the therapist. Now put Jackie on the phone."

What I wanted to do was hang up. Instead I put the receiver in Jackie's hand. "Here."

"Yes, ma'am," Jackie said respectfully into the phone. Then she reached in her pocket, took out a pencil and piece of paper, and started writing. "Yes. All right. I'll tell her."

Jackie handed the phone to Neva Jean. "Edna wants to talk to you."

Neva Jean went through the same act, yessing and writing down directions. Then she hung up.

Jackie and Ruby went to the closet where we keep cleaning supplies and smocks, got their supplies, and headed for the back door. "Call me when you get done with these new people," I told them. "I may need you to fit in another house today."

Neva Jean loaded up her caddy with supplies and struggled into a pink smock that looked dangerously tight. "Edna mad at you?" she asked, trying to fasten the bottom button.

"You could say that."

"It's none of my business," Neva Jean said, "but you only got one mama in this world, and Edna is a good one. So if I was you, I'd call her right back and tell her I was sorry, and could she please come back home."

"You're right," I said. "It is none of your business.

Now I suggest you get going on what *is* your business."

When they were all gone, I puttered around the kitchen for a while, putting coffee cups in the dishwasher, folding the newspaper, and picking up stray Lucky Charms from the floor. I had a good idea there were House Mouse appointments I was supposed to keep today, but there was no way I was going to call Edna back and beg her to tell me what to do.

Instead, I sat down at the computer and called up my file on Patti's murder. I added the information I'd gathered yesterday and last night, then sat staring at the computer screen, willing the disparate words to form some answers. Instead I got more questions.

I got out the phone book and looked up the listing for Southern Life Fidelity. It was an 800 number. When the receptionist answered the phone, I asked her what city I'd reached.

"Nashville, Tennessee," she said proudly. "We're the home office."

It took a while, but I finally tracked down the head of claims investigations and told him what I wanted.

"Keegan Waller's down in Atlanta right now," the man said. "He calls in for messages, though, if you want to leave your number."

I did and I did. Then I sat and fiddled some more. The news of Aunt Jean's heart problem was depressing. If she got that upset over a visit from the cops, I didn't want to know how she'd feel about the suspicions growing in my mind about her son-in-law.

Maleck Tebbetts, I told myself firmly. He's the bad guy here.

How to get a fix on such a bad guy was the problem. If every cop in Atlanta was actively looking for him, what chance did I have?

Nichelle Lattimore.

I doodled a while. It frees up my left brain. Or maybe it's my right brain. I can never remember which side controls the creative thought processes. But I sketched cars and trucks, airplanes, guns, and little boys.

I thumbed the phone book. The worst places in the world to try to get information are bureaucracies. But of course the bureaucrats are the ones who have all the information.

And of all the bureaucracies in Atlanta to have to deal with, the Atlanta Housing Authority is one of the worst. No wonder half their low-income housing units are empty at the same time they have two-year-long waiting lists. The AHA seems to train their clerks and administrators to strive for mediocrity. Their idea of on-the-job-training probably consisted of staring, scratching, yawning, and gum-chewing.

"Nichelle Lattimore," I repeated for the fourth, or was it the fifth, time. "L as in lazy. A as in attitude. Double t as in double overtime, i as in illiterate, and then m-o-r-e as in more money."

"Oh," the male clerk said, a light bulb clicking on somewhere in the dimness of his consciousness. "Okay. Yeah. Here we go. Who'd you say you are again?"

"Venus McDonald at the Atlanta School Board," I said quickly. "Nichelle has put in to transfer schools and we need to discuss the matter with her legal guardian. But the information we have in our files seems out of date. The old phone number we dialed says the line has been disconnected. Is she still living with her mother in Grady Homes?"

"Not the mother," he said quickly. "We have her living with a grandmother, Mrs. Susie Battles. You got the new phone number?"

"Give it to me, please," I commanded in my best bureaucrat to bureaucrat voice.

After I hung up, I thought of all the reasons I shouldn't mess with a helpless old lady who was only trying to protect her granddaughter.

Then I thought about Patti, who'd been unable to

protect her own helpless children. And about that nail file Nichelle had used to stab her classmate.

"Mrs. Susie Battles," I said, keeping my bureaucratic voice. "Yes. Venus McDonald at the Social Security Administration here ... No, I can't do anything about the check you had stolen last month. But we do need you to come down to our office right away to sign some papers ... Yes. ... Well, it's probably an increase of about twenty a month. We can see you at three P.M. today. ... Yes, at the Richard Russell Federal Building on Spring Street. Fine. We'll see you then."

I hung up the phone, guiltily. I'd been at the Social Security offices with Ruby months ago, trying to help her straighten out her benefits. What should have been a fifteen-minute errand had turned into a day-long nightmare. Mrs. Battles wouldn't be home before suppertime tonight, if she was lucky.

But it would be hours before Nichelle was due home from school. And without my appointment book it was useless to try to conduct any House Mouse business.

Instead, I decided to give the rest of the day over to research. The Georgia Secretary of State's office was a giant step up in efficiency from the Atlanta Housing Authority. The girl in corporate records was actually helpful—darn near cheerful. I guess the state has better benefits.

"The Texas Tearoom, Inc.'s president is listed as Grady Stovall. Secretary is Luanne Stovall. Agent of record is Bruce W. McNair," she said.

It was pretty much what I had expected. But so what? Bruce was a lawyer. Lawyers handle incorporations all the time. Hell, if I recalled correctly, he was agent of record for my own company. I had her check the records for Boot Hill and The Laffactory too. All three had the same officers.

"Your records are computerized, right?" I asked. "Can you search to see what other corporations Bruce W. McNair is agent of record for?"

There was a pause. "I can, but it may take some time, and I have other calls waiting. Do you want to give me your number and I'll call you back?"

While I was waiting I went on a scavenger hunt for food. Mama Bear was gone and I was sure she'd left the cupboard bare out of pure spite. It was only eleven-thirty, but I'd had no real breakfast and my stomach was protesting, loudly.

In the end I found a can of chicken noodle soup. Since nobody was around, I ate it standing up, out of the can, dipping into it with some saltine crackers. The feeling was positively decadent.

I was just finishing when the phone rang. It was my friend at the secretary of state's office. "Got a pen? Mr. McNair represents eight different corporations that I could find."

I wrote as fast as I could, thanked her, and hung up. The House Mouse was, as I thought, represented by Bruce. As was a company called Stovall Enterprises, my cousin Jack's construction company, something called Georgia Sanitary Supply, and JXD Holdings.

JXD Holdings meant nothing to me, but Georgia Sanitary Supply rang a bell. I went into the supply closet and checked the shelves. We buy most of our cleaning stuff for the House Mouse from a wholesaler called Ajax Distributors, but I seemed to remember having seen the name Georgia Sanitary Supply.

On a shelf near the bottom of the closet I found it: a dust-covered gallon plastic jug of pine-scented floor cleaner. Edna had gotten a mailer about Georgia Sanitary Supply and had even shopped there once. But their prices were significantly higher than our regular wholesaler, and the girls had complained that the floor cleaner smelled more like squirrel piss than pine trees. We'd never shopped there again, as far as I knew.

I squatted down to look at the label on the cleaner. Georgia Sanitary Supply was located at an address off

Northside Drive not far from downtown. I got my notepad and wrote down the address. A shopping trip for cleaning supplies seemed to be in order today.

Then I tried to call back my friend at the secretary of state's office, but she'd gone to lunch. I left my name and number.

I was in the process of locking the back door behind me when I heard the phone ringing. I fumbled with the key in the lock, dropped the key ring, picked it up again, threw the door open and lunged for the phone.

"Hello," I said breathlessly.

"Keegan Waller here," a high-pitched man's voice said. "I got a message that you called?"

I told him I was interested in talking about Patti McNair's murder, which was fine with him, since he was in town investigating it. We agreed to meet at the Varsity. He told me to look for a man wearing a brown tweed coat, driving a blue-gray Ford Taurus with Avis tags. "Meet you at the curb-service area," he said. Keegan Waller had been to Atlanta before. "If you get there before I do, could you get me a double order of rings and an F.O.?" I asked. Chicken soup out of a can, standing up, does not count as lunch.

My mouth was watering as I pulled into the Varsity's parking lot. When I was a kid, my dad would take the whole family to the Varsity on Saturday afternoons for lunch. We'd pile in the family wagon, pull up at the big red and white fifties diner and have a grease fest: chili cheese-dogs, PCs (which meant plain chocolate milk) for my brothers, and FOs, or frosted orange drinks, for my sister and me. Everybody had an order of chili rings and a fried peach pie for dessert.

I buttoned my jacket against the damp March air after I got out of my car. I spotted Waller's car immediately, went over, and slid into the front seat.

He had a grease-spattered cardboard tray of food on the seat between us. The car reeked of fried onions. Divine.

The first thing you noticed about Keegan Waller was his eyes. They were big and brown and sorrowful, like a basset hound's. The second thing you noticed was his head. The man was tee-totally bald. And he wasn't that old either, maybe in his mid-forties.

We exchanged some mindless chitchat about the weather and differences between traffic in Nashville and Atlanta.

I nibbled delicately on my onion rings, waiting for the subject to come up. Finally, I couldn't stand it anymore. "What can you tell me about my cousin's murder?" I blurted out.

He shook his head and chewed on his hot dog. "I'm in the business of gathering information, not giving it away."

"The same is true of me, Keegan," I said sweetly. "But since Patti was my cousin, this is the exception to the rule. I thought we could exchange information. You know, I tell you something new, you tell me something. Unless your company has rules about that?"

He glanced around the parking lot as though he were afraid of being overheard. "On an off-the-record basis, right?"

I spread the lapels of my coat. "I'm not wearing a wire," I said, "and I'm not a lawyer. I just want to find out who killed Patti."

"As does Southern Fidelity," he said, wiping his hands on a napkin. "I don't know if you're aware of this, but your cousin had a substantial life insurance policy with us. For $1.2 million, to be exact."

"Really?" I said, feigning surprise rather nicely, I thought. "Isn't that quite a lot for someone like Patti?"

"Precisely," Waller said. "But in your cousin's income bracket, it's not unusual for a couple to have major coverage. Frankly, the facts of the case are what caused us to postpone settlement of the claim."

"What facts are those?" I asked.

Waller frowned. "You're a private investigator. What makes you think it wasn't just an ordinary homicide?"

"The main thing is the location of the murder," I said. "Have you been out to the crime scene yet?"

"That's where I'm headed after I leave you."

"Well, it's in a bad part of town," I said. "Right near a public housing project with a pretty high crime rate. Patti had almost a phobia about driving anywhere out of her own corner of Cobb County. She wouldn't even drive to my house alone."

"Maybe she was lost?" he suggested.

"That's a possibility," I admitted. "But the more questions I ask, the more I have. Patti's life had really changed in the last few months."

"How do you mean?" he asked.

How did I mean? Patti was nearly forty. She had a right to make changes in her life, didn't she? It didn't necessarily mean her husband had killed her.

I took a deep breath. "She and Bruce had been fighting. They'd been in counseling. There were money problems all of a sudden. One of her best friends is convinced Patti was having an affair."

"And she'd seen a lawyer about a divorce," Waller added.

"What?" I said, startled. "Who? What lawyer had she seen?"

Waller brought a small notebook from his coat pocket, leafing through the pages before stopping. "Updegraff. Beverly Updegraff. Ever heard of her?"

"Bruce's former law partner," I said.

"She wasn't very forthcoming," Waller complained. "She did say Mrs. McNair visited her in her office six weeks ago for some preliminary advice about divorce proceedings. She was concerned about custody issues."

"My God," I said. "I had no idea things were that bad. She never said a word."

"Mrs. McNair was supposed to come back to see Ms.

Updegraff the following week, to start drawing up papers. But she called and canceled the appointment," Waller said. "She told Ms. Updegraff she'd decided to make the marriage work, for the sake of the children."

"Well, her priest said that they'd been in counseling, and he thought they had patched things up," I said. "Of course, this is the same priest Patti's brother Michael said he thought Patti was in love with."

"Really?" Waller said. "What's the priest's name?"

"Martin Covington, Our Lady of Lourdes church," I said. "He'll talk to you, but he'll just tell you what he told me. That he was Patti's spiritual advisor and nothing more."

"I'll just bet," Waller said, winking. "You mentioned Mrs. McNair's brother. I'd like to talk to him."

"Michael Rivers," I said. "But he doesn't live in town. He lives in Charlotte."

"I'll find him," Waller said. "Any other relatives as nosy as you?"

"Not hardly," I said glumly. "Everybody else just wants to get the investigation over with and forget about it. I've got the entire family alienated. This morning my own mother moved out without telling me. And I can't say I really suspect Bruce of murder. I don't want to suspect him."

Waller took a sip from a cardboard cup of coffee. "Homicide will tear up a family. Even when it's a stranger-on-stranger case. It tears families apart just when they need to stick together most."

I smiled bitterly. "The FBI and the Cobb County police have a suspect, you know, a black crack dealer who's head of one of the local gangs."

"But they haven't ruled out Bruce McNair as a suspect either," Waller said. "I spoke with Charlie Fouts just this morning. McNair isn't in the clear on this yet."

"I hope he will be," I said, and I meant it.

"If my company didn't have $1.2 million riding on

this thing, I'd say I hope you're right," Waller said. "But money talks, you know. And your cousin's husband has more than a million reasons for wanting his wife dead."

19

THE CAR PHONE RANG as I was leaving the Varsity.

"Callahan? Does it cost extra to call you in your car?" Ruby's voice was hesitant, apologetic.

"Don't worry about it as long as it's business," I said. "What's up? Are you and Jackie finished already?"

"My goodness, yes," Ruby laughed. "These new folks got a little bitty baby, and the woman, she keep that house 'bout as tidy as you please. Me and Jackie want to know do you have something else for us to do?"

A thought struck me. "Tell you what. Jackie can go on over to Mrs. Tobin's condo in Ansley Park. That's Edna's job, but it won't take Jackie but an hour or two. How'd you like to do some detecting work with me?"

She hesitated. "It ain't nothin' dangerous, is it? Because I've got my Missionary Circle at seven tonight and it's my turn to give the devotion."

Ruby Edwards is the sweetest, churchiest woman, black or white, I've ever met. She supports her husband, who retired on disability from the railroad, and her daughter and three small children on her House Mouse paycheck with never a word of complaint. When she's not working for us or doing for her family, she's at the tiny Pentecostal church across the street from her house.

"No, it's not especially dangerous," I said. "But I need to talk to a black teenager who lives in Grady Homes and I'm afraid it might look suspicious for me to be sitting outside her house by myself waiting for her to come home. I don't want to look like a cop and scare her."

Ruby laughed merrily. "Way I look in this raggedy old housedress today, I'll fit right in over at that housing project. I can have Jackie drop me at the MARTA train and you could pick me up at the Georgia State station. Would that be all right?"

When I saw the dingy yellow brick mass of Grady Memorial Hospital looming to the right, I knew we were near Grady Homes. The proximity of the housing project to one of the largest public hospitals in the country was serendipitous. Victims of the frequent shootings, stabbings, and drug overdoses could crawl, if necessary, to the emergency room a scant few blocks away.

A cluster of men, boys some of them, stood huddled around the door of the Family Superette on Bell Street, laughing and sipping from crumpled brown paper bags. It was two-thirty on a Thursday afternoon. I guess these guys hadn't heard the latest figures claiming that unemployment was a thing of the past in Atlanta.

Ruby tsk-tsked at the sight. "Shame on them," she said. "Got nothing better to do than drink their lives away."

I swung a hard right into the red brick maze of the housing project and slowed down, looking for Susie Battles's apartment. Both sides of Bell were lined with parked cars. I drummed the steering wheel in frustration. Looking in the rearview mirror I saw a car pull out of a parking slot four cars behind me. I let it pass, then backed up illegally and wedged the van into the space.

Apartment 407 was two doors from where we were parked. The afternoon had gotten dark and overcast, and someone had turned on the porch light. "This is the place," I told her.

While we waited I explained why I wanted to talk to Nichelle Lattimore.

"All these children over here have babies while they're still babies themselves," Ruby said, shaking her head in disapproval. "My husband's little niece lives over here. Pinky's not but sixteen and got two babies by two different boys. Now if her mama had raised her in a good Christian home, it'd be a whole different story."

"Um-hmm. We might be here a while," I warned.

"That's fine," Ruby said. She reached in her battered leather pocketbook and brought out a well-worn Bible, thumbing through the tissue-thin paper 'til she reached a page marked with a grocery receipt.

"Matthew," she said. "That's the lesson I've chosen. Don't you just love Matthew? So full of wisdom."

"Uh, yeah," I said, watching the door of Susie Battles's apartment. I'd arrived early to make sure she was out of the way before I attempted to see her granddaughter.

At two forty-five, the apartment door opened and a heavyset woman emerged into the gloom. She wore a blue wool hat with a jaunty pompom on top, a dusty black coat, heavy orthopedic stockings, and the same kind of clinic shoes the House Mouse girls wear. She walked slowly toward the bus stop, moving gingerly, as though her feet hurt. I felt guilty all over again.

"There goes the grandmother," I said. "The coast should be clear." A bus paused at the curb a couple of minutes later, and when it pulled away, Mrs. Battles was gone.

"That's nice," Ruby said. Her finger moved over the page, and she got an envelope out of her pocketbook and jotted down some notes.

I'd called the high school and found out school dismissed at three. Now all I had to do was wait for Nichelle to come home. I sat back in the seat and closed my eyes.

Ruby was reading softly from her Bible, moving her finger down the page. "'Blessed are the poor in spirit, for theirs is the kingdom of heaven. Blessed are they who mourn, for they will be comforted. Blessed are the meek . . . '"

Thirty minutes later, I woke up when I heard voices. A school bus had stopped at the corner of Decatur and Bell, and a dozen or so teenage kids came spilling out. A handful came sauntering down the sidewalk toward me, chattering loudly as they walked. One, a boy of about fourteen, dressed in an expensive-looking set of black warm-ups, went into the apartment next to Mrs. Battles's. The others kept walking.

I frowned. Where was Nichelle? I hadn't considered that she might not come home after school. Damn. She could be anywhere. A job, a friend's house. Maybe the gang was having a sock hop. Maybe she was at detention. I didn't even know if schools still had detention. Probably not. The ACLU had probably put a stop to it.

Ten more minutes. Mrs. Battles had probably found the Social Security office by now, and was probably waiting in line to get a number to wait in line. Unless she'd already found out she'd been scammed.

"You sure we got the right address?" Ruby asked mildly, looking up from her scripture study.

"Come on," I said. "Let's see if anybody's home."

I walked briskly to the door and looked around. Ruby caught up as I was ringing the doorbell. From inside I could feel a thumping, buzzing bass beat, and then a baby's cry. So that's where Nichelle was. Home with the kid.

The door opened a crack and a young girl peered around the edge of the splintered turquoise door.

"Yeah?" Her eyes were bleary and she wore what looked like a faded flannel robe.

"Are you Nichelle Lattimore?" I asked, trying, not very successfully, not to sound like a cop.

"If you from the school, my grandmama called up there this morning. She told ya'll. I got a cold and my baby got a cold."

She did look fluish. "No, I'm not from the school," I said. "I'm a private investigator, and this," I said, turning to include Ruby, "is Mrs. Edwards, my assistant. We'd like to talk to you about a friend of yours."

"Who?" she said belligerently.

"If you'll let us come in out of the cold, I'll tell you," I said.

She shrugged and opened the door to admit us. "Ain't talking to no cops," she muttered.

We stepped inside and I pulled the door closed behind us. The living room was small, with bare linoleum tile floors, a worn, pulled-out sofa bed, a television, and a battered armchair with the stuffing leaking out. The television volume was turned to sonic-boom level and a menacing looking rap singer was writhing around in a school yard, holding his crotch and acting tough.

"Isn't this nice?" Ruby said, glancing around. Her eyes widened when she saw the baby perched on Nichelle's bony hip. The child's dark hair stood up in tufts, his eyes were as red and bleary as his mother's, and his button nose was crusted and running. But his snowflake patterned pajamas were new and clean, and he had the fat healthy look of a baby who was the apple of somebody's eye.

"Oh, what an angel," Ruby exclaimed, holding out her arms to him. "That's the prettiest child!"

Nichelle shifted the baby but didn't offer to let Ruby hold him. She looked at me suspiciously. "Who you wanna know about? You gonna pay me?"

Linda Nickells had said the girl was sixteen, but I'd have guessed thirteen or fourteen. She was petite, no more than five two in her bare feet, and sparrowlike, with skin spotted with teenage acne and a wicked scar beneath her left eye. She was missing one of her front teeth, too.

She put out a hand for the money and I noticed her forearm was still wrapped in an Ace bandage.

"Maleek messed you up pretty good," I commented.

The hand was snatched back and wrapped defensively around the child on her hip.

"What you want with Maleek?" she said, eyes narrowed.

I dug around in the pocket of my jeans, pulled out a twenty, and held it out to her.

"Let's sit down and talk, okay? If you don't want to tell me what I need, you can still keep the money."

She grabbed the bill and put it in the pocket of her robe.

The thumping music didn't seem to bother Nichelle or the baby, but it was giving me a headache and making it hard for me to think. "Can we turn that down?" I asked, gesturing toward the television.

She picked up a remote control from the arm of the sofa bed and clicked the television off. The room was quiet now, the air hot and stale and smelling of baby powder and Vick's VapoRub.

Nichelle took the baby and set him in a wind-up swing near the front window. She wound the crank and set the swing in motion. It made a rhythmic clicking noise each time it went backward or forward. The child shoved a chubby fist in his mouth and began sucking. His eyes drooped and then closed. Nichelle gave him a pat, then sat down on the pull-out bed.

"What's that sweet baby's name?" Ruby said. "I could just eat him up."

"Cedric," she said, wiping her nose on the sleeve of her robe. "How I know y'all ain't cops?"

Ruby got up and moved over to the swing. She leaned down and stroked the child's cheek softly. "Cedric," she cooed. "That's a beautiful name."

I pulled one of my business cards out of my pocket and handed it to her.

She read it. "Huh? What's a House Mouse?"

I'd handed her the wrong card. "My cleaning business," I said, searching for one of my P.I. cards. "I used to be a cop a long time ago. Now I'm a private detective, and I run a cleaning business. Mrs. Edwards works with me."

"Here." She gave me back the card. "What you want with Maleek?" she repeated.

I didn't have a lot of time, so I decided to be straight with her. "My cousin was shot, killed, in a carjacking last week. In front of her own little boy. The police think Maleek and your gang might have been involved."

"I ain't in The Wrecking Crew no more," she said quickly. "Maleek, he hurt me. Beat me up bad. Now my grandmama say she put me out and take Cedric away if I don't go to school and act right."

"You quit the gang?"

The baby gurgled softly in the swing. Ruby sat in a straight-backed wooden chair, her eyes never leaving the child.

"I was gonna quit anyway," Nichelle said, coughing in a deep, racking spasm. "You know, it was fun for a while. Got some bad clothes. Peoples be scared of us. Maleek be buying me stuff after I had Cedric." She pulled a heavy gold chain away from the skin around her neck to show it off. "Twenty-two-carat gold," she said proudly.

"But they be doin' stuff that scare me, you know? I got a baby. I don' wanna go to jail or get killed."

"What kind of things?" I asked.

She shrugged off-handedly. "You know. Like one night, we were ridin' around, and Maleek, he say we goin' to a house party. But we went to this big old house in some rich neighborhood. Maleek and Street, he's one of Maleek's crew, they got shotguns out of the trunk and went and busted in the door of that house. I stayed in the car. But I heard shootin' and when Maleek and Street come runnin' out, they got a pillowcase full of guns and money and jewelry and shit. Maleek say he shot a dog that was barking. But Street said later they shot this man when he tried to call the police."

Ruby looked shocked. I was afraid she'd break into a

Bible verse any second. So little Nichelle had witnessed one of Maleek's home invasions. I wondered if Cedric had been along for the ride.

"And this other time, Maleek, he had this big old black truck. So we went down someplace near the airport. Jonesboro, I think it was. It was real late, like three in the morning, and Maleek, he drove that Jeep right into the window of a pawnshop. Busted right through it, and glass and shit was everywhere, and the burglar alarm was ringin'. And they went and just grabbed everything they could. Gold jewelry, and some beepers and a car phone and some guns. Lotsa guns. But Maleek was mad 'cause they didn't have no Desert Eagles. That's what he was lookin' for."

"Desert Eagle?" I said dumbly. "What's that?"

She sniffed and gave me a pitying look. "I know you ain't no cop. Desert Eagle. You know, that big old gangsta gun. Like they got in the movies with Sylvester Stallone and Arnold Swartzenegger."

I hadn't seen many movies lately, and I'd never seen anything with Sly Stallone. It was a point of honor with me.

"What about carjackings?" I asked. "Did Maleek ever pull any carjackings?"

She rolled her eyes slyly. "All I know is, Street and Maleek and the rest of the crew, they be driving all different cars all the time."

I leaned forward. "Listen, Nichelle. This is important. Did Maleek say anything about trying to steal a black Lexus last Friday night out on Bankhead Highway? Anything about shooting a woman and hitting her little boy in the head?"

"I ain't seen that muthafucka," she spat out. "Not since he beat me. He supposed to bring some money for Cedric, but my grandmama, she say she gonna call the police if he comes around here. Street say he stayin' with some crackhead bitch—"

A car backfired loudly outside and then the glass in the front window erupted into a million pieces. Boom. Plaster fell from a hole in the wall inches above where Nichelle was sitting. Boom. Another hole opened in the wall by the television.

"Get down," I screamed, throwing myself at Ruby and pulling her out of the chair and onto the floor. The baby screamed, and Nichelle screamed, and there were more booms. Three more. Smoke filled the room and flakes of plaster rained down on my head. My arms were thrown across Ruby's back, and I could hear her muffled voice, praying calmly.

"'The Lord is my shepherd, I shall not want. In verdant pastures he gives me repose; Beside restful waters he leads me. . . '"

"Jesus," Nichelle screamed. "Mama. Jesus. Mama. Jesus."

When the shooting stopped I looked up from my place on the floor. Nichelle had managed to wedge herself under the sofa bed, and she was sobbing and shaking. I wondered why the baby had stopped crying.

I crawled on my stomach toward the window. Little Cedric was still in his swing, but he was tilted awkwardly to one side. His snowflake-patterned jammies were drenched in blood. The swing kept clicking and moving. Back and forth. But Cedric didn't move.

"My baby," Nichelle screamed, running for the swing. "My baby's shot."

"Ruby, call nine-one-one," I hollered, racing for the door. I flung it open and dashed for the curb, just in time to see a black Trans-Am with tinted windows careen around the corner on two wheels and disappear into traffic on Decatur Street.

Heads popped out of the apartments beside and across from Nichelle's. "Somebody call nine-one-one," I screamed. "Get an ambulance. The baby's been shot."

20

S USIE BATTLES STEPPED off the MARTA bus just as the ambulance roared up to her door, siren wailing, lights flashing.

She elbowed her way through a throng that had gathered at the curb and on her porch. The crowd, which had been buzzing moments before, fell silent when they saw her arrive. "Hey, Miz Battles," a pigtailed girl sang from the sidewalk across the street. "Nichelle's boyfriend done shot Cedric."

I'd gone out of the house to flag down the ambulance and was standing on the porch. The look of horror that crossed Susie Battles's face stabbed me like a knife.

"My baby," the stricken woman whispered. "What they done to my baby?"

A uniformed Atlanta cop tried to bar the apartment door, but she rolled over him like a Sherman tank.

"My baby," I heard her shriek from inside, and then Nichelle's sobs joined her grandmother's. Moments later the emergency paramedics pushed a gurney out the door, carrying the tiny form of Baby Cedric, covered with blankets, an oxygen mask covering most of his face. Nichelle and her grandmother clung to the gurney, weeping and moaning as they wheeled it to the curb and the waiting ambulance. Ruby stood by Mrs. Battles's side, her arm thrown protectively across the other woman's shoulders.

The crowd parted reluctantly to let them through. The men loaded the gurney into the ambulance and the paramedics gently peeled the two women away from the vehicle before it pulled away.

Nichelle and Mrs. Battles stood at the curb, the teenager's head buried in the older woman's arms. Ruby shook her head, ashen-faced.

I touched Mrs. Battles's shoulder. "I have my car right here," I said. "We'll take you to the emergency room."

Too dazed to ask who I was or why we were there, she nodded yes. Someone in the crowd gave Ruby a green Army fatigue jacket, and she put it on over Nichelle's robe the way a mother dresses a child.

I had to toot the horn several times to clear the crowd out of the street. Nichelle and her grandmother clung to each other in the backseat as I inched the van through the maze of police cars and gawkers.

"My baby gone die," Nichelle cried. "Maleek done killed my baby. The Crew done killed Cedric."

"Hush," her grandmother said. "You need to be praying to Jesus right now. Pray he spares that sweet baby."

"That's right," Ruby said. She turned to the women and reached her hands out to them, and together they prayed. They were oblivious to me and to how lost I'd gotten.

I'd turned left at the bottom of Bell Street, and craned my neck forward, trying to keep the hospital in sight. Grady, built in the 1890s, then rebuilt some time in the 1950s, sprawled across a big chunk of downtown Atlanta, hunkering alongside Interstate 75 like a hog at the trough. As a cop, I'd spent more hours in its emergency waiting room than I cared to think about. Now the place was undergoing a drastic renovation, costing, I'd read somewhere, more than $300 million. The streets around the hospital had become a nightmare of dump trucks, cranes, scaffolding, and makeshift walkways. Streets that had been navigable six months ago had been suddenly dead-ended or made one-way. Despite the chill in the early evening air I felt a bead of sweat trickle down the side of my face, and my stomach churned precariously.

Where the hell was the emergency room entrance? The construction had me badly disoriented. I finally saw a sign pointing to the "trauma center admitting area." Talk English, dammit, I thought. I sped down the block, turned in the direction of the arrow, and saw the ramp off to my right.

The van wheezed as I urged it up the ramp. I stopped in front of the double sliding doors and turned to the women. "Go to the admitting nurse and tell her your baby was just brought into the trauma side by ambulance," I said. "I'll park and be right back."

I found a parking space in front of a fire hydrant half a block away, scrawled a note that said "Emergency Police Business—No Tow" on it, and stuck it inside the windshield.

I dug in my pocket and pulled out a dollar bill and shoved it in Ruby's hand. "You go on home," I said. "We're likely to be a while."

"I want to stay," Ruby said. "This poor child needs some powerful praying."

I gave her a little push. "No, go on home. You and your circle can pray. I'll call you as soon as I know something."

Ruby looked doubtful. "Go," I said.

Then I sprinted back to the hospital. Nichelle and Mrs. Battles sat huddled in some plastic chairs pushed against the wall, clutching each other tightly.

"Did they tell you anything?" I asked, still out of breath from my run.

Nichelle blew her nose noisily on a tissue. "A nurse came out and said he in surgery. They won't let me see him." She was crying again.

Her grandmother patted the girl's knee. "He's in the Lord's hands now." Then she looked up at me and for the first time realized she had no idea who I was. Susie Battles was from the old school: too polite to confront me, too frightened to tell me to go away.

I sat down next to her. "Mrs. Battles," I said, searching for words. "I'm a private investigator. I came to your house today to ask Nichelle about Maleek Tebbetts. The police think . . . well, I think too, that he may have killed my cousin last week. Shot her and tried to steal her car."

She sucked in her breath. "That boy is the devil. I told Nichelle. He the devil, and the devil and all his works are in that Maleek. Yes they are."

While she ranted on about the evil ways of Maleek Tebbetts, I saw two Atlanta police detectives walk into the waiting room. They spoke briefly with the admitting clerk, who pointed toward us.

The older of the two wore a checked Bear Bryant–type fedora and a heavy topcoat. He was tall, about six foot three, and the hat gave him a strange, scarecrow appearance. His name was Warren something. I recognized him from seeing him at so many crime scenes on the eleven o'clock news. His partner was younger and white, with fat, ruddy red cheeks, thinning wheat-colored hair, and a reddish walrus mustache. I'd never seen him before.

"Miss Lattimore? Mrs. Battles?" the older one said. "I'm Lieutenant Warren Belden. This is Detective Blackwood. We'd like to talk to you about the shooting if we could."

Susie Battles drew herself upright, ready for a confrontation. "We're staying right here where we are until somebody tells us something about Cedric," Mrs. Battles said. "Right here."

The two men exchanged glances.

"All right," Belden said affably. "There's a conference room right out in the hallway there. It's quiet and private. We'll tell the clerk that's where we'll be. All right?"

Mrs. Battles set her jaw. I'd seen that look before, on

the face of my own mother. It's a sure sign of pending intransigence.

"I told you, we're staying right here," Mrs. Battles said. "Now what do you want? I didn't see nothing. Got off the bus and the ambulance came right then. My baby was inside bleeding already. My house shot all up. Where was the police when that happened? People shooting and killing all the time around there. Where are the police at when we need help?"

The younger one, Blackwood, started to say something, but Belden gave him an almost imperceptible shake of the head.

"We have regular foot patrols on your street in Grady Homes," Belden pointed out. "But the police can't stop crime or make arrests without the help of the community. Now what about you, Miss Lattimore? Did you see anything?"

The girl scrubbed at her tear-stained face with clenched hands. "I was talkin' to this lady here, and all of a sudden, shootin' started. We got down on the floor. But Cedric, he was in his swing by the window, he too little to get down. They shot my baby," she whimpered.

I was thankful she'd forgotten to mention Ruby. The last thing she needed was to be dragged back downtown for a police interrogation that would yield nothing more than what I could tell the cops.

"Who shot your baby?" Belden said, impatient now. "Miss Lattimore?"

"She don't know," Susie Battles said defiantly. "She don't know nothin'."

Belden sighed. He'd heard it all before. He looked at me then with newfound interest.

"Who are you?"

I stood up. "Let's go get some coffee from the machine outside. Mrs. Battles, Nichelle, can I get you some coffee or something?"

"No thank you," Mrs. Battles said.

We pushed through the swinging doors and walked out into the vestibule. It was noisy and cold, but there was a bank of vending machines lining the wall: sodas, crackers, candy, coffee, cigarettes, even stale-looking sandwiches. Unfortunately, each machine wore a hand-lettered "Out of Order" sign.

"Damn," Blackwood muttered.

"Who'd you say you were again?" Belden asked.

"Callahan Garrity," I said. "I'm a private investigator. I was with the APD for ten years, up until around nineteen eighty-nine. I'm a friend of your captain's, C. W. Hunsecker."

That didn't cut much ice with Belden. He leaned against the coffee machine and folded his arms across his chest. "That still doesn't tell me what you're doing here, or what you were doing at Grady Homes this afternoon."

"Look," I said. "You'd better call Linda Nickells in Vice. Ask her to come over here right away. I'll give you a statement, but I don't feel like going over it twice. Okay?"

Belden gave Blackwood a nod. "Give Nickells a ring. She's the captain's lady. And see if you can find us a cup of coffee somewhere in this godforsaken joint."

Blackwood scowled, but he went back inside the waiting room to use the phone.

When Linda got to the hospital, I was still sitting in that same chair, watching a hospital-produced video on cancer prevention on a closed-circuit television set. I'd already found out all about healthy diet tips and the seven early warning signs of cancer. Nichelle was curled up on her chair with her head on her grandmother's lap. Mrs. Battles's head was tilted back, her eyes closed, snoring softly. Blackwood and Belden, the two cops, came in and out of the room intermittently, using the phone and talking to the admitting clerk.

It had been an hour since a doctor had come out to say that Cedric had been taken into the operating room.

Nickells hurried into the waiting room, stiletto heels

clicking noisily on the tile floor. She was in burgundy wool today, a business suit, sheer hose and matching suede shoes. She stopped in front of me, looking down.

"You had to do it, didn't you?"

"I told you I was going to go see her," I said, standing to stretch. I felt knotted up, and my skin felt too tight for my bones.

"You were supposed to wait for me," Linda said sharply. "How's the baby?"

"In surgery."

Blackwood and Belden strolled over. "Now can we talk?" Belden said with mock politeness.

We closed the door to the tiny conference room just outside the waiting room. Blackwood took out a miniature tape recorder and set it on the tabletop and we all arranged ourselves around the table. Linda got out a notebook and pen. Blackwood and Belden got out cigarettes and lit up. I guess they'd missed that cancer video.

Then I told them why I'd gone to see Nichelle Lattimore, and what she'd told me. I left out some stuff, like how I'd found out about Nichelle and how I'd gotten the grandmother out of the house. I wasn't proud of that part. I told them what Nichelle had told me about the gang, and how they'd started with home invasions by staking out well-dressed women going back to luxury cars in the parking lot at Lenox Square Mall, Atlanta's biggest, richest monument to retail therapy. Maleek and his crew followed the women home, and watched them enter. Later at night they'd come back, prepared to rape, rob, and plunder.

"Nichelle claims she stayed in the car," I said. "I have no idea whether or not she's telling the truth."

I told them about the black Trans-Am I'd seen speeding away from the apartment moments after the shooting.

"You didn't get the tag?" Blackwood asked, scorn dripping from his voice.

"It was at the end of the block by the time I got to the street. It was getting dark outside and the windows were tinted," I said evenly. "That's the best I could do."

"What about Tebbetts?" Linda asked. "Does the girl know where he is?"

I rubbed my eyes. I was tired and the cigarette smoke made them sting and burn.

"She hasn't seen him since he beat her up," I said. "The grandmother is terrified of Tebbetts. That's why she wouldn't let Nichelle talk to you. She knew he'd come back."

"Looks like the grandmother was right," Linda said.

"He must have been watching the apartment," I said wearily. "What can I say? I'm sorry. Sorry it happened. Sorry the baby got shot."

"Neighbors say they've seen the Trans-Am cruising the neighborhood in the past few days. They saw it cruising past earlier in the day," Blackwood said. "They all thought it was an undercover cop."

"What about Nichelle?" Linda asked. "Tell us exactly what she said about Maleek and The Wrecking Crew."

"She'd quit the gang because of her grandmother. Plus she was scared. Armed robbery, burglary, and car theft apparently didn't phase her, but when Maleek made the step up to assault and murder, it offended her sensibilities," I said. "Nichelle's scared of Maleek all right, but she's also pretty mad about getting beat up, and Maleek hasn't paid any child support either. She finally told me she's heard Maleek is shacked up with some 'ho,' as she put it, out in Smyrna. In an apartment."

"Shit," Belden said, reaching over to snap off the tape recorder. "There's only, what, about two thousand apartment complexes out there? That gives us a lot to go on."

"It's more than we had before, though," Linda admitted.

Belden and Blackwood stood up, threw their

cigarettes on the floor and ground them out with their shoes. I made a mental note not to invite them over to my house.

"We'll be in touch," Blackwood said. I bet he'd been practicing saying that line all through the police academy.

Linda let them leave the room while she fiddled with putting her notebook away. When they were gone, she stood up slowly, walked over to where I was sitting and picked something out of my short, tangled hair. She held it out for me to see: a half-inch shard of glass from Susie Battles's window.

"So was it worth it?" she said. "Was it worth getting yourself shot at and a baby nearly killed to find out something about Maleek Tebbetts? Do you think he's the one who killed your cousin?"

"I'm sorry, Linda," I said. And I meant it. I couldn't answer the question about whether or not I thought Maleek had killed Patti.

"You think it's my fault that baby was shot today, don't you? You think Maleek opened fire because he saw me go in the house. You think he thought I was a cop, don't you?"

She picked a chunk of plaster out of my hair and let it fall to the floor. "No, Garrity, I don't blame you. I think Tebbetts is a psycho who just decided to do a fly-by and waste everybody in that house today. You did the grandmother a favor getting her out of there. No way she moves fast enough to have gotten out of the line of fire the way you and the girl did. How'd you get her out of the house, anyway?"

"What makes you think I did?"

Linda laughed a big gum-bearing laugh, the kind a woman does when she's talking on the level to another woman.

"I know you, Garrity. Look, girl, you'd better get on home and get cleaned up. You look like a train wreck, you know?"

For the first time, I took a look at myself. My hands were crisscrossed with cuts from the flying glass, and there was plaster dust and blood on my shirt and jeans. I put my fingers to my face and found a half-dozen places where the blood from more cuts was drying.

"I'll go to the ladies room and wash up," I said. "I want to stay with them. Until they hear something about the baby."

Linda took me by the shoulders and shook me, once. "Go home. Hear? I'll stay with them. Who knows? Maybe the grandmother will let the girl talk to me now. Go home and I'll call you as soon as we know something."

21

FRIDAY MORNING I found the appointment book placed squarely in the middle of the kitchen table. No note, just the book.

Edna must have dropped it by some time the day before, but when I'd gotten back from the hospital Thursday night I'd gone straight from the bathtub to bed.

I flipped the book open to today's date. Nothing out of the ordinary. The girls were all supposed to be at their regular Friday jobs. And Edna was supposed to be helping me do payroll.

Oh well, I thought, setting my coffee cup in the kitchen sink. I'll just be like the Little Red Hen. I'll do it myself.

I'd called Grady first thing to check on the status of Cedric Lattimore. "He's in serious condition," the nurse said. "What's that mean?" I asked. "Better than grave, worse than guarded," she said.

For a moment I considered calling my sister Maureen to ask her to check on the baby. But she works night shifts on weekends, and besides, I was pretty sure she was among the family contingent who weren't currently speaking to me.

I got out the company checkbook, my calculator, and the girls' time sheets and set myself up on the kitchen table.

There was a rap at the kitchen door. I looked up to see Bruce McNair standing there.

He was dressed for work in a tweed sport coat, blue dress shirt and striped blue and burgundy tie, with neatly pressed khaki slacks and polished loafers. His longish hair had been trimmed recently, but there were dark circles under his eyes.

I opened the door and invited him in. We both knew this wasn't a social call.

"Coffee?" I asked, indicating the half-full pot.

"No," he said sharply. "I've got an appointment downtown. I can't stay."

He circled the kitchen nervously, tugging at his tie. He was seething with anger, trying to keep it in check.

"Okay," he said finally. "Callahan, I want to know what the hell is going on with you? You've been sneaking around town, asking embarrassing questions about me and Patti. I want to know what you're getting at."

"What do you mean?" I asked, stalling for time.

"I was in The Texas Tearoom last night with a client. The bartender told me somebody had been in asking about me, and he described you perfectly. Just who do you think you are, prying into my business affairs? It was bad enough that you interrogated poor Dylan as though he were a common criminal. The kid had to be sedated when you left, did you know that?"

Now I was getting pissed. I was tired of being blamed for Dylan's temper tantrum over a toy. "Bruce, all I did was ask—"

"No," he said. "I don't want to hear it. I just want to know why you've turned on us. Why do you want to destroy me and my family?"

"Whoa," I said. "Now you listen, Bruce. I'll tell you what I'm trying to do. I'm trying to find out who killed Patti, goddamn it. You may not care, but I do."

His face reddened. "You think I don't want this guy caught?"

"I don't know what you want," I said hotly. "In fact, I'm beginning to think I don't know anything at all about you, Bruce. If you were so concerned about Patti's whereabouts last Friday, why didn't you call the cops and report her missing? Your wife and son had disappeared and you never notified the police."

His face turned a purplish color then. "Jesus, Callahan. You think I killed Patti, don't you? My God, that's what this is all about. You're trying to implicate me in my own wife's murder. I don't believe it."

"Why didn't you call the cops, Bruce?" I asked, calmer now.

He turned and gripped the back of the kitchen chair so hard his hands trembled.

"We'd had a fight," he said. "On the car phone. She wanted to send Dylan to a speech therapist, to the tune of a hundred dollars an hour. Jesus. The kid was already going to a speech school that cost more for one year than my whole college career and law school cost. I told her absolutely not and she went berserk, crying, accusing me of not caring about my only son. She hung up the phone. I tried calling back but she wouldn't answer. When Caitlin and Megan called to say Patti wasn't home, I just assumed she'd taken off again and gone up to the lake house. She'd done it before."

"Your marriage was in trouble," I said accusingly. "You'd been fighting. There were money problems. Did Patti have any life insurance?" I knew exactly how much she had, but he didn't need to know that. "Think how it looks, Bruce, and not just to me, to the cops, too."

"You think I killed her for money? Well, fuck you," he exploded. "I loved Patti. And I love my kids. We were having problems, yeah, but we were working things out. I don't give a rat's ass what you or the cops think. I had nothing to do with Patti's murder."

"You'd been having an affair, hadn't you?" It just popped out, but I wasn't sorry it had.

The color drained from Bruce's face. "You are one vicious bitch," he said slowly. "I guess if you look under enough rocks, you'll eventually find some dirt. Yeah, I'd had an affair. Not that it's any of your business. By the time Patti found out about it, it was history. That was one of the issues we were dealing with in counseling. And let me tell you something else, Callahan, Patti wasn't perfect either."

"What's that supposed to mean?"

He waved his hand dismissively. "None of your god-damn business. Patti's dead. It's in the past."

I wanted to shake him as hard as I could. "It's not in the past, Bruce. Somebody murdered her. If you really do want to find out who it was, help me. Help the cops. They have a suspect, you know. Let Dylan talk to the cops again, for God's sake. He's their only witness."

"No way," Bruce said.

"This guy the police are looking for is a killer," I said. "Yesterday he drove by his girlfriend's apartment and emptied a semiautomatic pistol into it. His own child, a ten-month-old baby, was shot in the chest. A baby, Bruce. Let Dylan talk to the cops, Bruce. Please."

"He has talked to the police. Twice," Bruce said. "Hell, they can't understand a word he says and we're not even sure Dylan himself understands what he saw. His therapist says all of this is aggravating his speech problems. He's totally traumatized."

"His mother was shot to death right before his eyes," I said. "Surely his therapist thinks he needs to talk about it. Dylan's the key, Bruce. If the police frighten him so badly, let me talk to him. I'm family. He trusts me. And I'll go slow."

"No," Bruce shouted hoarsely. "Stay the hell away from Dylan, Callahan. I mean it. Stay away from him and get the hell out of my business."

He turned and left abruptly, leaving the kitchen door wide open. The least he could have done was to have slammed it. The cold March wind whistled through the trees outside, leaving me shivering as I went to close and fasten the door.

After Bruce had gone, I called the hospital again. No change. I threw myself into my work. Like the song says, the eagle flies on Friday. And if the girls didn't have their paychecks by the end of the business day, there would be a minor revolt at the House Mouse.

Number-crunching is not my forte. So I wasn't pleased when the phone started ringing right when I was trying to figure out FICA for one of the girls. I almost let the answering machine pick up.

"What the hell," I muttered, tossing my pencil down. "Maybe it'll be a cemetery salesman. I could use a laugh right now."

But it wasn't a salesman. It was my clerk friend at the Georgia Secretary of State's office.

"Sorry it took me so long to call you back," she said. "The president of XBD Holdings is Xavier B. Draper."

I thanked her and hung up. I glanced down at my paperwork. One phone call wouldn't hurt. I'd get right back to the payroll as soon as I had what I needed.

"Deavers, homicide," he said.

"Want your apartment cleaned free this week?" I asked seductively.

"No," Bucky said quickly. "Whatever you're selling, I ain't interested."

I was hurt. "It's me, Callahan. And I just need one little favor."

"No way," he said. "I saw you on the eleven o'clock news at that Grady Homes shooting last night. I should never have introduced you to Tyler King. You're into this thing up to your neck, aren't you, Garrity? Belden and Blackwood were in the captain's office this morning asking about you. What were you doing messing with Maleek Tebbetts's girlfriend?"

"Don't you start too," I said wearily. "You know

what I was doing. Trying to find out who killed Patti McNair."

"That's Charlie Fouts's job," Bucky said. "You're going to get your ass shot off messing with these people, Callahan."

I glanced down at myself. "Yeah, well, that's just the part I need the most to lose. Look, Bucky, just tell me what I need to know about Xavier Draper and I promise to hang up and leave you alone. And clean your apartment next week."

"What's Draper got to do with any of this?" Bucky demanded.

"I don't really know," I admitted. "I think he's one of Bruce McNair's clients. Why, who is he?"

"Shit," Bucky muttered. "Let me call you right back."

I managed to fill out two paychecks while I waited for Bucky to call back. I felt right pleased with myself.

The phone rang. "Who is Xavier Draper?" I repeated.

"You're going to get you and me in a world of trouble," Bucky moaned.

"Tell me," I said.

"He's hometown talent, born right here in Atlanta, Gee-Ay. Used to be a small potatoes Dixie Mafia type. Got busted in the seventies for running illegal poker games and making book out of a little used car lot he owned out in Austell. He got out of the Atlanta Federal Pen, says here, nineteen seventy-eight. For a while after that we thought he was clean. Then in the eighties, your boy Draper started buying businesses. Some janitorial supply outfit for starters."

"Georgia Sanitary Supply," I said. "Is it legit?"

"Nobody's proven otherwise," Bucky said. "I got an intelligence report right here says the Georgia Bureau of Investigation ran a wire on him last summer. They think he's the off-the-books owner of some strip clubs down on

Stewart Avenue. There was fairly solid evidence that he's financing a cocaine operation running between Miami and Atlanta, but Draper's good. The GBI could never get enough off the wiretap to take to a grand jury."

"What's you guys interest in Draper?" I asked.

"He originally had a partner in the janitorial supply place and the strip clubs. Guy went to buy a six-pack of Miller Lite one night and never came home. Draper got sole control of the businesses."

"You think Draper killed the guy?"

"We don't think he got amnesia and forgot to come home," Bucky said. "Now tell me how you think Draper's connected to your cousin's husband."

I told him about the credit card receipts and about my trip to The Texas Tearoom.

"Hey, I've been out there," Bucky said. That's when I remembered the outfit he'd been wearing the night we'd met at the Yacht Club.

"It looks like your kind of place," I said. "You know anything about the owner, guy named Grady Stovall? Bruce represents him, too."

"Never heard of him, but I'll check it out," Bucky said. "Is that all you need?"

"I guess," I said reluctantly. "Was C. W. mad when he heard I was at Nichelle Lattimore's apartment yesterday? I hate to have him pissed off at me. Especially since it kind of involves Linda."

"Captain'll get over it," Bucky assured me. "Nickells has him totally whipped. Now about that cleaning appointment?"

22

THE PHONE RANG again as I was finishing the calculations on the last paycheck. I totaled the column I was working on and scribbled the figure on a piece of scratch paper.

"Callahan Garrity?"

"Speaking," I said.

"Garrity, this is Charlie Fouts at the Cobb Police Department."

"Oh." I steeled myself for what I sensed was coming.

"I just had a visit from two Atlanta homicide cops who tell me you're investigating my homicide for me."

"Now wait a minute," I started.

"No. You wait a minute. I've cooperated with you up until now, you being a member of Mrs. McNair's family and all, but you're way out of line now. You're lucky you didn't get yourself blown away down there in Grady Homes, you know. You've got no business meddling in an active homicide case. I want you off this case and away from my witnesses. You understand that?"

"Hey," I said. "I'm the one trying to get Bruce McNair to cooperate and let Dylan talk to your people."

"You're doing a great job," he drawled. "I called McNair this morning and he informed me that neither he nor his son would be available for questioning and that any further communication would have to come from his attorney."

"He won't let me talk to Dylan again, either," I said. "Say, did Belden and Blackwood tell you that Nichelle Lattimore says Maleek is living with a new girlfriend in Smyrna?"

"They did," Fouts said. "We'll find Tebbetts on our own, Garrity. You stay out of it, or I'll report your butt to the state licensing board."

I hung up the phone and fumed. Some days you get the tiger and some days the tiger gets you. It wasn't noon yet but I was already feeling like tiger bait.

The back door opened and a strong gust of wind blew in along with Baby and Sister.

"Ooh, it is so cold out there," Sister said, unwrapping what looked like an eight-foot wool muffler from around her neck. "You know it didn't used to be this cold in March in Georgia when we were young'uns, did it, Baby?"

"What's that?" Baby asked, helping Sister out of her mothball-scented coat.

"I said it's unnaturally cold," Sister hollered.

"I know that's right," Baby said, hanging the jackets on the coatrack near the stove.

"You know, weather ain't been right since those mens walked on the moon," Baby said. "They done messed with nature, and now nature's payin' us back."

"What you talkin' 'bout, walked on the moon?" Sister said. "Our daddy said that weren't nothing but a gov'mint conspiracy. Ain't nobody really walked on the moon. That was just one of them television tricks. Like that talking horse they used to have. What was that horse's name, sugar?"

"Mr. Ed," I said. "Can I get you ladies a cup of tea?"

Baby and Sister sat themselves carefully down at the kitchen table. "Yes, ma'am, tea would be real nice," Sister said.

"Look a-here, Sister," Baby said. "Callahan's got our paychecks already wrote out for us."

Uh-oh. I'd forgotten the Easterbrook girls had worked for us at the McNairs on Monday, and that I'd promised a bonus for the fruits of their snooping. "Well, uh, I just need to finish a couple of things before yours is done," I fibbed.

I set the teacups down in front of them along with a plate of Fig Newtons I'd found at the back of the cupboard.

"We'll wait right here," Sister said, pouring milk into her cup.

I switched the calculator on, added up their hours, and quickly figured their pay. It's easier with the Easterbrooks; we pay them off the books and don't deduct taxes because it would mess up their Social Security benefits. I got my own checkbook out and wrote them each a check, tucking them into envelopes with their names written on them.

"Here you go," I said with a flourish. Two hands reached out simultaneously and plucked the envelopes from mine. Baby tucked her pay in her housedress pocket, Sister's was slipped inside the neck of her sweat-shirt.

"Ooh, now here's the other thing I wanted to give you, sugar," Sister said, drawing out a small white business card. "This here was in little Dylan's pants pocket when I was washing clothes over there Monday. Put it in my bosom and forgot all about it 'til I put my nightdress on that night."

"She probably had a bunch of your kinfolks' other stuff stuck down in there too," Baby said accusingly. "She bad to pilfer, Sister is. Where you get that new coat from, anyhow?"

All three of us turned to look at the cherry red wool coat with the gray fox collar that Sister had been wearing. Come to think of it, the coat was a surprisingly stylish number.

"One of them girls at Callahan's cousin's house gimme that," Sister said.

"Uh-huh," Baby said, unconvinced.

"Sister?" I asked.

"Swear to the Lord," Sister said, holding her hand in a pledge over her heart. "That red-headed one, I forget her name, she say it were her mama's, and she don't want her aunt wearing it. She done give it to me, and that's the truth."

I looked at the business card. Dr. Nancy Cook, MSW. Psychotherapy for Children, Adolescents. "So that's who Cookie is," I said. "She's Dylan's therapist."

"What's that, Callahan?" Baby said. "You say something was missed?"

"No," I said, absentmindedly. "You girls did a great job." I turned the card over. There was a note in tiny, precise handwriting. "Call me here or at home, 272-0112, if you need me."

I wondered if Dylan had told his therapist anything useful about his mother's murder. She probably wouldn't talk to me; therapists have as many bullshit ethics rules as lawyers these days. But it wouldn't hurt to call her. I tucked the business card in Patti's case file.

The girls had finished their tea and devoured the cookies and were up now, putting on their winter wraps and discussing the evening's entertainment.

"American Legion," Baby said loudly. "It's double jackpot night and they got no card limits."

"Nooo," Sister said. "Moose Lodge gots a free buffet and fifty-cent beer tonight."

"And then on the way home I got to stop the car every block and let you out to pee," Baby complained. "This girl got a bladder no bigger than a thimble, Callahan. Besides, we went to Moose last week. Didn't win nothing."

The ladies kissed me fondly and left. I could hear them bickering all the way to the car.

After the girls left I buckled down and finished all the payroll paperwork, putting each check in an envelope with the employee's name written on it. I looked over the book. Edna had made an appointment at two o'clock for me to talk to a woman in Ansley Park about cleaning her house and her elderly mother-in-law's condominium. Bruce McNair's old law offices were five minutes from Ansley Park, in midtown. I wondered if his former partner had kept the old offices.

Beverly Updegraff had stayed put. She said she remembered me from a dinner party at Patti's when we'd played Trivial Pursuit 'til three in the morning. "You were the one who knew all the Mercury Seven astronauts," Beverly said. She said she was planning on having lunch at her desk. "I'll bring the sandwiches," I said.

I stopped at the Superette down the block and went in for sandwiches. A Korean family bought the place a few years ago, and they've got a little deli counter in the back. Mrs. Yee, the owner's wife, makes a mean tuna salad sandwich on whole wheat bread. I added a couple of bags of potato chips and two Little Debbie Snack Cakes to the picnic bag.

After I got in the van and headed for midtown, the car phone buzzed. I've had the thing a while now, but I'm still startled when somebody calls me in my car.

"Callahan, you little sneak," Liz Whitesell said.

"What am I accused of now?" I asked. "Everybody else in town is pissed at me, Liz. What's your beef?"

"Aw, I'm not really mad," she said. "You did me a favor. After you asked about Father Mart, I got curious myself and put some feelers out."

"What did you find out?"

"Well, the hot gossip is that Father Mart is going on a year's sabbatical."

"Which means what?"

"You are out of it," Liz said pityingly. "It's like time

off for good behavior, usually. But sometimes people take sabbaticals right before they leave the priesthood."

"Hmm," I said. "Did Father Mart ask to take this sabbatical, or is that something the archbishop decides?"

"Good question," Liz said. "I've got a friend at the diocesan office who says it wasn't Father Mart's idea at all. She says some old Cuban lady was calling and calling the archbishop's office all week, trying to bend his ear. She was Father Mart's housekeeper. Of course the secretary wouldn't put her through, especially after she found out Father Mart had fired the old lady. She thought it was a labor dispute the archbishop wouldn't want to mess with."

"So what happened?" I asked impatiently.

"It would have been dropped, except that the old lady had been referred to Our Lady of Lourdes by Catholic Social Services. And the old lady went back there and told her caseworker, a woman named Alberta Oetgen, who is a real firebrand, how she'd been treated unfairly and fired.

"The social worker called the archbishop and raised such a stink that they decided to listen to the old lady."

"And?"

"And the next thing you know, not only is Mart Covington no longer a candidate for monsignor, but there's also talk that he's leaving the church."

"Jeez," I said. I'd reached the block where Beverly Updegraff had her office; now I needed a parking space. "Do your spies have any idea what the old lady told the archbishop?"

"Not so far," Liz admitted. "But it must have been juicy. I do know Father Mart intends to announce his departure at mass this Sunday, because we were asked not to put it in this week's paper until he's notified the parish. I'll let you know if I hear anything else."

"Wait," I said, "don't hang up. Do you happen to know the housekeeper's name?"

"That I can help you with," Liz said. "Estella Diaz.

No phone, but she lives with her son in the Pine Tree apartment complex on Buford Highway. Somebody there can tell you where exactly; everybody there is from the same village in Cuba."

"Thanks, Liz," I said. "Really."

"You can buy me lunch sometime," she said.

I'd circled the block once, searching for a parking space. On the second time around I relented and pulled into a pay lot.

The heavy outer doors to Beverly's office still had the firm's old name, McNair-Updegraff, in gilt letters over the doorway. I pushed the doors open and stepped into a small but tasteful reception area. The parquet floors were covered with worn but good Oriental rugs and a large Audubon print of a woodstork was placed over a camelback sofa. The receptionist's desk was empty, but the door behind it was slightly ajar.

I poked my head around the door. "Hello?"

"Back here," Beverly called. "Last door on your right."

Beverly's office was large and square with floor to ceiling windows that gave her a knockout view of midtown Atlanta's new glamour high-rises: The IBM building, NationsBank Plaza with its popsicle-stick tower ornament, and the pink marble Campanile building.

Beverly herself wasn't quite as glitzy looking. Her dark, shoulder-length hair was grayer than I remembered, and the thick black-framed glasses she wore on the end of her nose made her look like a prison warden. She wore a sensible black wool suit and a plain white blouse with a cameo pin at the neck.

She got up to clear a stack of files and papers off the chair facing her equally cluttered desk.

"Excuse the mess," she said. "We're still dealing with the effects of splitting up the firm. What'll you have to drink?"

"Diet Coke, if you've got it."

She patted her hips where the skirt fabric was a little

too snug around the pockets. "I live off the stuff," she said, opening a small refrigerator and taking out a couple of cans.

She set the cans and two glasses with ice on the desktop, and I handed her a sandwich.

We concentrated for a couple of minutes on getting our lunches set up—two busy career women in a nice midtown law office talking about the not-so-nice subject of murder.

"So why did you and Bruce break up the partnership?" I asked, looking around at all the boxes on the floor and the credenza.

She took a cautious nibble at her sandwich and chewed while she thought about it. "Did you ask Bruce?"

"No," I said. "Bruce is not very happy with me right now. He thinks I should mind my own business and let the police find Patti's killer."

"Shouldn't you?" Beverly asked, not unkindly. She reached in a desk drawer, pulled out a paper packet of salt, lifted the top of her sandwich, and sprinkled the salt liberally on the tuna salad.

"Maybe," I said. "But I can't."

She nodded her understanding. "I guess you could say Bruce and I split over a difference of opinion. I didn't like some of the new clients he was representing, and he didn't like all the nitpicky civil work the firm was handling."

"New clients," I said. "You mean like Xavier Draper and Grady Stovall?"

"You know about them, huh? Yes, that was part of it. When we left Sheffield, Stephens, Ringel, and Simpson we set up a real mixed practice with some criminal, some divorce, and some civil. We weren't getting stinking rich, but we were doing okay. Or at least I thought so. Then about eighteen months ago, Xavier Draper hired Bruce for some corporate work, and he introduced him to Stovall. Bruce was fascinated with these guys and he loved the whole club scene. They were taking up all his time.

But what could I say? Bruce was the real rainmaker for the firm."

"Did you know about the big insurance policy he had on Patti?"

"That was another reason for the split. When we set up the firm, we bought medium-sized insurance policies, the kind where if one of the principals dies, the benefits go to the firm. Standard stuff. Then, this year he tells me he wants to take out a bigger policy with each of us insured for $2.5 million, and with Patti, who he wants to name as an administrative assistant, insured for $1.2 million. Patti never worked a day in this office. I hit the ceiling when he suggested it. In fact, I was trying to get up the nerve to suggest dissolving the partnership when he came in one morning and announced he'd decided to go into solo practice."

I put my sandwich down on the wax paper wrapper, tore open the bag of chips and nibbled on one. "So there wasn't a fight or anything. He just left?"

"Along with a lot of files, one of the firm's computers, and about a quarter of our law library," Beverly added. "I thought I knew Bruce McNair, but I guess I was kidding myself."

I could say the same thing, but I didn't. "I understand Patti came to see you about a divorce."

She poured more Diet Coke into her glass and sipped at the foam. "That's right. Did she tell you that?"

"No," I said. "She never even hinted at it to me."

Beverly sighed. "Patti was one unhappy lady, that I can tell you. She came to see me right after New Year's, but I could tell she'd been struggling with the idea for a while. She came in asking about divorce, but at the same time she kept telling me she didn't believe in it."

"Catholic," I said. "If she didn't believe in it, why'd she want one?"

"She said Bruce didn't love her. She'd found out he was having an affair."

"Did she know who the woman was?"

Beverly nodded slowly. "I'm sure she did, but she never told me who it was or how she found out. All she said was that the marriage was over, that she didn't think she loved him anymore. In fact, she said she was almost afraid of him."

"Afraid of what?" I wondered. "Bruce McNair never struck me as being the sinister type."

"Patti didn't know exactly. She just said he'd started getting funny phone calls. He'd started wearing a beeper. They'd be out to dinner with friends, he'd get beeped and he'd leave without any explanation. He'd bought a gun, too."

"Bruce?" I was startled. "Mr. Anti-NRA had a gun?"

"Patti found it in the glove box of his car," Beverly said. "She was furious with him; Dylan could just as easily have found it as she did."

Beverly wasn't the only one who was discovering how little she knew about Bruce McNair. The man she was describing was not someone I'd known for the past eighteen years.

"Did you think there was any basis for her fears?"

"Not at the time," Beverly said. "Now I'm not so sure."

I balled up the wax paper my sandwich had come in and threw it in the trashcan.

"Did Bruce know Patti had seen you about a divorce?"

"Oh yes," she said ruefully. "They had another fight, about money, the night she was here. She blurted out that she wanted a divorce. And she told him that she'd get money out of him one way or another, and that I would help her. Worse, she told him she'd get the kids because she could prove he was an unfit father."

"Oh no," I said.

"Oh no is right," Beverly said. "Bruce called me the next day and let me have it. He threatened to take me before the bar association, to sue me for money he claimed I owed him from the firm's assets, all kinds of stuff. He got really ugly about it."

"But Patti never followed up on the divorce, did she?"

"No," Beverly said. "That happens all the time. A client gets steamed up about something, wants a divorce. The next day, everything's fine and they want the whole thing dropped. You wouldn't believe how many unbillable hours divorce work entails."

"What exactly did Patti say?" I asked.

"She called to cancel our appointment. She was sorry to have caused problems for me with Bruce, and they'd patched things up, for the children's sake. I could tell she was embarrassed that she'd confided in me at all."

I glanced at my watch. I needed to get to my next appointment. "Beverly," I said, standing up, "did you tell any of this to the cops?"

She shifted in her chair. "I told them Patti had consulted me about a divorce and had later changed her mind."

"That's all?"

She blushed. "Look, Callahan, I don't know anything, not really, about Bruce's clients. Patti was upset. Who knows if she was telling the truth? I don't need to have my name thrown around in court in connection with a homicide. Especially when the victim is my ex-partner's wife."

"What if your ex-partner killed his wife, or had her killed? What then?"

Her eyes met mine. "You really believe Bruce is responsible?"

"You tell me," I said.

She looked tired. "All right," she sighed. "You're right. I'll call that detective. What's his name? I'll tell him what I told you. Okay?"

I flashed her a smile. "His name is Charlie Fouts. Better not mention we talked. He thinks I'm meddling."

"You? Nah."

23

ON ANOTHER DAY I could have tolerated Anita Lindermann. Some other day her Southern accent, so thick it oozed, her tiny pointed chin and huge doelike brown eyes, her china-doll perfection, might not have made me want to slap her into the next county.

This was not one of those days. "And hay-yuh," she said, throwing open two frosted-glass French doors, "is the mastuh bath. These tahls are French, hand-painted, so I want the flo-wah and tub surround hand-washed and waxed ev'ruh week."

I dutifully added this latest requirement to the list of Anita's cleaning dos and don'ts. She didn't want any scented cleaners, aerosol sprays, abrasive scrubbing powders, or shoes of any kind on her priceless Oriental carpets. She did want all the silver polished, the drapes vacuumed, the baseboards damp-wiped, and the oven disassembled and cleaned every week.

"Now," she said brightly, leading me back to the bowling alley-sized kitchen where we'd started the tour. "Your muthah said you'd quote me a price. I was thinking somewhere around forty dollars. How would that be?" She blinked her eyelashes rapidly and beamed at her own selfless generosity.

"Well actually, Mrs. Lindermann," I said, "for all the intensive weekly cleaning you want in a house of this size, we'll need two girls and our minimum charge would be a hundred and fifty dollars."

"Good heavens," she said, her finely tweezed eyebrows shooting heavenward. "That's absurd. Why, we only paid Dixielee, our old maid, thirty dollars a day, and she did my husband's shirts, too. If I told Preston I wanted to pay you people a hundred and fifty dollars a week, I believe he'd have my head examined."

I wrote the price I'd quoted on the bottom of my list, signed my name, dated it, and handed it to her. "We're a professional, licensed cleaning business," I said. "Our girls work extremely hard and they deserve a decent wage. If you can find someone to do as thorough a job as the House Mouse for less money, I invite you to do so."

She held the estimate, scanned it and pursed her teensy little lips. "Seventy-five. And I'll have to pay it in cash so Preston won't know what I'm spending."

I snapped my estimate pad closed. "Better call Dixielee," I said. "Thank you for your time."

I let myself out the back door and made a beeline for my pink van, congratulating myself on my cool demeanor.

"Thirty fuckin' dollars a day," I said, backing the van down the Lindermanns' steeply sloped driveway. "Bet she probably thinks she deserves a medal, too, for lettin' poor old Dixielee have all the family's cast-off clothes and leftover dinner party food. These people give me a pain."

I sped down the Prado and headed toward Piedmont Park. At the light, a black woman dressed in a white nurse's uniform pushed a fancy English perambulator slowly across the street.

Cedric. I'd called the number so many times today I'd memorized it. I dialed the number, saying a quick prayer. "Let him be okay, God, please let Cedric be okay."

The nurse didn't say Cedric Lattimore was okay. "He's stable," she said.

"Is that better than serious?"

"Yes," she said.

"Thanks," I said fervently. And I wasn't talking to the nurse.

It was only three o'clock—the shank of the day, really. Instead of heading home to do battle with more satisfied House Mouse customers, I decided to pick up some supplies.

I got on Interstate 75 at 14th Street, went up a couple of exits, and got off on Howell Mill Road. There's a fancy new shopping center right there at the exit, but the farther west you go on Howell Mill, the grittier it gets.

I passed the Atlanta Waterworks with its quaint red brick buildings and placid retaining ponds and the not-so-quaint Atlanta Union Mission for Women, a grim-looking building that always reminds me of something right out of Dickens.

Farther west I hit what bureaucrats like Mac call a light industrial area. Auto scrap yards, machine shops, a salvage yard, and blocks and blocks of anonymous, run-down warehouses.

There were plenty of package stores, too, and a couple of new strip joints had popped up since I'd last been over this way. With fresh paint and glittering neon signs, the clubs had an oddly respectable look about them compared to the run-down neighborhood. Club Exotique advertised itself as a United Nations of Nudity while The Erotic Zone proclaimed itself home of the two-dollar table dance.

Georgia Sanitary Supply was wedged in between an auto transmission shop and a place that fabricated burglar bars. All three businesses in the single-story block were good patrons of the burglar bar business.

A small sign on the door instructed me to buzz for entry. Through the glass I saw a man behind the counter look up, annoyed at the interruption. He set down the newspaper he'd been reading and walked slowly to the door.

"We don't do no retail business," he said after unlocking the door. He turned his back and walked back to his perch behind the counter. He had a gray, military-style crew cut, and his sweatshirt had the sleeves cut off at the shoulders, exposing a set of beefy tattooed forearms.

"I'm a wholesale customer," I assured him. "We have a cleaning business."

I looked around me. As showrooms go, this one wasn't much. Big cardboard cases resting on wooden pallets had been pushed into makeshift rows, some of them displaying gallon jugs of cleaners, solvents, mops, buckets, and industrial-sized metal waste baskets.

I walked up and down the rows, glancing back at the sales clerk. He'd picked up his newspaper again and was ignoring me.

It didn't take long to check out the merchandise. The company only stocked a couple of dozen items, and many of the cases had never been opened. The merchandise had been strung across the room with little regard for convenience or aesthetics. A set of metal double doors at the back of the concrete-floored room looked like it might lead to a loading dock.

The room was damp and chilly, with the only apparent heat coming from a kerosene-burning heater the clerk had propped on top of the counter facing himself.

A hand truck leaned against a wall. I got it, walked back down the rows, and racked my brains for something to buy. I found a case of window-cleaner concentrate and loaded it on the hand truck along with a gallon jug of toilet bowl cleaner.

I pushed the truck over to the counter and stood there, waiting to be checked out. Crew Cut lowered his paper.

"That it?"

"Well, uh, do you have any non-aerosol dust spray?"

"You see it over there?" he asked, pointing toward the boxes.

"No."

"Then we're out. Anything else?"

"I guess not," I said.

"You got an account?"

I had no idea whether or not we did, but I didn't want this guy knowing who I was anyway.

"No," I said, "but I was planning on paying cash. Is that acceptable?"

"Cash is good," he said. "We can do that."

He leaned over the counter and looked at the stock I'd loaded onto the hand truck. "Twenty dollars," he said.

No adding of figures, writing down of stock numbers, or figuring of sales tax. Nothing. Georgia Sanitary Supply ran a pretty informal operation.

I handed him two ten-dollar bills and he opened a drawer in the counter, tossed the bills in, and shut the drawer again. "'Bye," he said.

He didn't offer to help me load my purchases. "You got a loading dock I can pull around to to put this stuff in my van?" I asked. I wanted to get a look at the back of the business, too.

"Nope," he said.

Well, all right. I took the hand truck out front and loaded the supplies myself. Out of meanness, I left the hand truck leaning against the front door.

I had to wait for the light to change before I could back onto Howell Mill again. While I waited I thought about what I'd just seen and what I hadn't seen.

A nearly empty storefront, only one employee, and a very casual attitude toward customer satisfaction. In some neighborhoods it might mean business was off. In this neck of the woods, I had a feeling it meant Xavier Draper was running a shell business to hide the profits from some other more lucrative, and probably illegal, business.

Bucky had said he thought Draper had a stake in some strip clubs as well as Grady Stovall's clubs. I wondered which ones. I dialed Bucky's number at the cop shop but the homicide secretary said he'd left for the day.

"Gone home?" I said hopefully.

"He had his gym bag," she said. "I think he was planning to go work out for a while."

Next I called Nickells at the vice squad. She was gone for the day, too. And here I was, still slogging uphill. It's hell working for yourself.

The phone buzzed as soon as I set it back in the cradle.

"Callahan?" Despite the static on the line I recognized Neva Jean's voice. She sounded panicky.

"What's wrong?"

"You moved your gun," she said in an accusing tone. "It's not in the oatmeal box anymore."

"It's here in the van," I said, glancing at the carefully locked glove box. "But if you plan to shoot Swannelle, I think you'd better do it with your own gun, Neva Jean. And don't tell me about it, either. I don't want to be a party to a conspiracy."

"It's not for Swannelle," she said, near tears. "There's a man parked across the street from your house. A big ole black man. He's been sittin' in his car, watchin' your house since we got back here at three. Me and Ruby and Jackie are scared, Callahan. I think Ruby's blood pressure might be up. She's got a bad headache and keeps talking about seeing some baby get shot. What if it's the same guy who killed your cousin?"

"Now don't get hysterical," I said. "Maybe the guy's just visiting Mr. Byerly next door."

"He ain't visiting nobody," Neva Jean said. "Mr. Byerly's car is gone. And I'm tellin' you, he's a-watching this house. And it's giving us the creeps. If Swannelle wasn't so sick, I'd call him and have him come run this guy off with his deer rifle."

"Never mind the deer rifle," I said sharply. "You all just stay put. Make sure all the doors are locked. I'm five minutes away."

"Shouldn't we call the police?" I heard Jackie say in the background.

"No," I said. "I'll be right there. Go on in my bedroom and lock that door, too. Make Ruby lie down and elevate her feet. Tell her to take some of her medicine. You all just stay put."

The streets in midtown were clotted with traffic. I wove in and out of every side street I could find, working my way back east toward Ponce deLeon and Candler Park.

I ran the light at Ponce and Oakdale, squeezing the van through the intersection just as an ancient pickup truck whizzed through, honking its horn at me in justified anger.

I had to pull over to the curb to unlock the glove box and fish out my pistol, a nine-millimeter semiautomatic Smith & Wesson. The loaded clip was tucked inside a rolled-up map. I loaded the clip with shaking hands. Patti had met her death unarmed, a defenseless lamb. Whoever was watching my house would find himself looking at the business end of my pistol. I'd felt helpless long enough.

At the stop sign at Oakdale and McClendon I spotted the car Neva Jean had seen. It was a battered white Nissan. With Cobb County license tags, parked directly across the street from my house.

The normally busy street was eerily quiet. I stepped on the gas and pulled parallel to the Nissan with the nose of the van blocking the street in front of him. I hopped out, ran around to the driver's side, and tapped the rolled-up window with the pistol.

"Okay, asshole," I said, sounding braver than I felt. "Who are you and what do you want?"

The man in the car dropped the paperback book he'd been reading propped up on the steering wheel. His mouth moved rapidly, but no sounds were coming out. He was black and young, no more than twenty-four, with a baseball cap jammed backward on his head. He wore mirror-lens sunglasses, a beat-up leather jacket, and an expression that said "Oh shit."

He started to reach for something on the seat beside him. "Leave it," I said, pointing the gun directly at his head. "This gun is loaded. Now tell me who you are and what you're doing staking out my house."

"I'm a process server," he said. "What the hell is with you, lady?"

That's when I noticed the title of the paperback book he'd been reading, *Law Review for the Georgia Bar Exam*. If he was a gang member or a carjacker, he was a pretty damned ambitious example of the species.

"What kind of papers?" I asked, lowering my pistol but not putting it away.

"I'm getting it now, all right?" he asked. He took a sheaf of typewritten papers from a folder on the car seat beside him, rolled the window down, and shoved them at me. Then he got another piece of paper and offered that, too.

"You've got to sign to show you were served," he said, spitting the words angrily.

I scribbled my name on the certificate of service and handed it over. "Sorry about the gun," I said lamely. "We've had a violent death in the family recently. My employees in the house saw you sitting here and they were frightened. We're all a bit jumpy these days, you know?"

He turned the key in the ignition. The engine coughed, then died. He tried again. "Yeah. You see a nigger in a car in Atlanta, you lock the doors and load the gun, right?" He rolled the window up, threw the Nissan in reverse and backed away from the van, then floored it.

My knees wobbled noticeably as I walked to the van. I got in and pulled into the driveway, cut off the motor, and sat there for a while looking at the gun on the seat beside me—the loaded pistol I'd just pointed at a poor innocent process server. A law student, for Christ's sake. "Get a grip, Callahan," I told myself. I unloaded the clip, and put it and the gun inside the glove box and locked it up.

It was only then that I thought to read the papers I'd just been served.

It was a TRO, a temporary restraining order. Bruce McNair had gotten a TRO to keep me away from Dylan.

Specifically, I was being ordered to stay at least one thousand yards away from the minor child Dylan Daniel McNair at all times. I was further enjoined from attempting to communicate with such child, either by telephone or in person, or through written communication, for the child's best interests.

"My ass," I muttered, folding the paper and sticking it in my purse.

When I got in the house, Neva Jean and Jackie were huddled together on one side of the bed, watching a black and white rerun of "Leave It to Beaver." Ruby was stretched out on the other side, her feet propped up on a stack of pillows.

"How are you feeling, Ruby?" I asked anxiously. "Do we need to take you to the doctor?"

"I'm all right, Callahan," she said. "Took my pill like you said. I'm just a little scared. I been rattled ever since we left Grady Homes. I called the hospital this morning, they said little Cedric's getting better. Now who was that man outside? Did he try to hurt you?"

"Yeah, who was he?" Jackie asked. "Did he pull a gun on you?"

I put my purse and clipboard on an armchair and sat down on the edge of the bed with them. "Actually, I pulled a gun on him. Fortunately, he wasn't the criminal type. Unfortunately, he was a process server who wanted to hand me some bullshit legal papers."

"What kind?" Jackie asked. She'd been going to school nights studying to be a paralegal.

"A TRO," I said, pulling off my black suede flats and massaging my tired toes.

"That's a temporary restraining order," Jackie said proudly. "Who put that on you, Callahan?"

"Bruce McNair, my cousin's husband," I said. "He's convinced some cockamamie judge in Cobb County that I was harassing Dylan. So now I can't go near the kid. Can't call him, write to him, or speak to him. I can't even get within a thousand yards of him."

"What'd you call that thing again?" Neva Jean wanted to know.

"A TRO," Jackie said.

"You think I could put one of them on Swannelle's mama?" she asked.

24

THE HOUSE WAS TOO quiet. I had a throbbing headache but somehow I craved noise, action, conversation. I shook the last three tablets out of the aspirin bottle and swallowed them with a gulp of water from the kitchen sink.

Then I made myself a cup of tea and sat on my bed to watch the six o'clock news. As they had been doing every night since Patti's death, the investigative team on channel six had an "exclusive" story on the sensational murder of Cobb housewife Patti McNair. Their exclusive showed footage of Patti's car being towed away from the murder scene on Bankhead Highway, an old photo of Patti, Bruce, and the kids taken three years ago for their church directory, and a tape of Charlie Fouts saying his department had several strong leads, but that the case was being hindered because the only witness to the murder, nine-year-old Dylan McNair, had not been allowed to make a statement to the police. The television camera zoomed in then and showed a close-up of Dylan's latest school picture.

"Oh good," I said aloud. "Show the kid's photo in case the gunman decides to go back and get rid of the only witness."

For the first time, I started to consider that Dylan

actually could be in danger. I wondered what, exactly, he had seen.

I switched on the computer and called up Patti's file. Typing rapidly, I made a list of people I needed to see and questions I needed answered. Bruce could keep me away from Dylan for the time being, but he couldn't stop me from doing anything else. Yet.

At the top of my list of things to do was a visit with Nancy Cook, Dylan's therapist. I'd looked her up in the phone book. Although she kept offices in Marietta, near Cobb General Hospital, there was a Nancy Cook listed as living on Los Angeles Avenue in Virginia Highlands, less than two miles from me.

I also wanted to ask Bucky or Linda Nickells about the strip clubs Xavier Draper was involved with, and I needed to see if Bruce and Draper could possibly be connected with Maleek Tebbetts. The one thing I did know about Patti's killer was that he was a young black male driving some kind of truck. I needed to talk to Nichelle Lattimore again.

I thought about what Liz Whitesell had told me about Mart Covington's firing his former housekeeper, and about his abrupt decision to take a sabbatical. Maybe the housekeeper knew something about his relationship with Patti. Maybe she'd like a visitor.

And what about Bruce? Beverly Updegraff said Patti knew who Bruce had been seeing on the sly. If he was involved in Patti's murder, maybe he had confided in his girlfriend.

By the time I heard a knock on the back door I'd been working for over an hour.

"It's me," Mac yelled.

I padded into the kitchen in my worn bedroom slippers, switched on the light, and peered out the window. Mac stood there, rubbing his arms against the cold.

"Glad to see you're finally starting to take security seriously," he said after I'd unlocked the door and let him in.

"It's kind of creepy being here all alone," I said, kissing him. His face was ruddy from the chill, his lips chapped. "I hate to admit it, but I kind of miss Edna. You want a beer or a drink or something?"

"I thought maybe we'd go out to dinner, maybe catch a movie," Mac said, opening the refrigerator and getting a beer. He held one up for me, but I shook my head no.

"That sounds great," I said. "But I was just making a list of things I need to do on this case. Mac, I'm starting to think maybe Bruce arranged for Patti's murder."

He popped the top of the beer, took a pilsner glass from the cupboard, sat down at a table, and poured the beer out. The foam made a soft fizzing noise. "What makes you think Bruce was involved?" he asked. "I thought the cops said they thought some black gangleader did it."

Mac obviously hadn't seen yesterday's news about the gangleader suspected in the drive-by shooting at Grady Homes. And I didn't plan to tell him about my involvement in it. I reached over and took a sip of his beer, which was a mistake because it made me want more. A beer wouldn't help my headache.

"He's gotten mixed up with this guy named Xavier Draper. The guy's an ex-con, small-time hood, Bucky says. The cops think Draper murdered his ex-partner, and he's probably laundering drug money or something through this phony janitorial supply business. Bruce is his lawyer, they hang out at clubs together."

"So Bruce is a crook," he mused. "Or he just likes to work for crooks. He's a lawyer, Callahan. That's what lawyers do."

"I wish that was all there was to it," I said. "He's deliberately keeping Dylan from cooperating with the police. He had me served with a TRO today to keep me away from Dylan. That little boy knows something, Mac. They showed his picture on the news tonight. He could be in danger, too."

"Let's say he did have Patti killed," Mac said. "Bruce wouldn't harm his own son. If he'd wanted to do that, the gunman probably would have killed Dylan in the car."

"Maybe the gunman didn't have time. I wouldn't have thought Bruce was capable of any of this, up until now."

"So what's the motive?" Mac demanded. "Even if you hate your wife, why have her shot to death in front of your kid? Why not just get a divorce like everybody else?"

"Money. Patti wanted a divorce. I think Bruce talked her out of it. They'd been having financial problems. Then Bruce took out a huge insurance policy on Patti just six months ago. Beverly Updegraff, his former partner, says she thinks Patti was afraid of Bruce. Maybe she knew too much."

Mac crumpled the empty beer can in his hand and tossed it toward the trashcan. It fell an inch short. "Gotta work on my hook shot," he said. "Come on. Get dressed and let's go out to eat. I bet you haven't had a real meal since your mother took off."

"Not tonight," I said stubbornly. "There are some people I need to talk to. Give me a rain check, will you?"

He got up, picked the beer can up, and slammed it hard into the trashcan. "Your mother's right, you know. You're obsessed with this thing. It's not healthy."

I handed him his jacket. "I know it. And I'm sorry. Call me tomorrow?"

He took his jacket and went to the door. "No. You call me when you're ready to let go. I can't deal with you when you get like this."

The phone rang. "Wait a minute," I said. "Don't go yet. Just let me—"

But he stalked out the door, shutting it noisily behind him. And the phone kept ringing.

"I heard you were looking for me," Bucky Deavers said.

"What?" I said, momentarily distracted. I could see Mac's headlights backing down the driveway.

"You called me," Bucky repeated. "What's shakin'?"

Back to business. If I couldn't have a love life, I could always keep busy with work. "Oh yeah," I said. "I was wondering if you know the names of those strip clubs you said Xavier Draper owns."

"I know the names," he said. "But I don't know that I need to tell them to you."

"How about Club Exotique or the Erotic Zone? Are those the ones?"

"Not bad," Bucky said. "How'd you know he owns Exotique? I don't know about the other one."

"Just a guess," I admitted. "They're both just a few blocks from that bogus supply business."

"You checked that out, huh? See anything interesting?"

"Just that there's no way that's a legitimate business," I said. "You've probably got as many cleaning supplies under your sink as he does in his warehouse. And none of his stuff is priced accurately, and he doesn't charge customers a state sales tax or write up receipts. And Charlie Manson's twin brother is the office manager."

"Yeah, that's pretty much what the latest intelligence report says," Bucky said. "Now if you could find Jimmy Lee Rakestraw's body in that warehouse, or the gun that killed your cousin, we'd be cookin'."

"You busy tonight? I thought maybe you'd like to go riding with me. Kind of like old times."

"Except you're not a cop anymore, and you got no business messing with people like Xavier Draper, and this is a Cobb County case that I've got no business messing with," Bucky said. "Anyway, I can't. I've got a date."

"So buy her a Happy Meal and drop her off at Kindercare," I said. "C'mon, Bucky, please?" I hadn't realized until just then how desperate I was for company.

"I'm at her house now," Bucky said. "And for your information, Niki happens to be twenty-two. She's a nurse. She's working tomorrow, though, so we're making it an early night. If you're still on the streets after midnight, call me on my pager. Maybe we'll get together at the Yacht Club or something."

I was taking the number of his pager when my call waiting button beeped. I clicked the receiver twice.

"Garrity? Keegan Waller. You doing anything tonight?"

25

WALLER WAS STAYING at the Holiday Inn in Decatur. Nancy Cook's house was on the way. I decided to stop in to see her. Nothing ventured, nothing gained.

The woman who answered the door at the dark green cottage on Los Angeles Avenue didn't look like my idea of a shrink. She had long blonde hair piled haphazardly on top of her head, a generous nose, and green cat's eyes. She wore a paint-spattered sweatshirt and cut-off sweatpants.

After I told her who I was and what I wanted, she frowned. I thought she was about to chase me off. "Come on in," she said finally. "The place is a mess. I'm remodeling."

Her house was of approximately the same vintage as mine, the 1920s. But someone had thoroughly modernized, knocking the ceiling out to expose old wooden beams, stripping the old plaster down to bare brick in the living room.

She had a fire going in the fireplace and the place smelled of wood smoke and wet paint. The dining room was furnished with a ladder, paint buckets, rollers, and drop cloths.

All the furniture had been pushed into the living room. I followed her to a couple of beat-up armchairs near the fire.

"Can I get you a glass of wine?" she asked. "I was going to take a break from painting anyway."

"Sure," I said. Maybe the wine would make her easier to talk to, I reasoned.

She poured us each a tumbler of Chardonnay, sat down and held the glass between both hands, twirling the glass absentmindedly, letting the fire light the pale yellow liquid.

I reached into my oversized purse and brought out a notebook. She looked startled.

"I can't tell you anything specific about Dylan," she said. "Not about his sessions with me, or my diagnosis, or my conversations with his father. Patient confidentiality. I thought you understood that."

"Maybe there are some things I should tell you," I said. "Things about the family and what I've learned about Dylan's mother's death."

"This isn't a swapping situation," she said quickly.

"I'm not offering a swap. But I think you should know that there's a possibility that Bruce McNair arranged his wife's murder."

"Arranged?"

"Hired a man to kill her and make it look like a bungled carjacking," I said. "Patti had a $1.2 million life insurance policy. Bruce is the beneficiary."

"I see," she said slowly.

"There's more. I don't think Bruce planned for Dylan to be in the car when Patti was killed. I think her killer expected that Patti would be alone. And I'm concerned that the killer might decide to eliminate the only witness to Patti's murder."

"Dylan." She kept twirling the glass. Her Chardonnay was getting warm. I was sipping mine. It was a much better grade than I usually buy.

"Unless the police can catch the guy and arrest him," I said. "But Bruce won't allow Dylan to talk to the police. He won't let them show him a photo lineup of suspects. He keeps saying Dylan has been traumatized enough and that his therapist has told him to help Dylan forget."

Her head jerked slightly at this last, and she stopped twirling the glass.

It was the cue I was waiting for. "Did you tell Bruce not to let Dylan talk to the police?" I asked.

"I can't tell you anything I discussed with Bruce McNair," she repeated.

"Fine," I said. "Let's talk generalities. In general, would you say it's best to keep a child from talking about or thinking about a parent's death?"

"Never," she said firmly. "Children and adults need to confront reality. I don't believe any responsible therapist would advise anyone to try to repress such memories. My job as a therapist is to help the patient work through any feelings they have about such an event. It's absolutely destructive for a child to be encouraged to forget."

I set my empty glass on the floor beside my chair. "That's the exact opposite of what Bruce is telling the police and the rest of his family," I said. "Tell me. What, in general, happens to a child who is trying to repress such memories or feelings?"

"In general, right?" she said. "The child internalizes things. There might be behavior problems, at home or school. Acting out, explosive or irrational behavior. When a child acts out it's because he can't express his feelings through more acceptable outlets."

"A kid like Dylan already finds it nearly impossible to communicate with others," I said, thinking out loud. "Then he's told by someone he loves and trusts that he should shut up and forget the most disturbing thing he's ever experienced."

Nancy Cook pushed long paint-stained fingers through her tangled hair. "God, what a mess."

"How do you get a child like Dylan to talk about something like a parent's murder?" I asked.

She leaned forward, her eyes glowing with enthusiasm. "Play therapy. We'll let the child use toys to act out something that's on his mind. Or through art. We'll ask the child to draw his family, or to draw the thing that gives him his biggest problem. A child who can't really articulate his feelings in words will often be more open and expressive in play about what is on his mind. Even a very young child can take a crayon and sketch a picture of himself, or hold a doll to act out a family argument."

It didn't seem like the kind of therapy I'd always seen on television or movies: beetle-browed shrinks urging neurotic types to lie back on the couch and open up about their feelings of ambivalence toward their fathers.

"What can you tell me about the rest of Dylan's family?" Nancy Cook asked.

Her question surprised me. I would have assumed Bruce had told her all that. "It's a fairly close-knit family. You know Dylan has two older sisters, Megan and Caitlin, they're sixteen and eighteen, I think. They're maybe resentful of all the attention their brother gets because of his language problem, but I think they do love him. Dylan's maternal grandmother, my aunt Jean, lives not far from them. She's a widow, a very warm, loving type. Bruce's father lives in Florida, I believe. Um, Patti's brother Jack lives here, too, and his kids, and her sister DeeDee recently moved back to Atlanta. She's staying at Bruce's, helping with the kids. And the other brother, Michael, lives in Charlotte."

"And you're certain that Bruce, Mr. McNair, is involved in his wife's murder?" She leaned forward again and studied my face.

"Certain? No. If I were certain, I'd be on the phone with the police. But now that I've talked with you I am certain that Bruce is hiding something, and that Dylan may be in danger."

Dr. Cook stood up abruptly. "And what do you intend to do about all this?"

"Me? I intend to find out who killed Patti and why, and I intend to try to keep Dylan from being harmed again."

She gathered our empty glasses. "You sound like a vigilante or something. Have you ever seen the view of downtown from around here?"

I was disconcerted by the sudden change of subject. "No. Is it particularly good?"

"Spectacular," she said. "Go out the kitchen door onto the deck if you'd like to look. I need to call a patient for a moment. I'll just be a minute."

The kitchen was in disarray, too. Dishes, pots and pans, and food cartons were stacked in the center of the floor. A long, narrow table was covered with rolls of wallpaper and a plastic water tray.

I stepped out onto the deck. The front of the house had a small, level lot that stretched to the street, but the back of the house dropped forty feet away from the grade. The deck was cantilevered out from the house, leaving you the feeling that you were in a tree house. To the west I could see the lights of downtown, with tiny dots of jets twinkling in the skies as they headed for the airport further south. It was bitterly cold, and I could see my breath forming puffy clouds of vapor, but the view was irresistible.

Nancy was suddenly standing beside me.

"This house is built on the highest lot in the neighborhood," she said. "I added the deck as soon as I bought the house. I never tire of looking at the city like this."

We both gazed at the city skyline. The Hyatt Regency's big blue lozenge-shaped revolving lounge had once been the highest thing in Atlanta. I'd had my first peach daiquiri there on prom night. Now other skyscrapers dwarfed it. "It doesn't look like a dangerous place at all," I commented. "It's like watching a cocktail party in somebody else's house, while you're standing in the street or walking by. Everybody looks all happy, like they're having the time of their lives."

"And when you get closer, reality sets in," she said. "Maybe that's why I live here and work out in Marietta. Maybe I like looking at Atlanta, but I'm afraid to really experience it."

I glanced down at my watch. "I'd better go." I handed her one of my business cards. "If you change your mind, if there's anything you can tell me about Dylan, please call."

Keegan Waller was dressed for action: blue jeans, running shoes, and a gaudy teal Charlotte Hornets satin warm-up jacket.

He eyed the van with disdain. "You expect me to drive around Atlanta in this pink piece of shit?"

"It's the perfect camouflage," I pointed out. "Who'd think we were detectives?"

"We'll take my rental car," he said, as if that settled it.

I got my purse and notebook out of the van, and after some hesitation I opened the glove box, got the Smith & Wesson and the clip and added it to my purse.

Keegan had seen the gun. "You're not playing, are you?" he asked, buckling his seat belt.

"I've been shot at once this week," I said, "and where we're going, a gun's just another accessory."

"Where to?" he asked as he headed out of the motel parking lot onto Clairemont Road.

"Let's go see Estella Diaz in Chamblee," I suggested. "I'd like to know what she told the archbishop about Mart Covington."

Waller made a face. "Come on, Garrity. No priest had Patti McNair killed. We're wasting time with the old lady."

"Humor me," I said. He followed my directions, though, and half an hour later we pulled into the Pine Tree Apartments on Buford Highway.

In the seventies, when I was getting out of high school, Buford Highway was swinging-singles heaven, new apartment complexes, shopping centers, bars and fast food restaurants. In the past twenty years, though, the highway had become internationalized. The singles got married, divorced, and remarried, and moved to the suburbs. In their place came waves of immigrants—Mexicans, Cubans, Chinese, Koreans, Vietnamese. Barbecue restaurants and hotdog stands were transformed into dim sum palaces and drive-through taco joints.

The Pine Tree apartment complex had sagging cedar-siding buildings with tiny balconies sprouting from each small unit. Some buildings were numbered, others weren't. A group of teenagers clustered around a basketball pole whose backboard and hoop were long gone. They bounced a ball and passed it back and forth.

I rolled my window down. "Hey, kid," I called to the nearest. A low murmur came from the group. The kid took a step away from the pole, but came no closer. I guess he'd been told about messing with strange Anglo ladies.

"You know where Mrs. Estella Diaz lives?" I asked.

The kid shrugged. "*No se.*"

My Spanish was pathetic, but I knew *no se* because that's what I spent most of my time telling my teacher, Senor Harris, in high school Spanish class.

"He doesn't know," I told Waller.

"Let's go," he said, pulling into a parking space in order to turn around.

A middle-aged man waited by the sidewalk in front of us as his leashed German shepherd squatted squarely in the middle of the pavement. Big dogs poop where they want. It's a law.

"Lemme just ask this guy if he knows her," I said. I

was getting annoyed with Waller. We'd been working together only thirty minutes and he was already cramping my style.

"*Señor*," I said, struggling to remember the phrases I needed. "*Dónde está Señora Estella Diaz?*"

He smiled and pointed up the street and rattled off a sentence that seemed to include the *calle* and *veinte-cinco*.

"Up here, apartment twenty-five," I said smugly. "*Gracias*," I told the man, but he and the dog were headed down the walk for a smoke.

Apartment twenty-five was on the bottom floor, at the back of the building. A young girl of about fifteen answered our knock.

"Estella Diaz?" I asked.

"Mama," the girl called. She shut the door in our faces.

A moment later, her mama opened the door again. She wore a maid's uniform and a name badge that said Radisson Hotel. Anna.

"We're looking for Estella Diaz," I said slowly. "Does she live here?"

"Yes," Anna said. "She has her papers. What do you want?"

Waller and I exchanged glances. "We'd like to talk to her about the man she used to work for, Father Covington," I said.

Anna shrugged. "She don't speak no English."

"Maybe you could interpret," I suggested.

She shut the door in our faces. Again. "Now what?" Waller griped.

"We wait."

Five minutes later the door opened again. Estella Diaz was large and square with very black hair and enormous black eyes set in concentric circles of wrinkles. She wore a bright purple sweatsuit and gold lamé house shoes.

She said something to the younger woman in rapid Spanish.

"Tia Estella say Father Covington is a sinner. She say he got ladies in his house all the time and he say bad words to her when she tell him he's going to hell. He fire her, and now she can't make the payment on the sofa."

The old lady gave us an appraising look and a shy smile, then fired off another round of comments.

"She tell the archbishop on him and Father Covington get fired. Tia wants to know do you need a good strong housekeeper. Three hundred a week and you buy the MARTA card."

Estella Diaz didn't work cheap. "Tell her no thanks, but ask her if she saw a woman with Father Mart, a woman named Patti McNair." I pulled a snapshot of Patti and Bruce out of my pocket and showed it to them.

Mrs. Diaz shook her head and said something further.

"Tia don't know. She don't want to talk about it no more."

This time when the door shut we heard it being locked on the other side.

"That's it," Waller said. "Let's go."

We got back in the car, and he turned on the engine and let it warm up a little. "Now what?"

"I think she probably recognized Patti," I said. "Maybe she was pissed because I wouldn't give her a job."

"Forget it," Keegan said. "I thought we were going to go see Maleek Tebbett's girlfriend."

"Oh yeah," I said. On the way to Grady Homes we swapped info.

Waller was fascinated with the idea that Bruce McNair apparently had some criminal connections. "We link him up with the shooter and my company's off the hook for that $1.2 million. Plus I'm claims investigator of the month. A free golf weekend for two in Sarasota."

"Don't start packing your clubs yet," I cautioned. "We still don't know who the shooter is, or how Bruce is tied to him. I can't get to the only witness, and neither can the cops. You get anything from Charlie Fouts yet?"

"I got some reports and stuff in my briefcase in the backseat," Waller said. "Tell me what exit I need to get off on." We were on Interstate 75, headed downtown.

"The next one up, for Grady Hospital," I told him.

When we stopped on the street outside Susie Battles's apartment, Waller looked uncomfortable. He gestured toward the plywood boards nailed across the blown-out windows. "You think it's safe here?"

Cars cruised slowly down the street, music blasted through closed windows, and from not far away we could hear the wail of the Grady Hospital ambulances.

"Hell no, it's not safe," I said, picking up my purse. "But it's early yet. Maybe we'll just be lucky. If you can't be good, be lucky, my daddy always said."

Waller smiled weakly.

Nichelle Lattimore just nodded when I introduced her to Waller. She was dressed now, her cold apparently on the mend. She invited us in, then sat down at the tiny dinette table and resumed eating from a paper take-out box of fried rice and bright orange sweet and sour pork.

"Ya'll find Maleek and put his sorry ass in jail yet?" she asked.

"Girl, close your nasty mouth," her grandmother called out from the bedroom. She walked into the living room and looked at us solemnly.

"Our Cedric going to be all right," she said. "Doctors said they're going to move him over to the Hughes Spalding Pavilion maybe Monday or Tuesday."

"That's the children's hospital," I told Waller. "That's wonderful, Mrs. Battles. But I don't think the police have found Maleek yet. That's one of the reasons we came to talk to your granddaughter."

"She don't know where that boy's at," Mrs. Battles said sharply. "Nichelle's done with that mess now."

"What we were wondering," Waller said politely, "was whether Maleek ever knew or talked to a man named Bruce McNair."

"He's a white guy, a lawyer who lives in Cobb County," I added. "He drives a white Mercedes, has kind of longish hair." I showed her my snapshot of Patti and Bruce.

Nichelle looked at the photo with interest. "Is this your cousin that got killed that you told me about?"

"Yes," I said. "This is her husband. We think he might have hired Maleek or someone else to kill Patti and make it look like a carjacking."

Nichelle picked up an egg roll, dipped it in a plastic tub of duck sauce, and bit off the end. "I ain't never seen this dude before," she said.

"She been in school," her grandmother said. "She ain't had no time to know who that boy knows or what evil he does."

"We mostly rode around at night, went to the Showcase to party, stuff like that," Nichelle admitted. "I don't think I ever saw him with a white dude in a Mercedes. I'd of remembered that."

"And you don't have any idea where Maleek might be hiding?" Waller repeated.

Mrs. Battles heaved herself up off the sofa. "This child don't know nothin'," she said angrily. "I done tol' y'all that."

As we pulled away from the curb, Susie Battles stood in her doorway like a sentinel, hands on hips, watching us go.

"An old lady like that," I said more to myself than Waller, "she just might be able to keep Nichelle straight. She just might."

26

I T WAS NINE O'CLOCK. "How about we get some dinner?" Waller said. "My stomach was growling to beat the band when I smelled that girl's Chinese food."

"I'm hungry too," I admitted. "But look, let's go out to Kenneyville Court, maybe talk to some of the kids who hang out at that youth center. Covington told me they have some gang activity out there. Maybe there's a connection to Maleek or his crew."

"Are you still on that kick?" Waller asked.

"I want to check it out," I insisted. "You don't want to go, drop me off at your motel so I can get my car and I'll go by myself."

"Forget it," he said, relenting. "We'll go. But when were you planning on eating?"

"Just as soon as we finish at Kenneyville," I assured him. "I know a place nearby. We can grab a bite there. They stay open late."

He turned on the radio and started mashing buttons, flipping from AM to FM and back again. "What's the all-sports station here?" he wanted to know. "NC State's playing Vanderbilt tonight."

"You too?" Mac was probably watching ACC basketball on television at home right now, a beer in his hand, Rufus's head on his lap where my head should have been. Should have been if I hadn't been so damn stubborn. I felt like I'd been running in place all week. I'd been dashing around all night and so far we'd accomplished nothing.

I fiddled with the dial 'til I found the faraway crackling sound of a basketball game in progress. I had no interest in the game, but the sound was sort of soothing.

"This the turn?" Waller asked twenty minutes later. I sat up and tried to shake myself awake. I recognized the area. "Yeah, turn right here."

Kenneyville was fairly quiet tonight, not like Grady Homes. Curtains were drawn tight at the apartment windows and the streets were deserted.

Lights blazed at the Youth in Action club. Waller looked around with alarm. "You sure know some nice places," he said.

"Hey, this is the Ritz compared to some other housing projects around Atlanta," I told him. "This youth club is pretty cool. They've got all kinds of organized activities to keep the kids busy."

Waller looked dubious.

We went inside. The basketball game was still in progress and the same group of girls was practicing cheers. We stood at the edge of the floor and watched.

"Hotty-totty. Good God Almighty. Who's the best? Of the rest? We are. Whoop. There it is," the girls chanted, leaping and twirling in the air.

When they fell laughing on the bleachers, I wandered over and sat down beside one of the teenage girls. She was pretty, with cocoa-colored skin and hair slicked into the nineties equivalent of a French twist.

"Y'all are pretty good," I said. "Do you have uniforms and cheer at regular games?"

"Shiiiit," she said, making it a three-syllable word. "We're just messing around. Real cheerleaders be ten times better. You ever see the Lakers Girls? That's what I wanna do."

She looked at me with unmasked curiosity. "You from Father Mart's church?"

"My aunt goes there," I said. "I'm sort of doing some research about gangs, for the newspaper. I'm a reporter. You know anything about gangs around here?"

She looked down at her shoes and then back up at me. "Yeah. Some boys around here be in gangs."

"Like which ones?"

She slumped down with the small of her back against the bleachers. "Like the Crips and the Aces and The Wrecking Crew and the Thirty-eight Posse."

"The Wrecking Crew?" I said. Mart Covington had told me he'd never heard of them.

"Yeah," she said. "And then the new one, that's the Street Warriors."

"What's your name?" I asked.

"Valerie."

I pulled a ten-dollar bill out of my pocket. Waller was still standing at the edge of the basketball court, hands in his pockets, fascinated with the fast-moving game.

"Valerie, do you know anybody here tonight who's in The Wrecking Crew?"

She eyed the bill and licked her lower lip with the tip of her tongue. "Uh-uh. They don't be playing in the gym. This is Street Warrior turf."

Damn. "Do you know anybody here who might know something about The Wrecking Crew?"

"My brother Earl, he be knowing some of 'em," Valerie said. "He's over there playing. You want to talk to him?"

I handed her the bill. "Sure."

Valerie darted to the opposite end of the gym and called out to her brother. Earl was the same cocoa color as his sister, and not much taller, but he was powerfully built. He wore baggy black shorts that hung below his knees, high-top sneakers with the shoelaces trailing, and a red, black, and green striped knit hat that reminded me of the one worn by the cat in *The Cat in the Hat.* She showed him the ten-dollar bill and pointed my way.

He strolled toward me, grinning, hitching his shorts lower on his hips. It was a look, I guess.

"How you doin'?" he said, sitting down beside me.

"Okay," I said. "I'm interested in finding out about The Wrecking Crew."

"You ain't no cop," he said flatly.

"I'm a newspaper reporter," I told him. "What can you tell me about The Wrecking Crew?"

"Those mutha-fuckas ain't shit," he sneered. "What you want with them?"

"I'm really just interested in one. Maleek Tebbetts. Do you know him?"

"I know the mutha," Earl said.

"You know where he is?"

"Nowhere around here," Earl said, laughing. "Father Mart, he run the crew off. They be dealin' crack to the little kids, man. Stealin' old ladies' checks, shit like that. Father Mart got the cops after 'em, they split. Hey, you know Father Mart?"

"Yes."

"He's all right," Earl said. "Hey. You think he ever got any pussy?"

I felt myself blush. "I wouldn't know," I said stiffly.

Earl shook his head. "Man say he don't want none, he be lying or crazy."

It was an interesting theory about chastity, one my friends and I had often discussed in our parochial school days, but not from the obvious authority that Earl had.

I fished in my pocket and came up with another ten-dollar bill. Waller would have to spring for dinner.

I held it out. "I really need to find out where Maleek Tebbetts lives for this story I'm working on. My editors will fire me if I don't get this story."

He plucked the bill from my fingertips. "Be right back."

Earl ran downcourt, inserted himself into a knot of players, and conferred with them.

When he loped back he was grinning again. "My man Maleek stays over to Smyrna. You know where Atlanta Road is?"

I had a vague notion. "Yes."

"Don't know the name of the place, but they got a big old rock wall with a waterfall coming down it outside," he said. "He stay with some bitch named Eddie. Light-skinned girl works at a car place over that way."

"Thanks," I said, and headed toward Waller and the door.

"Hey, lady," Earl yelled after me.

"What?" I said, turning.

"You ever hear of a Desert Eagle?"

I felt my scalp prickle.

"What about it?"

"My man say Maleek got him one," Earl said. "He hit a sporting goods store last night and scored one." He made a gun barrel of his left forefinger and pointed it at me. "Boom." Then he blew the imaginary smoke away through pursed lips. "Be cool now."

"Can we eat now, please?"

"You like fried chicken?" I asked. Stupid question. All men love fried chicken. It was nearly ten. I was hungry and tired. We had a lead on Maleek Tebbetts, though, and that was something. I'd stopped at a gas station to phone Charlie Fouts, but the police dispatcher said he was on the road, out of radio range. I left a message. With Tebbetts in possession of a cannon-sized weapon I had no intention of trying to track him down on my own.

Waller glanced over at me. "What have you got in mind?"

"Get back on 285 and go south," I said. "Let's go to

that Popeye's on Bankhead Highway. I want to see those reports of yours, and get a look at the crime scene again. I still need to do a door-to-door out there, but it's too late tonight."

A beat-up station wagon with a cab light on top was parked in the lot at Popeye's, and the driver, a shrunken-looking man wearing an outsized Atlanta Falcons baseball cap, was the only other customer in the restaurant.

The waitress and cook were a different crew than the pair I'd encountered earlier in the week. The waitress was a well-padded black woman of fifty or so, the cook a muscular teenaged kid with raging acne. "Don't order the iced tea," I warned Waller.

We got our food and sat down at a window facing Bankhead. I could see the stop sign at the corner of the street, could still see bright yellow remnants of crime scene tape.

Waller put the briefcase on a chair beside his, unsnapped it, took out a sheaf of papers and handed them over.

I took a bite of chicken and started reading one of Charlie Fouts's supplementary reports. His investigation seemed to parallel mine, with the exception of the fact that there was no mention of Bruce's connection to Xavier Draper or Grady Stovall.

Stapled to the back of a report I found the transcript of the first and only interview with Dylan at the hospital.

The sentences were fragments, the impressions hazy. From what I could make out, he'd told Fouts he'd been asleep after Patti picked him up at school, and that he'd felt the car stop and heard his mother say something. Then a man's voice, then his mother screamed. When he heard the screams, Dylan said, he'd sat up, and seeing his mother being shot had screamed also.

"Blood. Mama's head. Broken."

I set my chicken down. It suddenly tasted rancid.

The man opened the back door and hit him on the head with the gun.

Dylan's description of the man was that he was black. Scary looking. No mention of any beard.

Fouts's report said he had taken an Ident-i-kit to the hospital, but the doctors had refused to let him show it to Dylan.

Waller was busy cleaning the meat off what looked to be an entire chicken carcass. He had a morsel of coleslaw on his upper lip.

"Nothing much here so far," I said.

The car inventory sheet listed a boy's blue blazer with Dylan's name marked on the label, a child's book bag with schoolbooks and papers and an empty lunch box, a paperback copy of *Waiting to Exhale* by Terry McMillan, a paper sack containing two nearly full drink cups and a bag of french fries, and a box containing various CDs and the car phone.

"Did the cops give you a list of the calls to the car phone?" I asked.

"Right there," he said.

I leafed through the papers. The computer printout listed six calls and the time of day each was made. "I made notes of what the numbers were," Waller said. "Nothing out of the ordinary that I could tell."

The first call listed had come in at 10:55. Miller-Shipley School. "That's when they called to say Dylan was sick," I said. The next call had Sherrill Mackey's number on it. "Sherrill said Patti called to cancel their tennis match."

At 12:20 there was a call from Bruce. "That's the office number," Waller pointed out.

"Bruce told me Patti called him," I said. "The printout says it's the other way around."

Waller stopped chewing. "Yeah?"

"It was the morning after Patti's murder that he told me that, though," I said. "He'd been up all night. Hadn't had any sleep. Maybe he forgot who called who."

"Maybe," Waller said, taking a bite of biscuit.

At 1:15 there was a call made to the rectory at Our Lady of Lourdes. At 1:45 Patti had called Bruce again.

"Did the cops get a record of Bruce's calls from the office?" I asked.

"They're working on it," he said. "Fouts promised I could see it when they get it."

I stared out the window and sipped at my drink. "Bruce is behind this," I said. "I just wish I knew how to prove it."

"Me too," Waller said. "You done?"

We rode most of the way back to Decatur in silence. Out of boredom, I picked up the reports Waller had given me and switched on the dome light to read them over again. The car inventory sheet caught my eye.

An inventory of my van would have taken pages and pages to list all the equipment and trash I carry around with me. But Patti's car was fairly new and fairly fastidious.

Except for the Popeye's bag.

"The day manager and cook who were working the day of the murder swore to me that they never saw Patti or Dylan," I said. "So why was there a Popeye's bag and two nearly full drinks and an order of fries in the car when she was killed?"

"Maybe they just forgot they saw her."

"I don't think so," I said. "They saw the ambulance and the police come, and they made a point of telling me they never saw Patti."

"What about the drive-through window?" Waller said.

"That's got to be it," I said. "I forgot about the drive-through. If Dylan was sick, and she was scared of the area anyway, Patti wouldn't have gotten out of the car."

"After my kid was born we didn't go to a sit-down restaurant 'til he was almost six," Waller said. "We went to drive-through liquor stores, restaurants, dry-cleaners, you name it. Anything to keep from dragging him inside."

"The manager told me that she and the other crew

member, Kwante, were the only ones working that day, but if she was at the counter and he was cooking, somebody else had to be at the drive-through. The manager must have forgotten about it. It's probably in a booth off to the side."

"You don't want to go back there now, do you?" Waller asked, obviously alarmed.

"No. The drive-through person probably works the day shift anyway. I'll go back tomorrow."

Waller pulled alongside the van to let me out. "You want me to go with you on the door-to-door tomorrow?"

I really wanted to do it alone, but I'd never get as much done by myself as I would with his help. "Sure," I said.

"Call me in the morning when you're ready to leave," he said.

I started to unlock the van.

"Hey," he said. "You left this. It must have fallen out of your purse."

He held up a videotape in a clear plastic case.

"That's not mine," I said. "You sure it's not yours?"

"Positive," he said. "This is a rental, remember? We don't have a VCR in the motel."

I took the tape and turned it over. No label. "Maybe it did fall out of my purse," I said. "Let's take it to my house and have a look."

"Not me," Waller said. "I've still got reports to write tonight. You take a look and tell me about it tomorrow."

27

THE TAPE QUALITY was poor: grainy, black and white, it was barely better than those 7-11 hold-up tapes they sometimes show on the six o'clock news.

There was a time and date stamped on the bottom of the screen, 10:30 A.M., Monday.

A little boy was sprawled on the floor of a carpeted room. He looked like Dylan. He hummed to himself as he pushed a toy car along the floor.

"Who is in the car, Dylan?" I heard a woman's voice ask off camera.

He kept humming and didn't answer. "Who. In. The. Car?"

The boy looked up, his face solemn.

"Mama. Dylan."

"And what happens when Mama and Dylan are in the car?"

"Mama goes to store."

"Did something bad happen?" the woman's voice asked. It was Nancy Cook's voice, I was sure. She must have slipped the tape into my purse when I'd gone out onto her deck.

"What happens?" she repeated.

Dylan got up and trotted over to a box of toys and dug

until he found another car. He took both cars to a table and stood beside it, his face puckered in concentration.

He thought a while, then crossed back to the toy box and got what looked like a toy telephone. He picked up the receiver, and in a deepened voice said, "Go get watch."

Then he took the phone, switched ears, and in an uncanny falsetto cried, "No. No. No watch. Car lost." Then he turned to the camera, put his fingers to his lips and said, "Shh. Dylan. Don't tell Daddy."

The little play made no sense to me, but Nancy Cook was a better interpreter. "Did Daddy call Mama and tell her to go get a watch?"

Dylan nodded, pleased with himself.

"Did Daddy know Dylan was in the car with Mama?"

He smiled, giggled almost, at the secret he and his mother shared, and shook his head no.

"The bastard," I said aloud. That phone call Friday from Bruce at the office. He must have sent Patti on that errand, something about a watch, out to Bankhead Highway and her waiting killer. Only he hadn't known Patti had just picked Dylan up from school.

Nancy Cook was talking again, asking questions. "Are you still in the car now? Are you sick?"

The little boy's face clouded. "Dylan bad."

"Why?" she asked gently. "What makes you think you were bad?"

"Not sick," he whispered. "Lied."

"You weren't really sick at school that day?"

Dylan hung his head in shame.

That's why the kid was so reluctant to talk. He thought he'd killed his mother because he'd played possum at school. He'd somehow made himself responsible for Patti's death.

The tape kept rolling. Now Dylan had the cars again. He made one car stop, then brought the other car up behind it and stopped it, too.

"What can you tell me about when Mama was hurt?" Nancy asked.

He bit his lip and thought. "Car stopped. Mama said 'No. No. NOOOOOO.'" His screams made me jump in my chair.

"NOOOO," he screamed again. Then he took one of the cars and bashed the other with it. "No. NO. No. Bad. Hurt Mama."

Dylan burst into sobs then, and finally, the off-camera voice came on camera, with a grainy black and white Nancy Cook enveloping the child in her arms.

There was a blip, and a bit of blank tape. Now Dylan was seated at the table, calmly examining a box of crayons.

"Could you draw your family for me now, Dylan?" she asked.

The child nodded, picked up a crayon and started to work. His strokes were bold, and he furrowed his brow as he furiously covered the page with figures. At one point, he pressed down so hard that the crayon snapped in his hand, and he threw it in a box and chose another.

The film stopped again, and when it resumed, the voice was asking him to show his picture. Dylan held the sheet of paper in front of him, smiling shyly.

"That's a very nice picture," Nancy Cook said encouragingly. "Could you tell me about it?"

It was hard to tell much about the picture because of the poor quality of the tape, but I could see a large distinct stick figure of a man dominating the page. He was smiling. There were two stick figure girls in skirts, and a little stick boy, standing apart from the others. The little boy had a head and neck and torso and legs, but no arms. Odd. Standing on the other side of the man, away from the children, was a figure of a woman wearing a skirt, smiling and showing a jagged row of teeth.

"Can you tell me about this drawing?" Nancy asked again. "I see someone who looks like a man. Is that Daddy?"

"Yes," Dylan said haltingly.

"And the little boy, is that you?"

"Uh-huh."

"And your sisters?"

"Yes."

"Who is the lady, Dylan?" Nancy asked. "Is that your mama?"

He shook his head violently. "Mama died. She went to heaven."

"Is that Mama in heaven?"

Dylan looked angry. "No. Aunt DeeDee. She stays here now."

"Oh," Nancy said. "She looks nice. Is Aunt DeeDee nice?"

"Yeah," Dylan said reluctantly.

"Dylan," the voice said. "Are you sometimes angry with Aunt DeeDee?"

He shook his head no.

"Shall we read a story now?" Nancy Cook asked. She came into camera range again, and sat cross-legged in front of Dylan. She read to him from a book. A story about a little dog who loses his best dog friend and is sad all the time and won't play with any other dogs. So one night in his dreams his old dog friend comes to him and tells him not to miss him, that he can keep the dog friend in his heart.

Dylan listened raptly. When she was done telling the story, he moved closer. "Again," he said.

And the tape ran out.

I re-wound the tape, took it out of the VCR, and looked at it. No writing anywhere.

It was nearly midnight, but I dialed Nancy Cook's number anyway.

The phone rang and rang. I winced each time. "Hello?" The voice was groggy.

"Nancy? It's Callahan Garrity."

"Who?" she said. "What time is it?"

"It's nearly midnight. I'm sorry to call so late, but I just watched the videotape. I wanted to thank you and ask you what some of it means."

"What tape?" she said sleepily.

"The tape you put in my purse tonight of your session with Dylan McNair," I said.

"I don't know what you're talking about," she said. "Please don't call me again." And she hung up.

28

THE WOMAN IN MY dream wore a diaphanous white gown, feathery wings, a sparkly gold halo, and a tennis bracelet. I could see her up there in the clouds, hovering over us, watching down. There was a little boy in the dream, too; he had a face but no mouth and no arms. And a man came in, impossibly tall, two stories high, wearing a Grateful Dead shirt. There was a woman with him, and she was laughing and baring jagged, endless rows of teeth. And the little boy kept crying, "Nooo, don't hurt my mama."

In the morning, after I got up and had coffee and toast, I watched the videotape again. Then I got out the telephone book and called Beverly Updegraff at home.

I got right to the point. "Do you keep the firm's old telephone bills?"

"I was audited by the IRS three years ago," Beverly said. "I don't throw away so much as a Lillian Vernon catalog. Why, what do you want with the phone bills?"

"I'd like to look for some phone numbers to see if Bruce called them. Are the bills in a place where I could get to them?"

"They're in a shoe box in my hall closet. I ran out of storage space at the office," she said. "You're welcome to come and look at them if you want. I'll be out this morning, but back after lunch."

"I'll call before I come," I promised. "Thanks."

Charlie Fouts wasn't in his office. "It's Saturday," the woman who answered the phone pointed out. "I know, but this is really important. Could you call him at home and ask him to call Callahan Garrity. Tell him it's about Maleek Tebbetts."

The bait worked. Fouts called back five minutes later.

"Didn't I make it clear that you were to stay out of my homicide investigation?" he asked.

I decided to ignore him. "Do you know an apartment complex in Smyrna, on Atlanta Highway, one that has a rock wall with a waterfall coming down it?"

"Millstream Trace," Fouts said promptly. "Place is a snakepit. Why?"

"I talked to a kid at Kenneyville Court who claims Maleek is living there with a girlfriend, a light-skinned girl named Eddie who works at some auto place in Smyrna."

"Eddie Collins," Fouts said. "We know about her. She was seen with Maleek in Atlanta a couple of days ago, but we don't have a current address on her. Okay, that's good. We'll check it out. Thanks," he said begrudgingly.

"Say, Fouts," I said. "You ever hear of a Desert Eagle?"

"Yeah, but I'm a cop," he said. "How do you come to know about it?"

"The kid says Maleek knocked over a pawnshop and got one the other night."

"EZ-Pawn up in Kennesaw was hit Thursday around three A.M. Somebody drove a stolen pickup truck through the front window, jumped out, and while the alarm was ringing, cleaned the place out. The shop owner had just gotten a Desert Eagle."

"Sounds like Maleek," I said.

I dialed my aunt Jean's phone number with dread. Edna answered the phone.

"It's me," I said.

"What?" She was obviously still pissed.

"Now listen," I said. "I know you're hacked off at me, but this is really important. I'm almost certain Bruce had Patti killed for her insurance money. Over a million dollars."

"That's ridiculous," she hissed. "He's a lawyer, he doesn't have to kill his wife for money."

"He had a new law practice and money was tight," I said. "And Bruce was having an affair. He admitted it to me and Patti admitted it to the lawyer she went to see about getting a divorce."

"I don't believe it," she said.

"Patti told the lawyer she knew who Bruce was seeing. I think it's possible that DeeDee was the other woman."

"What?" Edna said. "That's the sickest thing I've ever heard. I'm hanging up."

"Mom," I said urgently. "I swear to you, this is for real. I'm dead serious. You know I'm good at what I do, don't you?"

"Up until now," she said. "But now I think you've lost your mind. And I don't want to listen to any more of this mess."

"You've got to listen," I shouted. "Honest to God, I'm afraid for Dylan. He's the only witness to Patti's killing. They showed a picture of him on the news last night. What if the killer decides to go back and finish off the job?"

I heard voices in the background. "What? Yes, I'll be right there."

"So do you believe me?" I said. "Please, Mom. I know you're mad at me for investigating this, but think about Dylan. Hell, think about me. Are you going to believe in Bruce McNair or in your own daughter?"

She didn't say anything. "That's what it comes down to, Mom," I insisted. "Me or Bruce."

"Listen," Edna said. "I've got to go. We've got to go

to the drugstore to pick up some medicine, and then I'm taking Jean to the beauty parlor. A permanent and a rinse will make her feel worlds better."

"Wait," I said. "Can you do me a favor? Get me DeeDee's old phone number in Miami, home and work. It's probably written down somewhere around the house there. Oh yeah, is Michael still in town?"

"Yes, but he's going back to Charlotte tomorrow," she said.

"Where's he staying?"

"He was staying here, but he moved over to Bruce's house this morning because he couldn't take the heat over here."

"Heat?"

"Your aunt keeps this place at a steady eighty-two degrees. She's so thin, she can't keep her body heat up. Me, I feel like a roastin' hen two hours overdone. I'm thinking about coming home today, to tell the truth."

"Can Aunt Jean stay by herself?"

"Oh, hell," Edna said. "Peggy's over here every minute of the day sucking up to her and babying Jean 'til you want to puke."

"Well, get those phone numbers, will you? And call Michael. Ask him to call me, but not from there. Give him my car phone number. Call me as soon as you can."

"I'll do it," Edna said, "but I still don't believe any of this."

"Give me a little help and I'll be able to prove it to you," I said. "Thanks, Ma. I missed you."

"Missed my cookin' is more like it," she said tartly.

Waller wanted to take his rental car, but I insisted on the van. "I'm expecting calls," I said, pointing to the car phone.

I told him about the videotape Nancy Cook had slipped in my purse, and what was on it, but he wasn't overly impressed.

"She'll deny she gave it to you," he said. "And there's

no documentation, no proof that the kid is Dylan or that the tape was of a counseling session between the shrink and the kid."

"It's a start," I said. "It's proof that Bruce deliberately sent her out to Bankhead Highway, where he had the gunman waiting."

"Did you tell Fouts about the tape?" he asked.

"No. I don't want him raising hell with Nancy Cook. But I told him where to find Maleek Tebbetts. I think the key is to find the gunman. Then maybe he'll roll over on Bruce."

"Yeah, we just gotta find a black guy on Bankhead Highway with a gun," Waller said. "Shouldn't be too hard."

I parked in the parking lot at Popeye's and Waller winced. "I burped up fried chicken 'til three in the morning," he said.

"So stick to the coffee," I suggested.

The morning rush hour was over, if they'd ever had one. I asked the girl at the counter if I could talk to whoever ran the drive-through window on weekdays, and she pointed to a trashy-looking bleached blonde woman who sat at a table drinking coffee and reading the want ads. "Her name's Marcia," the girl said. "She ain't working today, though."

Standing over her I could see two inches of black roots. The girl was in her early twenties, and she wore a thick layer of makeup, including shiny black eyeliner extended out beyond her eyes to make her look like a trailer park Cleopatra.

"Marcia?" I asked. "Could we sit down and talk to you?"

The girl gave us a sour look. "Ya'll from DFACS?"

"No," I said, "we're private detectives. We're looking into the homicide that took place here last Friday. You were working the drive-through last Friday, weren't you?"

"You won't tell nobody at DFACs, will you?" she said quickly. "See, Mama was sick Friday and couldn't keep the baby. And I can't afford no five dollar an hour day care. So I kept Buddy out of school and he watched Tara."

"We're not from Family and Children Services," I reassured her. I showed her the snapshot of Patti. "Did this woman come through the drive-through window last Friday afternoon? Maybe around two-thirty? She probably ordered two drinks and an order of fries and was driving a black Lexus with a little boy asleep on the backseat."

"I remember the kid," Marcia said. "I tol' her I wished I could get my kid to sleep that good in the car. The lady said he wasn't feelin' too good. He had a stomachache."

"That was Patti," I said. "What else did she say?"

"She just asked how to get back to I-285, said her husband had sent her out this way to pick up a watch he'd had fixed and she was lost. She didn't say it, but I think she was afraid of the neighborhood, you know, there's niggers everywhere out here."

"Was anybody else around? Did you see any trucks?"

"Like what kinda trucks? I mean, it was Friday, so they was trucks in and out of here all day. See, there's a truck freight yard on up Bankhead and those boys come here all the time, and then we got trucks of our own, delivering stuff. You know, the meat truck and the bread truck and the Coke man; he was here cause the Mister Pibb tap wasn't doing right."

"Were all the drivers regular customers? Did you see anybody strange, or acting suspicious?"

"You ever seen a route truck driver didn't act strange or suspicious?" Marcia demanded. "All of 'em's squirrelly as they come. I oughta know 'cuz Tara's daddy drove a UPS truck."

"Did you see or hear anything after they left? Like the gunshot?"

Marcia turned around and pointed toward the kitchen and her drive-through station. "You see that window there? I can see the car driving up and the car behind him. That's it. I'm wearing a headset and people are screaming into it about they got a coupon or they don't want no thighs or how come extra biscuits cost extra. Then I got no-count niggers in here actin' like they doing the world a favor coming to work. Tell you the truth, when the cops showed up, I told Margeneeda I was sick and had to go home. All I need is DFACs on my butt about my kids. That's all I need."

She turned back to her newspaper then. Waller got us two cups of coffee to go, so we went.

"Real high-quality employees they got here," he commented.

"They pay four twenty-five an hour and make their people wear hair nets and take lie detector tests," I pointed out. "Let's go across the street and see if anybody saw anything."

"The place is huge," he protested.

"We don't have to do the whole thing. Just the front bank of apartments that face the street. You take one end and I'll take the other, and we'll meet in the middle."

The first four apartments I tried I met with the same answer, "I wasn't home. I didn't see nothing." At the last two units the tenants merely hollered a plain "Get the hell out of here" from behind locked doors.

I finished my bank first, so I walked over to join Waller at the doorstep he was standing on.

A little boy of three or four came to the door, opened it and peered out at us. He wore a too-small T-shirt and what looked like soggy training pants. "What y'all want?" he asked.

"We'd like to see your mama," I said.

"My mama's sleeping," the child said.

"Tell your mama that there are two detectives here who want to talk to her," Waller said. "Here." He took a pack of gum out of his pocket, offered a stick to the little boy, took one himself and gave me one. All three of us unwrapped the gum and popped it into our mouths. The boy disappeared inside the house, leaving the door open.

A minute or two later, a highly irritated woman came to the door, wrapping a threadbare terrycloth robe around her waist. Her face was sleep-swollen and she was trying to drag a brush through her mussed hair.

"What ya'll want?" she asked, her inflection the same as the little boy's. Her voice was deep and husky, a Jim Beam and Camels kind of voice. A voice that would have sounded like a man's on the telephone to a police dispatcher.

"We're investigating a homicide that happened across the street there last Friday," I said. "The woman was my cousin. She was shot in the head while her little boy watched. Can we come in? It's cold out here."

She motioned us in, then turned to her son. "Go on in the bedroom, Bennie," she said.

"I want to watch cartoons," he protested. "I wanna see the Ninja Turtles."

"You gonna be seein' stars, I'll slap you so hard," she said, popping his backside with the flat of her hand. The boy skipped into the other room.

"My name is Callahan Garrity," I said, extending my hand to shake hers. "This is my colleague, Keegan Waller."

She ignored my hand, sat down in a wooden kitchen chair, and lit a cigarette. "Adalene Prather," she said. "What you want with me?"

Uninvited, I took a chair near hers. "We think you're the anonymous caller who reported the shooting to the police. I'd like to ask you to tell me exactly what you saw."

Adalene Prather's eyes were fixed on her front window. "What makes you think I saw anything?"

I pointed to the window. "You've got the best view of the corner. The police thought the caller was a man. But at all the units I went to either the man was at work Friday or there wasn't a man there. I think you called."

"I don't need none of this shit," she growled. "I mind my own business, get along fine."

"You saw something last week," I suggested. "Do you have a telephone?"

"Southern Bell cut it off a month ago," she said.

"So you ran across the street and used the phone at Popeye's."

"I was at Popeye's," she said finally. She massaged her temples with her fingertips as though she had a headache. "Man, I don't need none of this."

"He shot my cousin in the head," I said. "Blew her brains all over the car. Her nine-year-old son was in the backseat. His father won't let him talk to the police. You're the only other witness we know about."

She got up, went to the refrigerator, got a can of Colt 45 Malt Liquor, popped the top, and sucked back a long time.

"I didn't see it happen," she said. "I went across the street to get me a Coke. Coming out, I heard this loud popping noise. Bennie, he was hollerin' about wantin' a Coke too, so I had to get in his face about how we only had enough money for one Coke. I look up, I see a guy parked at the corner, slamming the hood of a truck down. He gets in and takes off. Fast. Soon as that truck is gone, I notice the car behind it, one of those fancy cars. See, I thought the guy in the truck was fixin' it. A minute later, I see a woman cross the street, she actin' real antsy, she move over to the curb side, and I see her take the hubcaps off that car."

"That's when you called the cops?"

"Yeah," she said. "Should have kept my damn mouth shut. Ain't none of my business."

"Did you see the woman take anything else?" Waller asked. "Mrs. McNair's purse and some jewelry were missing."

"Time I got off the phone was a whole mess of folks standing around that car. Anybody could have taken that shit. Fancy car like that draws a crowd like stink on a dog around here. I went on home and shut my door."

"Tell us about the truck," I said. "Was it a pickup

truck or some other kind? What color? Did it have any writing on it? And how about the driver—can you tell us anything about him?"

She tapped the bridge of her nose. "Glasses been broke six or seven months. Can't see far away worth shit. The dude that got in the truck was skinny and black and he was wearing dark pants and a jacket, that's all I could tell. The truck wasn't no pickup, more like a van kind of thing. White. Had some kind of writin' on the side, but I couldn't say what it was."

Waller had been taking notes furiously while Adalene Prather talked. "Ms. Prather," he said. "Did the police come here and ask you about this? Why didn't you tell them what you've just told us?"

Bennie poked his head around the corner. "I wanna see the Ninjas," he started, but his mother made like she was coming after him and he darted back inside the bedroom.

"Police come here, I tol' them I was asleep, didn't see nuthin'," she said.

"Why?" Waller asked.

She took a gulp of beer. "My phone got cut off 'cause I was in the county lock-up for shoplifting and writing bad checks," she said. "My little boy went to stay with my sister and she like to beat him to death for messin' in his pants. I'm done with the police, mister. You got that? They leave me alone and I'll leave them alone."

"Ms. Prather, the police will be coming back, asking you questions again," I said, standing up to go. "They won't lock you up because you witnessed a crime. It's important that you tell what you saw. Please?"

She scowled and took a drag from her cigarette. "Y'all got any money I could get for some groceries?" she said casually.

Waller looked at me and I shrugged. He reached in his pocket for his wallet and extracted a twenty, which he laid on the kitchen table.

"Is there anything else you remember?" I asked.

She put her head back and examined the ceiling. "Seem like I seen a truck like that before over there. That worth twenty bucks?"

"Yeah," Waller said. "I'd say that's worth twenty bucks, if it's true. Especially if you'll tell the cops the same thing when they come back."

"Ain't studyin' no cops," she said.

Back in the van, Waller looked excited. "She saw a truck at the murder scene. You said Maleek Tebbetts used a truck in that pawn shop break-in."

"That was a pickup truck," I pointed out. "This sounds more like a commercial truck of some kind, if there was really something painted on the side of it. She'd seen it at the restaurant before. Maybe it was a delivery truck."

The car phone buzzed. Waller picked it up and handed it to me.

It was Edna. "I had to go through Jean's purse while she was under the dryer at the beauty shop to get DeeDee's numbers," she said. "I don't like this, Jules, you know I'm not a sneaky person."

She is the single sneakiest person I have ever met in my life, but I thought it prudent not to mention that at this juncture.

"Take these numbers down," I told Waller as Edna dictated them.

"Did you talk to Michael?"

"I did," Edna said. "Bruce and DeeDee took the girls shopping at the mall and then they were going to a Tech basketball game, so Michael is baby-sitting Dylan. He said for you to come on over if you want to talk."

"I can't," I said. "Bruce got a damned temporary restraining order against me. I'm not supposed to go anywhere near that house or he could have me arrested."

"He did what?" Edna said, her voice rising. "You didn't tell me he got the law after you."

"Well he did," I said, enjoying the sensation of tattling. I thought for a minute. "Could you call Michael back and ask him if he'd come over to the house this afternoon?" I looked at my watch. I still had to go by Beverly Updegraff's house and look at her phone records, and there was one other stop I hadn't mentioned to Waller. "Ask Michael to come over around one. I should be home by then."

"I still don't like any of this," she grumbled. "All this sneaking around. Still, if Bruce got the law after you, he must be hiding something." She sighed. "I'll see you at home. I never thought I'd miss my own bed and my own thermostat this much."

After I hung up the phone I smiled. Maybe I'd have a shot at talking to Dylan after all.

"One more stop in Cobb County and we'll head for Beverly's house in Dunwoody," I told Waller.

"Are you going to see Fouts?" he asked.

"Not just yet," I said. "I want to go see Father Mart. He's going to announce tomorrow at mass that he's leaving and I'll bet he leaves town right afterwards. If I don't see him today, I won't see him at all."

"Aw, Garrity," Waller said. "This whole priest business is a load of shit. I thought we agreed that the husband hired the gunman. The priest has nothing to do with it."

"I want to talk to him," I said. It was one reason I had decided to take my car today, so that Waller wouldn't have veto power. "If you're not interested, stay in the van and work on your reports. It won't hurt my feelings."

"Fuckin' ridiculous," he groused.

"Look," I said. "I realize Southern Life has an interest in proving Bruce McNair had Patti killed. But my interest is in finding the truth. Mart Covington was close to Patti. Too close maybe. Maybe she wanted him to give up the priesthood for her, maybe she threatened to tell the archbishop about their affair. Maybe Father Mart got one of the gang members at that youth club to find somebody to kill Patti. It's farfetched, but it ain't impossible."

Father Mart was in his office in the rectory, packing books and papers into cardboard cartons.

"It's Saturday morning," I said, standing in the doorway. "Shouldn't you be hearing confessions?"

"I have two assistants doing just that," he said. "Was there something I could do for you today?"

The bookcases were half empty and other cartons had already been filled and taped.

"I talked to Estella Diaz," I said bluntly. "She tells me you and Patti were having an affair."

He laughed and sat down in the chair at his desk. "Mrs. Diaz told the archbishop I was sleeping with Sister Mary Gerald, who is seventy and incontinent, with Rosellen Finnegan, our two hundred and eighty-pound choir director, and with Amy Harris, our nineteen-year-old youth leader. I think she has me mixed up with one of those televangelists."

"But the part about Patti was true," I said. "You weren't just her confessor and marriage counselor, were you?"

He picked up a string of rosary beads on the desktop and fingered the rosewood beads. "No," he said quietly. "No, we were more than that. But less than lovers."

"I don't believe you."

"It doesn't concern me anymore about what you or others believe. Patti and I cared deeply for each other. If I had wanted a physical relationship, she would have readily agreed. Bruce had hurt her very deeply, you know."

"By sleeping with her younger sister," I suggested.

"I don't know who the woman was," he said. "Patti wouldn't tell me. But the marriage was broken, irretrievably I suspect. We had a lot in common. We enjoyed each other's company. She probably thought she was in love with me." He looked at me steadfastly. "We were never intimate."

"Then why are you leaving the church?" I asked. "Isn't the archbishop forcing you to take this sabbatical?"

He laughed. "You lapsed Catholics love to think all

priests are sex-crazed, power-hungry, money-grubbing deviates, don't you? If one pharmacist forges prescriptions, nobody assumes all pharmacists are drug addicts. But let one poor tortured devil look up the skirt of some parochial school kid and the whole world suddenly turns against everybody wearing a cassock and surplice. I asked to go on sabbatical. It was one of the things Patti and I had been discussing. I really feel a calling to do marriage and family counseling, to try to heal fractured families. But the demands of a huge parish like this one never stop. The fund-raising never stops. The sick and the dying and the spiritually bankrupt never stop."

"And the horny women, do they ever stop?"

He shook his head. "Patti told me you were outrageous. I might appreciate your candor more if it weren't directed at me. We were not having an affair. Okay? We did not sleep together."

He was charming, funny, what he said made sense. I still didn't want to believe him. "Patti lied to Bruce about where she was going and what she was doing when she was with you," I pointed out. "And you told me she was at the monastery, meditating, which I totally don't buy."

"You're pretty damn smart, Callahan Garrity," Covington said. "We went to movies. To plays. To the mall. To dinner. Once we went rafting down the Chattahoochee. Things Bruce didn't have the time or inclination to do. She needed someone to talk to her, to appreciate her for what she was. I needed—I guess I needed to relate to someone as a man instead of as a spiritual leader. It was wrong, but it seemed harmless."

Against my will, I was starting to believe him.

"I think Bruce McNair hired someone to kill Patti," I said. "You were his priest. Do you think that's possible?"

"I've been wondering that myself. There was something there that I missed. I thought it was guilt over his own infidelity, and anger at Patti for her unwillingness to forgive, but I see now there must have been more."

"I think Dylan may be in danger," I said. "Is there anything you know about this that you haven't told the police?"

The rosary was wound tightly around his fist, and he held the cross, rubbing his fingertips over the raised silver figure. "She was afraid of him lately. God help me, I told her to forgive and forget. And she went back to him, and now she's dead."

I got up to leave. Waller had been right. This priest hadn't killed anybody.

29

"YOU LIKE STRIP CLUBS?"

Waller blushed, then shrugged. "I've been to a few. Guy like me, travels all the time, sometimes you get bored. It's no big deal."

"Hey, I don't care if you work the door at a live sex show," I said. "Reason I ask is, we need to check out those clubs Xavier Draper owns. If I go in a place called Club Exotique, the United Nations of Nudity, people are gonna start to wonder, me being a woman and all. I thought you could check 'em out."

He thought about it. "Check 'em out for what exactly?"

"I don't know, just look around. Spend a little money and people answer your questions. If you go this afternoon, it should be sort of slow. See what you can find out about Draper, ask if they've seen Bruce McNair in there." I handed him the snapshot of Bruce and Patti.

"Okay, but home office is gonna have some questions about a fifty-dollar bottle of champagne."

"So drink beer," I said. "It's probably only ten dollars."

After I dropped Draper off at his motel I went over to Beverly Updegraff's place. She lived in one of those two-story town house deals that look like little Charleston row houses.

She led me into the dining room, where she'd stacked three shoe boxes. "These are the phone bills going back to nineteen ninety-one," she said. "What exactly are you looking for?"

I pulled the slip of paper with DeeDee's phone numbers out of my pocket, then opened one of the boxes and took out an envelope. "Phone calls to the three-oh-five area code. I think maybe Bruce was having an affair with Patti's sister DeeDee, who just moved up here from Miami about a month ago."

"Is that the sister who was in the bad car wreck?" she asked.

"If she was, it's news to me," I said.

"Bruce told me his sister-in-law was hit head-on by a Florida Power and Light truck and she had all kinds of injuries and was suing them. He said he was handling the case as a favor to Patti. There should be lots of phone calls to Miami. I think he made a couple of trips down there, too. And I know he did a continuing legal education course down at Boca Raton last spring."

"Some favor," I said dryly.

Beverly had sorted the bills in order, month by month, with each year in a separate box. Starting with the 1992 box, phone calls to DeeDee's office and home started showing up sporadically at first, then weekly, then daily. "What a family guy," I said to myself.

Beverly wandered in with coffee for both of us. "Find anything?"

"Looks like he was conducting an affair of the heart and charging the phone calls to the law firm," I said, showing her how frequently DeeDee's number came up on the bills.

"The son of a bitch," she said. "He had me completely snowed. Do I feel stupid."

"Don't," I said. "He had us all fooled. Hey, did you guys have a company credit card?"

She got up and headed back to the hallway. "American

Express. Those bills are in the closet, too. I can't wait to see what they show."

Bruce had gone down to Miami once in the winter of '92, once in the spring of '93, each time staying at a Marriott that charged $170 a night. There were plenty of bar charges, meals, and long-distance phone calls back to Atlanta.

Beverly had gotten out her calculator and was adding up the charges. "Do you believe this? Counting first-class plane tickets, which he also charged to the firm, Updegraff & McNair and Associates spent over thirty-eight hundred dollars so he could see his little girlfriend down there."

I'd separated out the phone bills with the Miami charges and the American Express receipts. "Can I take these and make copies?" I asked. "I'll see that you get them back."

"Help yourself," she said grimly.

Edna's land yacht was parked in the driveway at our house. And when I walked in the back door the kitchen smelled like home again. She was stirring a pot of chili on the stove at the same time she was opening the oven door a crack to look at a pan of corn muffins.

I wanted to tell her I was glad she was home. Instead I pointed out that the corn muffins were getting too brown.

"Smart ass," she said, but she took the pan out of the oven and set it down on the table.

"I been eating leftover funeral food all week," she said, apropos of nothing. "I don't ever want to see a platter of turkey or ham again."

We'd just ladled ourselves steaming bowls of chili when the phone rang.

It was Bucky Deavers. "Hey, babe," he said. "You done stirred something up. We got a call from Grady Stovall's girlfriend this morning; old Grady never came home last night. She thinks something bad happened."

"What? Run that by me again?" I walked over to the table, got a pen and paper, and started to take notes.

"Stovall went by The Texas Tearoom about one o'clock this morning, and he was last seen at the Laffactory at about three," Bucky said. "The bartender at the Laffactory said he came in, got the cash for the night's deposit, and left about three. But he never got home. The girlfriend called us when she woke up, at around nine o'clock. We just got a call from the cops in Chattanooga; they found Stovall's car, a nineteen-ninety black Cadillac Seville parked in a rest stop just off I-75. There's blood on the seat and no sign of Grady or the bank bag."

Edna was grating cheddar cheese into a bowl which she placed next to a bowl full of diced onions. She got two cold beers out of the refrigerator and poured them into frosted mugs. It was great to have a mom around the house.

"I appreciate your letting me know about Stovall," I said, "but I can't help but wonder why you're being so nice."

"The bartender at The Texas Tearoom saw Bruce McNair with Stovall when he was leaving there last night," Bucky said. "He wasn't seen at the Laffactory, but then Stovall just came in, got the money, and left. He didn't hang around and seemed in a hurry. We'd like to talk to Mr. McNair, but we can't seem to locate him."

"So you called me," I said. "He and his sister-in-law and the two girls, Dylan's sisters, were going shopping at some mall, and then to the Georgia Tech game." I looked at the clock. It was after one. "They're probably already at the game," I said. "Have you talked to Xavier Draper?"

"It's being taken care of," he said. "Talk to you later."

While we ate chili, I filled Edna in on what I'd discovered during the week. "Bruce was doing legal work for this Draper guy, who's a small-time crook and ex-con, and for Grady Stovall," I said. "The cops think Draper was the financial backer for Stovall's nightclubs and some strip clubs. They think he was using the clubs to launder drug money. If they're right, Bruce was probably involved. He was hurting for money not long ago, then suddenly he pays off all the credit card bills and buys Patti a fancy car. The money must not have been enough, though. I think he killed Patti for the insurance money. I don't know what Stovall's disappearance means. But the cops want to talk to Bruce about it."

Edna blew on her chili to cool it down. "Isn't this where you say 'I told you so'?"

I pushed a chili bean to the side of my bowl. "Not necessarily," I said. "We still don't know who Bruce got to do his dirty work. But is this where you tell me you're sorry for not having more faith in me?"

She sighed loudly. "You know how I am about family. If it was somebody deliberately hurting you or your brothers or sister, I'd have been the same way."

"But I wasn't deliberately trying to hurt them," I pointed out. "You think this has been fun for me? You think I like everybody hating me?"

"Seems to me you could have used a little more tact, that's all."

There was more that could be said, but neither of us was ready to say it yet. We ate our chili in silence for a while.

"You don't think DeeDee was involved, do you?" Edna asked. "Jean couldn't take that, Jules, it would just put her in the grave."

I'd been trying to figure that out. DeeDee was a selfish little brat, but I couldn't see her having anything to do with a plot to kill her own sister. "I really don't think she knows Bruce had anything to do with it," I said.

Edna put her head in her hands and massaged her temples wearily. "This family will never be the same again," she said. "You can't put the pieces back together after a thing like this."

When Michael came in with Dylan, we were just putting the chili dishes in the dishwasher.

Dylan's cheeks were red from the cold, and he was smiling and laughing and tugging on his uncle's hand. "Just came from the pizza parlor and the video arcade," Michael said. "This kid is about to break the bank."

"Come on, Dylan," Edna said, taking his hand, "let's see what's on television in the den. After a little bit, I'll see about fixing you a snack, all right?"

Dylan nodded yes. "Cookies?"

"We'll see," Edna promised.

Michael and I sat at the kitchen table and drank our coffee. "Michael," I said, "what do you think about DeeDee's relationship with Bruce?"

"You know," he said flatly. "When did you find out?"

"Something Dylan told the therapist," I said. He looked startled. "I talked to her. Dylan drew a picture of the family showing DeeDee next to Bruce. Then I did a little digging and found all these long-distance phone calls and trips he'd been making down to Miami."

Michael looked miserable. "I was right in the middle, Callahan," he said. "Patti called me before Christmas, sobbing. She said I was the only one she could trust. Bruce had gone on some business trip to Palm Beach and somehow Patti found out DeeDee went up and met him there. She was devastated, but she wouldn't confront Bruce, and she wouldn't say a word about it to DeeDee. I wanted to throttle Dee, but Patti made me swear to keep quiet about it. She said it was as much Bruce's fault as DeeDee's."

"You're sure Bruce didn't know Patti knew who the other woman was?"

"Positive," he said. "We were all together at Christmas at Mom's this year. One big happy family. Patti sat at the table across from DeeDee and acted like nothing had happened. I had to choke down every bite. It was awful. I couldn't believe Patti could pull it off."

Edna came back into the kitchen and refilled our coffee cups. I felt like I'd already drunk a gallon of it, but

I couldn't get enough caffeine. "Tell Michael what you told me," she said.

"It looks like Bruce paid somebody to kill Patti," I said. "He had a huge insurance policy on her, $1.2 million. And he's got all these criminal connections. One of the men he's been working for disappeared early this morning, and the police think he's been killed. They want to talk to Bruce about it."

"My God," Michael whispered. "Callahan, you don't think DeeDee knew about any of this? She wouldn't. She loved Patti. Looked up to her. Jesus, this is going to kill Mama."

We were all quiet for a moment or two. Then Edna spoke. "Jean's a stronger woman than we all realize," she said. "She lost your dad and survived that, and she's dealing surprisingly well with what happened to Patti. She's got a lot of faith, Michael. No matter what happens, the rest of us will be there for her, and we'll see her through this."

None of us wanted to bring up the subject we were all thinking about: what would happen to Dylan and the girls if their father was arrested, tried, and jailed for the murder of their mother?

"We're a family," Edna repeated. "We take care of each other."

When a car pulled into the driveway, Edna went to the front door to look out. "It's a good-looking black guy," she called out. "You expecting somebody?"

"Not that process server again," I said, coming to look. "He probably got a warrant out against me for assault with a deadly weapon."

"Doesn't look like a process server to me," Edna said. "Take a look yourself."

Tyler King was just getting out of a dark conservative-looking sedan. He wore corduroy slacks, a heavy knit sweater, and a suede jacket and looked like he had just walked off the cover of *GQ*.

"That's the FBI agent who's working with the Cobb police," I said. "He used to play football at Tech."

I opened the door before he could ring the bell. I introduced him to Edna, who stood waiting to see what he wanted.

"Could we go outside to talk?" he asked.

Edna was disappointed. We went out and got into King's car.

"Deavers called and told you about Stovall, right?"

I nodded yes.

"We had McNair paged at the Tech game. He was mad as hell, but he got real quiet when we told him Stovall had gone missing and was presumed murdered. I think he's pretty scared," King said. "We had a nice talk. He admitted he thinks Xavier Draper had his wife killed, and he said he's sure Draper is behind Stovall's disappearance."

"Wait a minute," I said. "Bruce said Draper had Patti killed? Why?"

"McNair was the one who brought Stovall and Draper together. Draper needed a front man to run the nightclubs; he couldn't get a liquor license because he's a convicted felon. Draper has what McNair calls 'business interests' in South Florida. He needed a place to launder money. Strip clubs, night clubs, comedy clubs, they all have a right nice cash flow. Then, according to McNair, Draper became convinced that Stovall was dipping into the till, and that McNair was helping him skim and cook the books."

"Were they?"

King laughed. "Well now, McNair says Stovall might have been, but his hands are clean. You ever know a lawyer who'd admit doing any wrong? When Draper discovered how much money was missing, and it was a lot, Stovall told Draper that it was McNair took the money. He pointed to McNair's fancy new car and fancy new law offices and fancy little girlfriend who was also driving a new car."

"Where does Bruce say the money came from?" I asked.

Tyler King smiled wide. "A loan from Stovall."

"You guys don't buy that bit about Draper having Patti killed, do you?"

King shrugged. "McNair says it was a warning from Draper. That's why he wouldn't let the kid talk to us; he's been terrified Draper would come after the kids."

"That's a crock," I said. "Did you arrest Bruce? Where are DeeDee and the girls?"

"Still at the game, probably," King said. "Tech's kicking the living shit out of Maryland. I would have stayed myself, but duty calls. No, we didn't arrest McNair. He's agreed to cooperate and help us nail Draper. We've been waiting a long time to get this guy, and now he's ours. We don't have any evidence to suggest McNair's involved in his wife's murder."

I was floored. "Bruce had Patti killed, I'm sure of it. Dylan just told us that Bruce called Patti on the car phone that day and asked her to drive out to Bankhead Highway to pick up some watch he was supposedly having repaired. He had the killer waiting there at that Popeye's. A guy in a truck. I found a witness at Garden Homes who said she saw the truck peel off right after she heard the shot."

King looked annoyed. "Still meddling in police business? Charlie Fouts is very unhappy with you, Garrity. How about calling him and giving him the name of this witness? And we know about the watch. McNair gave us the repairman's name and address. One of Charlie's guys went over there. The guy still had the watch. McNair tells us he's sure Draper had the killer trail Patti that day."

"You're wrong," I said. "Bruce did this. You make a deal with him, you're letting a murderer go free. I don't intend to let that happen."

Michael and Edna looked at me expectantly. "Well?" Edna said.

"Bruce has got the cops convinced Xavier Draper had Patti killed. He's working some kind of sweetheart deal to turn state's evidence against Draper, who the cops have been dying to nail. Unless we can prove otherwise, he'll get away with it."

"Shit," Michael said. Edna got up, went to the top shelf of the pantry, took down a flour canister and opened it, and took out a bag of Pepperidge Farm chocolate-chunk cookies.

"Hey," I said. "Why'd you hide the cookies? I was starving here while you were gone."

She took a handful of cookies out and put them on a plate, then poured a glass of milk. "You're supposed to be trying to diet," she said. "I knew you'd eat 'em if I left them where you could find them."

We followed her into the den where Dylan was sitting cross-legged on the floor, flipping channels. He flipped past an old episode of "Wild Kingdom" where Marlon Perkins was wrestling an anaconda, and paused. Past a John Wayne movie where Wayne was embracing Maureen O'Hara. "Ecch," he said, and flipped quickly past. He settled on the Comedy Channel, where a girl in a red dress was playing an accordion and making raunchy jokes.

"Here, Dylan," I said, "let me have the remote. Let's switch to another channel."

But the kid acted like he hadn't heard me. "This show is so gross," I told Michael and Edna. "I was watching this the other day somewhere and at the end of her act she moons the audience. Talk about a cheap laugh."

The girl ended her act, pulled her dress up again and showed her panties. "See," I said. She had just introduced the next act when the guy bounded on stage. He was wearing a brown leather tuxedo. At the sight of him Dylan seemed to visibly shrink, his face contorted with rage. "No, no, no. Don't hurt Mama, no." He was screaming and pounding the floor with his fists. "No. No."

Michael got on the floor and wrapped his arms around Dylan, who was now rolled up in a tight ball, rocking back and forth, screaming "NO, NO" over and over, in a chant.

"He did this the other day at home," I told Edna. "In fact, he was watching this same program. I guess they show stuff over and over again on cable. We thought he was having a fit because Caitlin took the Gameboy away from him."

I got down on the floor beside Michael and tried to talk to the distraught child.

"Dylan," I said, "that man on television who is upsetting you. Have you seen him before?"

He was crying now, limp in Michael's arms. He glanced at the television, where the comic was finishing his act. "He hurt my mama."

"Is that the man who shot your mama?" I asked.

He nodded. "He killed my mama."

30

"DID YOU CATCH the comic's name?" I asked Edna. Michael had taken Dylan into the kitchen for a cookie and milk refill.

"No, it happened so fast, and then he was screaming so loud I couldn't hear anything," she said. She picked up the *Constitution*'s television listing guide and paged through it for the Saturday listings.

"It just says 'Live at the Joker's Club,'" she said, throwing the guide to the rug. "This damn paper is worthless."

"I'll call the cable company; surely they have a detailed list of what they're showing on these different channels."

I went into my bedroom and called the cable company, keeping my fingers crossed. Instead of a human being I got a recording directing me to call another number if I wanted to schedule a hook-up or disconnection, and still another if I had a question about billing.

Dylan and Michael were sitting at the kitchen table dunking cookies into the same glass of milk. "I'm going to the cable company," I said. "I couldn't get an answer on the phone."

Michael walked out to the car with me. "It's close to four right now," I said. "You'd better get Dylan back home. And remind him in the car not to mention about going to

Aunt Edna's house or seeing me. Bribe him if you have to. I'll call you. Wait. No, I'll have Edna call you as soon as I find out anything. Keep an eye on him, Michael."

The cable company's offices were in a small one-story office building on Ponce de Leon, near the DeKalb Farmer's Market. The doors were locked, but there was a small white compact car parked in the lot, so I knew someone must be home. I pounded on the door and buzzed the buzzer until I heard someone unlatch the door.

"The business office is closed," said the woman who came to the door. She was dressed in jeans and a sweat-shirt, Saturday at the office garb. "You want a hook-up, you'll have to call Monday after eight A.M."

"I've got a hook-up," I said. "I need to find out some-thing about a program that appeared on the Comedy Channel this afternoon at three-thirty. The newspaper listings just give the name of the program; they don't tell the comedian's name. It's really important that I find out this guy's name."

She looked at me dubiously. "Come on in," she said reluctantly. "I'll see if we can find Comedy Channel's number in our program guide." While I stood in the tiny tile-floored reception area she leafed through a Rolodex on the receptionist's desk. "Here it is," she said. "It's long distance, though."

"I'll spring for a call," I said. She wrote the number on a slip of paper and handed it to me. "You must watch a lot of television for this to be so important," she said. "Usually we just get calls about recipes from that cooking channel. You wouldn't believe how many people—"

"Thanks," I said, cutting her off.

At home I dialed the number. Strike two. All I got was a recording telling me that the offices were closed on weekends but to leave a message which would be returned on Monday.

"Goddamn it." I slammed the phone down and paced

around the kitchen. "The program was called 'Live at the Joker's Club,' but where's the club? And who were the comics?"

Edna was working my crossword puzzle. "Maybe you could call one of the local comedy clubs and ask them if they've ever heard of this Joker's Club."

"Yeah, I could call the Laffactory, that's Grady Stovall's comedy club," I said sarcastically.

"No, what's the name of that one that runs all the radio commercials? The Punchline. Try calling them."

I leaned over and kissed her on the cheek and she pushed me away. "Gawdamighty, Julia. You got the worst chili breath I ever smelled."

The woman who answered the phone at the Punchline's box office did not want to let me talk to the manager.

"This is an emergency," I said hotly. "Now get the manager before I come down there and tear the place apart."

She must have sensed that she was dealing with a woman who had only a tenuous grip on her emotions. "Just a minute," she said.

While I waited I got out my Fantastick bottle and cleaned the last vestiges of chili grease off the stovetop. Nervous energy. I was about to scour the sink when the manager came on.

"Ronnie Carerra," he said.

"Hi," I said. "I'm trying to find out about a comedy club called The Joker's Club, I saw a special live from there on the Comedy Channel today and recognized a comedian I need to contact. Do you know where The Joker's Club is?"

"Sure. They're in Nashville," he said. "Is cable still showing that thing? It's about two years old if it's the one I'm thinking of. Who's the comic? Maybe I can help you find him."

Two years old. My heart sank. "I don't know his name,"

I said. "Skinny black guy wearing a brown leather tuxedo."

Carerra laughed. "Honey, all the comics at The Joker's are black, it's a black comedy club. Tell you what you do. Call Rich Reimer. He used to be the manager at The Joker's. He's managing a club in Oakland, California, now. A place called The Gas Station. Tell him I told you to call."

"Thanks a million," I said fervently.

"Come on out to the club sometime," he said. "Wednesday is ladies' night. I'll leave you a pass."

Edna looked up from the crossword she was working with an ink pen. "Well?"

"I think I'm getting warm," I told her.

And then I got cold again. The Gas Station had a recording too—saying that the club wouldn't open until five P.M., and to leave a message. I left a message and hung up.

"The club's in California and they don't open until five," I said despairingly. "That's another three hours out on the coast."

"Find something else to do," Edna said sharply. "You're about to drive me nuts pacing around here."

I got out the House Mouse appointment book and tried to concentrate on the week's bookings, but it was useless. I was too keyed up to concentrate. After fifteen minutes I slammed the book shut and picked up the phone again.

After six or seven rings Waller answered. He sounded groggy. "Yeah?"

"It's me, Callahan," I said, trying not to show my annoyance. "I thought you were going to call me as soon as you got back from the club."

Silence. "What time is it?"

"Almost five."

"Geez. I must have come in and fallen asleep. I've got a splitting headache from all that cheap champagne."

Now I was annoyed. "I thought you were going to stick to sipping a beer."

"I got in the club and a little Vietnamese dancer came over and sat down by me and started talking. She said she knew Xavier Draper but she wouldn't talk unless I bought her a bottle of champagne. Sixty bucks for a bottle of Cold Duck!"

"Was it worth it?"

"I don't know," he sighed. "Like we thought, Draper owns the club, but he only comes by every once in a while. Last night he came in before one and stayed until the last table dance at four. He sat at the bar and drank decaf—they keep a pot going just for him."

"Did Stovall come in?"

"No, and the girl said that was unusual. He usually stops by on Saturday night to make a cash pickup. Last night there was no sign of him."

"But Draper made sure everybody saw him. Probably establishing an alibi. Did the girl say she'd ever seen Bruce McNair in there?"

"Kim, the Vietnamese girl, she only started at Club Exotique a month ago," Waller said. "Another girl, big blonde who said she's from Norway, I showed her the picture, she said she thought she'd seen him a couple times with Draper or Stovall."

"Norway, my ass," I said. "Norcross is more like it. Anything else?"

"Oh yeah," he said, "do you know any sharp-dressing black cops working this case? Guy came in just as I was leaving, all the girls swore he was a cop."

"Sounds like the FBI to me."

"Call me later," Waller said suddenly. "I gotta go lie down again. Or maybe I better puke."

As it turned out, Rich Reimer got to The Gas Station early and called me at seven o'clock Eastern time. "Yeah, I remember the dude," he said after I'd described him. "I only know the stage name though. Rover Boy he called himself. Like a rap name, see?"

"You wouldn't have any records of his real name, or

a phone number or anything?" I think he sensed the despair in my voice.

"Lemme see," he said. His voice trailed off and I could hear a metallic sound like a file drawer opening. "I got an old photo here. Just says Rover Boy, managed by Kippy Washington Talent. Kippy's out of Atlanta, she manages a lot of talent around the Southeast. You know her?"

"No," I said. "How can I reach her?"

"Saturday night?" he asked. "Check any of the comedy clubs out there. She books acts into all of 'em, and she checks out the other talent, too."

"That photo you've got. Could you fax it to me?"

"Sure," Reimer said. "Like I said, though, it's two years old. I ain't used him out here. He ain't ready for the Coast yet. You mind if I ask what you want him for?"

What I wanted him for was homicide. What I said was, "I think somebody I know hired him for a job and I'd like to talk to him about it."

I picked up the fax at the corner drugstore. The paper was slick and the transmission wasn't too hot, but the photo showed the same guy we'd glimpsed on television today: a whippet-thin black man in his mid-twenties. His head looked oversized for his body and he had a long square jaw and slightly protuberant eyes. In the photo he wore his hair longish in one of those processed hairdos.

There was no way I dared take the photo over to show to Dylan. I called Waller from my car phone. This time he answered the phone a little faster, but he didn't sound much healthier. Before I could tell him what I'd accomplished, he was moaning again about his headache. "Don't even tell me what you want," he said. "I'm not going anywhere with this headache. Whatever it is you're into, let it wait until tomorrow. I'll talk to you then."

It was the first time I've ever had a man say "Not tonight dear, I have a headache." I called Edna and told her where I was heading.

Garden Homes was jumping tonight. It was still cold outside, but the wind had died down and there was no rain in the air. People had pulled chairs out onto their stoops and were listening to music, or were gathered in knots passing brown paper sack–covered bottles.

Adalene Prather had company. She shooed him into the bedroom when she opened the door and saw it was me. "Go on out of here," she hissed. "Peoples be thinking you the cops. I got to live out here you know."

I flashed the faxed photo. She held it up close. "Head shape is right, the boy had a big old head look like a loaf of bread, but it was too far away to be sure."

She thrust a hand out the door and waited. All I had was a five-dollar bill. She took it quickly and shut the door just as fast.

Margeneeda, the manager at Popeye's, was working a double shift. She looked at the photo, squinted, held it up to the light, shifted her chewing gum from one side of her mouth to the other. "He kinda looks like the dude drives one of the trucks come in here sometime," she finally said.

"Kwante," she called into the kitchen. He stuck his head through the window dividing the service area from the grill. "Don't you think this dude looks like Jerry?"

"Who?" Kwante asked.

"Jerry, the dude who drives the truck that brings the paper towels and napkins and stuff. Don't he look like Jerry?"

Kwante hooted. "Ain't never seen Jerry in no Jheri curl or no tuxedo."

"It's an old photograph," I explained. "Do you know Jerry's full name or the company he works for?"

"Naw," Margeneeda said. "He just comes sometimes, and I ain't seen him in a while. Maybe they changed his route."

"How about the day that woman was killed? Was he here that day?"

Margeneeda had lost interest. "I don' know," she said. "Told you we was busy."

The car phone was ringing when I got into the van. It was Edna.

"The shit hit the fan," she said. "Michael just called. As soon as he got Dylan home, and he saw Bruce, Dylan started crying uncontrollably. He told DeeDee he saw the man who killed his mama on television at Aunt Edna's house. He told her Callahan is gonna find the man who hurt his mama and put him in jail."

"And DeeDee told Bruce," I predicted.

"Who went into a rage at Michael for taking Dylan over to our house. Bruce got on the phone with his lawyer and told him what had happened and when he got off he told Michael they're going to get a judge to issue an arrest warrant for you for violating the TRO. Then he invited Michael to leave."

"Oh God. Where's Michael now?"

"On his way over here. He stopped at a gas station to call and warn me. He was apologizing all over the place. I told him he could stay with us tonight."

"Well, it's not all bad," I said. "The woman who called the police after she saw Patti's car made a semi-identification of old Rover Boy. And the manager at Popeye's said the picture looks like a truck driver named Jerry who sometimes makes deliveries there."

"That's the good news," Edna said. "Now here's some more bad. Linda Nickells called, too. She said you'd want to know Cedric Lattimore died this afternoon at Grady. She said he got some kind of staph infection and was too weak to fight it off. Who's Cedric Lattimore?"

I'd forgotten about Cedric. The excitement of the hunt. "He was a baby," I said. "An innocent bystander. A sweet little boy who never had a chance. Did Linda say anything about Maleek Tebbetts?"

"She didn't, but a guy from the Cobb County Police

called to tell you that Maleek is in custody, but he's not talking."

"He didn't kill Patti, but he did kill his son," I said bitterly. "I'll be home in a little bit."

"No," Edna said quickly. "If Bruce does get a judge to issue an arrest warrant they'll come right to the house to look for you. Go on over to Mac's and call me from there."

Mac hadn't called all day. I knew from his silence that he was still pissed at me. And he had a right to be.

"I've got to come home and get a bath and change my clothes," I said, looking down at my worn jeans and chili-spattered sweater. "I'm going out to some comedy clubs tonight, to see if I can track down this Rover Boy."

"Then park the van in Mr. Byerly's garage and cut through his backyard and come in the back door," Edna said. "I'll call him and tell him to leave the garage door open. And call me just before you get to Oakdale. If I see any strange cars around you can just go to the Yacht Club and call me. I'll bring your clothes over there."

31

YOU'RE NOT GOING OUT by yourself tonight." Edna said it as a statement, not a question. She stood in my bedroom door, watching me pull on my favorite black sweater, black stirrup pants, and black suede boots. I fluffed my hair and dabbed on some lipstick.

"I'm not going after this guy, Mom," I said. "I'm just going to track down his manager and see what I can find out about him, like his real name and where he lives. As soon as I find out, I'll call Charlie Fouts and Tyler King and they can be the heroes."

"You've been shot at already, working this case," Edna said. "They killed Patti, they'll kill you if they think you're getting close."

I turned to look at her. "How'd you know about what happened at Grady Homes?"

"Linda Nickells told me when she called. She told me I needed to sit you down and talk some sense into you."

"Ten years too late," I said airily. I got my pocketbook, reached inside and brought out my nine millimeter. "See, this is my gun. In my purse. That's what it's come to, living in Atlanta now. I'm carrying a gun and looking over my shoulder. Pretty soon I'll be like Patti, driving five miles out of my way to avoid making a left turn, afraid to go anywhere outside my own little frame of reference, afraid to leave a man who's cheating on me with my own sister." My eyes burned with unshed tears.

She went into her own bedroom and when she came back she handed me a small metal disc-looking thing. "Give me your key ring," she said.

She attached the thing to my key ring and handed it back. It looked like a tape measure.

"What's this for, in case I see a sofa I need to measure while I'm on a stakeout?"

"It's called Skreem-Away," she said. "After what happened to Patti, your cousin Jack went out and bought a half dozen of these things. He gave them to me, Jean, Peggy, DeeDee, and Maureen."

"I see he didn't bother to get one for nasty old Julia," I commented.

She had the grace to blush a little. "He knows you've got a gun."

I was intrigued with the thing, I'll admit. I turned it over in my palm. It was about a quarter inch thick, with an outer ring and an inner, slightly raised button.

"You press in that metal pad and hold it for about fifteen seconds," Edna said. "Jack says it lets out the gawdawfulest screeching sound you ever heard. He tested one at his office and it made such a racket somebody in the building next door called the police and told them somebody was being tortured over there."

I took my key ring back. "Listen. I'll be in the van on and off. If you're worried about me just buzz me, or I'll call you. I'm going to a couple of comedy clubs to look for this Kippy Washington woman. Giggles is out on Powers Ferry Landing near the river and Funny Bonz is on Roswell Road in Buckhead. See, that's my itinerary. Feel better?"

"Not much," she grumbled. "Don't forget to call."

"You and Michael have a good time tonight," I said.

"You reckon his mama knows he's gay?" she asked.

Talk about from out of left field. "I didn't know you knew it," I said.

"I'm old, Jules, not stupid. Now be careful."

The first show was about to start when I got to Giggles. I asked at the box office for Kippy Washington. "Haven't seen her tonight," the guy in the box office said.

Reluctantly, I handed over the seven-dollar cover and he handed me a token good for a drink.

I hurried in and glanced around the room. It was packed with Saturday night daters and what looked like a big bachelor's party crowd. Huge gold comedy masks were painted on the dark purple walls and the ceiling was covered with purple and gold balloons trailing long ribbon streamers. A big-screen TV was showing an old Abbott and Costello routine. I winced. I can't tell you how much I detest Abbott and Costello. The only thing unfunnier is the Three Stooges.

A waitress in tight purple satin shorts and a gold satin midriff top stopped at the tiny table I'd squeezed behind. "Get you anything?" she asked.

I told her I was looking for Kippy Washington. She stopped another waitress zooming by. "Susannah, have you seen Kippy tonight?"

"Not yet," Susannah said. "She likes to come after the opener, anyway."

I ordered a beer and gave the waitress my token. There was a bowl of popcorn on the table. Stale. But eating stale popcorn beat watching Abbott and Costello any day. A minute later, it seemed like, my waitress swooped down with my beer, set it on the table, and rushed off again. The lights dimmed and the emcee bounded onto the stage.

She was a tiny blonde ball of fluff, dressed in an oversized man's pinstripe suit and a black fedora. Her short routine seemed to consist mostly of riffs on her unhappy dating experience. "My sex life is so bad," she said, "I wouldn't have one at all if it weren't for my weekly visits to the gynecologist."

After that I didn't hear much of her act because I was busy watching the door for a black woman who looked like she might be named Kippy. I'd asked my waitress to let me know if she came in. I had to pay for another beer I didn't want, but that's show business.

The opening act was a ventriloquist whose dummy was Mexican and who did a third-rate José Jiminez routine. By the time he was done and they'd brought the headliner on, I was itchy to leave. The waitress came back to settle my tab. "No sign of Kippy tonight," she said sympathetically. "You might try Bonz or the Laffactory."

I left her a grateful tip and did a ducking run out the door. I was overly cautious going to the van. Edna had made me slightly paranoid with all her warnings and cautions.

I got back on Interstate 285 to follow its arc north to Sandy Springs and Roswell Road. Traffic was heavy; Saturday night in the biggest Saturday night town in the South. On the way I checked in with Edna.

"You find Rover Boy's manager?" she asked.

"Not yet."

"Well, Bruce must have gotten his warrant," she said. "I saw a beat-up yellow Chevy cruising real slow past the house just as soon as your car pulled out of Mr. Byerly's driveway."

"Did he see me leaving?" I asked.

"I can't be certain," she said, "but the car speeded up after it passed the house. Maybe he just didn't see the van in our driveway."

The parking lot at Funny Bonz was jammed. In the end I had to park in the lot of a dry cleaner's next door.

"Yeah, Kippy called and asked us to reserve her a table near the front," the girl at the box office said when I inquired. "She just came in a few minutes ago."

The headliner's act was already in progress. Now

that I was a comedy club regular I could tell she was the headliner because her jokes were funnier and people were actually laughing and clapping for her.

"She's up there," the door man said, pointing to a large black woman with a dramatic fall of beaded braids. Kippy Washington wore a gold lamé caftan and one of those Afrocentric pillbox-looking hats.

I slipped the guy five bucks and he helped me thread my way through the close-packed tables to where she sat engrossed in the show.

"Miss Washington," I started to whisper, but she turned to me with a stern face. "Hush up now and talk to me when this act is done."

Mollified, I sat down. Another waitress was at my side within seconds. This time I ordered a Diet Coke. I was working now.

With nothing else to do, I watched the headliner. The marquee outside said her name was Miranda Day. She was tall, mahogany skinned with a facial structure to die for. And she was pretty damned funny too. "Y'all white people," she said, "y'all are different from the brothers and sisters. That's all. Got those country singers with the big hair talkin' bout 'yore cheatin' heart.' Lemme tell you something. Ain't no sisters singin' about that mess. We catch our man steppin' out on us, we gonna get a knife and cut his cheatin' heart. That's all."

Kippy clapped her hands in delight, then surveyed the audience to see if their reaction was as strong as hers. "Child is smokin'," she crowed.

Miranda was indeed cooking. "My grandma got that old-timer's disease, we had to put her in a home," she continued. "Set her on the porch, rang the bell, and ran like a sumbitch. Didn't know whose home it was."

"Yes, yes," Kippy chortled.

When the act was over and Miranda Day left in a chorus of whistles and applause, Kippy beamed as if she'd just finished a huge, satisfying meal. "Tell the truth," she demanded of me. "Is she the next Whoopi Goldberg or what?"

"Very funny," I said, sipping my Coke. I introduced myself and told her I was a private detective looking for a comic she managed.

"Rover Boy, right?" She sighed deeply. "That boy and his ex-con mentality gonna screw up everything I ever did for him. I quit messin' with him after the last time. Told him to get hisself straight and then we'd talk. I can't book a boy puts stuff up his nose all night."

"What last thing?" I asked.

"Went in a seven-eleven all coked up and tried to put a six-pack of beer down his pants," she said with disgust. "Down his pants, now. Boy don't weigh a hundred and thirty pounds. Don't you think the clerk noticed a thing like that?"

"What's his real name?" I asked. "Can you tell me where I can find him?"

She looked at me closely. "Do I want to know how come you lookin' for him?"

Kippy Washington struck me as somebody I could be straight with. "My cousin was killed a week ago. Shot to death in her car while her nine-year-old son was in the backseat. The child saw an old comedy cable show today and as soon as he spotted Rover Boy he started screaming that he was the one who'd shot his mother."

Kippy shook her head, swinging her beads to and fro. "Mmm-mm-mm," she said. "I ain't sayin' he didn't do it, but why would he want to shoot some white lady he didn't even know?"

"For money," I said. "I think my cousin's husband might have hired him. Has Rover Boy ever worked at the Laffactory?"

She stared. "He's gone back to his real name now: Jerome Young. How'd you know about the Laffactory? Jerry did an emcee gig there about a couple months ago.

Mr. Stovall and Mr. Draper said they're gonna let him headline pretty soon."

It figured. "Does he have a day job driving a delivery truck of some kind?"

"Sweet Jesus," she said in a low voice. "You got the right boy. He been driving a truck delivering supplies for some company sells paper goods and cleaning supplies."

"Georgia Sanitary Supply?" I hadn't considered that there might be a double connection to Draper.

"Sounds like the name," she said uncertainly. "Jerry's in it bad, ain't that right?"

"Real bad," I said. "How can I find him?"

She reached down and picked up a suitcase-sized canvas pocketbook, rummaged around until she came up with a thick red address book. She got one of her business cards, looked up the address and wrote it down. "That there's his mama's address. Jerry don't stay there all the time, but when I got a gig for him, that's where I go looking."

I got up to leave. "You're right about Miranda Day," I said. "She's at least as funny as Whoopi."

32

I T WASN'T UNTIL I'D gotten in the van and was getting ready to pull out onto Roswell Road that I noticed the battered yellow Chevy parked directly across the street from the club. The car's windows were tinted, so I couldn't see the driver. I pounded the steering wheel in fury. God damn Bruce McNair. He was the one who had paid thirty pieces of silver for his wife's contract killing, but I was the one being tailed by the law.

The Chevy waited until I'd pulled into traffic and he let a couple of more cars get between us before he pulled out behind me. I wasn't really alarmed. My first instinct was to try to outrun him, but common sense told me it was useless. It was nearly midnight, but Roswell Road traffic was heavy, people coming and going from the bars, nightclubs and movie theaters that lined both sides of the street. My van was sluggish in cold weather, and besides, where would I go? I knew the inevitable. Sooner or later Bruce McNair and the process server would catch up with me.

I got back on Interstate 285 and glanced in the rearview mirror. The Chevy was still there. I guessed he planned to wait until I got home to arrest me.

At the I-75 interchange I turned south toward the city, the Chevy right on my tail. I took 75 into downtown

Atlanta and took the Boulevard-Jimmy Carter Library exit, then a right on Boulevard and left onto Austin Avenue. The roads are torn up there, with detour signs everywhere because they're building the much-hated Freedom Parkway there. The state has been trying for years to build a roadway through Inman Park over to the Jimmy Carter Presidential Library. The neighbors fought it and DeKalb County fought it, but in a road-building state like Georgia, the parkway was a foregone conclusion. Our school systems may rank third from the bottom in the nation, but we can build a damn road in Georgia.

The street was deserted. As I was passing a stretch of homesites that had been abandoned and cleared for the parkway, the Chevy rammed me from behind. My head jerked forward and bounced off the steering wheel. "What the hell?" If this guy was a process server he took his work mighty seriously. I thought about pulling over and showing him my Smith & Wesson the way I had the other guy, but then I decided that this stretch of kudzu and red clay was too isolated for that kind of confrontation.

I wasn't going to get a chance to pick my spot anyway. He sped up, pulled beside me, and rammed me from the side, forcing the van off the road and down into a shallow ditch. I cut off the ignition, crammed the keys in my pocket, and reached for my gun. But my pocketbook had been knocked off the seat beside me when he rammed the van. I was groping around on the floor desperately when the passenger side door was flung open. Rough hands grabbed me by the arm and jerked me upright.

"You playing with me, bitch?" My accoster had a strangely shaped head, protuberant eyes, and a nine-millimeter semiautomatic pistol. "A loaf of bread head" was how Adalena Prather had described him. Bruce hadn't bothered to send a process server after me once he knew Dylan could ID the gunman who'd killed his mother. Instead, he'd sent the gunman himself: Jerome Young.

I pulled away from him and dove again for my gun, but he jerked my arm again, so hard tears sprang to my eyes. He might have weighed only 130 pounds, but most of it was muscle.

"Get your ass out the car," he ordered. "You wanna ride? We gonna go for a ride." He had my arm twisted awkwardly behind my back and was pushing me toward the Chevy, which he'd left with the motor running.

He was opening the passenger side door with one hand when I made my move. I jerked away, turned and kneed him as hard as I could in the groin. He doubled over and screamed with pain and I lit off running. I could see the lights of houses on the other side of a kudzu-covered hill, so I headed that way. The ground was wet with dew and the kudzu vines tore at my ankles. Within seconds I could hear Young's breathing behind me. The field was open; they'd bulldozed all the trees, and there was no sanctuary except that hill and the houses beyond it. I took a deep breath and ran for my life. A kudzu-covered tree stump was my undoing. I hit it full-speed, ankle-high, and went down in a heap. Pain shot up my right leg.

"Got you, bitch," he said, yanking me to my feet. I nearly screamed from the pain. "I'm hurt," I cried. He put the gun under my chin, poking it into my skin until my bottom jaw ached. "You gonna be more than hurt in a little while. Now you wanna run some more and end it here?" I said nothing. He slapped me hard; my cheek stung and I felt my ears buzzing. "Huh?" he demanded.

Then he grabbed my hands and took a roll of tape out of his pocket, wrapping it around my wrists.

He poked me with the gun again, this time in the back of the neck. "Now move. We goin' for a ride."

Back at the roadside, he pushed me into the front seat of the car and locked the door. "Stay there or I'll shoot your white ass," he said. I could see him open the passenger side door of my van and bend over to retrieve something. My gun. My stomach lurched.

He got in the car again and I could see my Smith & Wesson tucked in the waistband of his pants. "Nice piece," he said. "Thanks."

He pulled away from the curb and sped back down Austin, back the way we'd come. "Where are you taking me?" I managed to say. My ankle throbbed something fierce. I was terrified.

He held up a credit card to show me. It said Julia C. Garrity. It was my bank card.

"We gon' do a little banking, Julia C. Then we gonna take a little Sunday drive. All right?"

"Do I have a choice?" I said bitterly.

"Sorry," he said, "you all outta choices. You had a chance to shut yo' bitch mouth and mind your own business, but you wouldn't do it. Kept on and kept on. Made a simple little job get all kinda complicated."

He drove up Austin to Boulevard, then took a right. He was doing the speed limit, thirty-five, and I considered trying to jump from the moving car. But with my hands tied behind me it was useless. Even if I made it out of the car without being shot, I'd surely be run over by one of the big tractor-trailer rigs that traveled that stretch of road going to the CSX Railroad piggyback freight yard.

At the corner of Boulevard and Marietta he turned right. It was a gritty urban neighborhood. Chinese take-out places with menus painted on the windows, self-serve car washes, liquor stores and storefront check-cashing operations. He pulled into a small strip shopping center with a run-down Kroger and a small bank with a drive-through window.

"Now look there," he said happily. "Ain't that nice we got equal opportunity banking in Atlanta? They even put instant teller machines on the Southside these days."

He pulled the car up to the curb in front of the machine and got out. Then he came around to my side and pulled me to my feet. "You try kneein' me in the balls again and they'll be picking up your brains with a broom and dustpan," he said. "We gonna walk over to that machine and you gonna stand in front of that camera looking just like you do: scared shitless."

He pushed me toward the machine. When I looked back he had pulled a navy blue ski mask over his head. He stood beside me, fed the card into the machine.

"What's the magic number?" he said.

My mind went blank. I couldn't remember my own name. He raked the gun barrel across my face. The pain was searing. Blood oozed down my cheek. "Seven-two-seven-five-seven," I said through clenched teeth. My birthday, my lucky day.

"Smile for the camera," he said.

He pushed the right buttons and the ATM gurgled and burped and spit out a wad of twenty-dollar bills. "Have a nice day" flashed on the monitor as it fed back my card.

Young stuffed the card and bills in his pocket. "Thanks. I will."

He shoved me in the car and then we were back on Memorial, headed toward the gold dome of the state capital.

"Is that what this is all about: armed robbery?" I said.

"Oh no, no, no," he chuckled. "You the victim of that bad Atlanta crime rate, Julia. Got bad dudes raping little schoolchildren and stealing cars and sellin' crack and shootin' up housing projects. And kidnapping smart-ass white whores who don't have the sense to stay home after midnight. Making 'em empty out their bank accounts and then shootin' 'em in the head."

"I thought you were supposed to be a comedian," I said. "Do you just do contract killings in between gigs?"

"Whatever pays the bills," he said.

"What did Bruce McNair pay you for popping his wife?" I asked.

He glanced over at me. "Now that was a two-part deal. He's gonna give me ten thousand dollars, and later on, I'll be booked as a headliner at the Laffactory he's starting up in Houston."

"But you don't get the money until McNair gets his wife's insurance money," I guessed. "And the insurance company ain't gonna pay. Not anytime soon."

"No, Bruce has the money already," Young said. "Kind of borrowed it from the bossman, you might say."

"Xavier Draper," I said. "What makes you think Draper will let either one of you get away with this shit? He'll kill both of you. He already killed his old partner and now Grady Stovall is missing, too."

Young laughed. "Mister Grady ain't missing at all. He's right where I put him last night: in an old well on the bossman's farm up near Ringgold. Got a thirty-eight bullet in his head from the gun I got out the bossman's safe at Georgia Sanitary Supply."

I felt a chill that had nothing to do with the temperature. "The same thirty-eight you used to kill Patti?"

"That's the one," he said. He slowed the car down as we neared the low brick and granite wall of Oakland Cemetery. At the corner of Memorial and Oakland he waited until a car passed, then turned right and stopped in front of the elaborate wrought-iron gates in the entryway.

"Stay right here," he said, locking the doors again. He stepped out of the car, looked around, then put a bullet through the big old iron lock. The gates creaked apart and he opened them wide enough to let the car through. He got in the car, pulled through, then got out again to shut the gates.

"So you and Bruce think you're smart enough to frame Xavier Draper for Patti's and Grady Stovall's murders," I said when he was back in the car. I didn't want to dwell on what he planned to do in the cemetery.

"Sure do," Young said. "You don't see Bruce in jail. He's at home huggin' on that sweet little thing he's shacked up with. After what he told the cops, I bet they're opening up that safe at Draper's place right this minute."

"You've forgotten about Dylan," I said. "He saw you on that cable special today. He had a fit as soon as he saw you. My mother and his uncle were there. He told them, too."

"Kid was hysterical," Young said. "Besides, he ain't tellin' the cops nuthin'. His old man's his legal guardian and he ain't lettin' the kid near no cops or lawyers. Kid can't talk or hear right anyway. Who's gonna believe a kid like that?"

He laughed again. I looked out the car window. The moon was nearly full, but the huge old oaks, pecans, and magnolias seemed to lean over the narrow asphalt road and shut out most of the light. Young came to a fork in the road. A sign pointed to the left to the visitor's center, but he was looking off to the right. I didn't think he saw the dim light in the visitors' building or the pickup truck parked at the roadside.

"I talked to Kippy Washington tonight," I said, trying to distract him. "I told her I was looking for you. When I turn up missing, she'll tell the cops who to look for."

He slowed the car to a crawl and hung his head out the open window, looking from side to side.

"Kippy don't know shit," he said. "When she managed me, I was Rover Boy, then Jerome Young. After tonight, baby, ain't no more Jerry. I cut my hair real close and color it red, get me some thick eyeglasses and grow a goatee. I got a new stage name too: Bones Malone. How you like that, baby? I got the idea right out here in good old Oakland Cemetery."

"So you're a history buff," I said dryly. Oakland was Atlanta's first graveyard. It's where Margaret Mitchell and Bobby Jones and all the finest Atlanta families and about 2,500 Civil War casualties are buried. I knew all this from field trips they used to take us on in elementary school.

"Yeah, I love old Oakland," Young drawled. "Used

to come out here with the Boy Scouts and clean graves to get project points. Can you imagine that—bunch of nappy-headed little colored boys cleaning the graves of Confederate generals? We used to take a leak on 'em when the Scout leader wasn't lookin'."

He'd apparently found the spot he was looking for. He stopped in the middle of the road and cut the motor. "There it is," he said, pointing to a marble structure two hundred yards away. "Malone family got the biggest—what you call those house-looking things?—out here."

"Mausoleums," I said, amazed I could conjure up any word at all, even as my teeth chattered and my knees quivered. It was a crossword puzzle word.

"Yeah, mausoleum. That's where you going to die," he said.

As he got out of the car I craned my neck to see if I could see the light of the visitor's center. My only hope was that the pickup truck belonged to a security guard and not the eighty-year-old caretaker who'd always been around on those school field trips.

Jerome opened the door and jerked me out. "Here you go, baby," he said. "Leavin' on that midnight train to Georgia." He put the gun in my back and shoved me forward. "Let's go."

I limped along the broken brick walkway, trying to keep the weight off my bad ankle. The moonlight shone dully on the waxy leaves of a giant magnolia and overhead I could hear the soft coos of doves nesting high in its branches. An owl hooted off in the distance. I tripped over the exposed magnolia roots that had pushed up through the cracked brick walkway, and cried out from the pain. Young bent over and pulled me to my feet. "Don't hurt yourself," he said, pushing me forward again.

We stepped up a foot or so off the walkway onto the Malone family plot. The Malones had had some money. Theirs was an elaborate raised affair, with the mausoleum looming in the background and two large Victorian angels flanking the central walkway. There were a half-dozen other smaller, raised rectangular headstones set in the grass.

I tripped again, but this time I rolled to the side and pressed with my elbows on the doodad I'd stuck in my hip pocket. Nothing happened. "Get up, bitch," Young said, leaning down to grab me. I rolled forward a little, and pressed again. Ten, fifteen, twenty, twenty-five seconds. Young's hands gripped my shoulder, his fingers tearing into my flesh.

Then the Skreem-Alert went off. EE-ee-EE-ee. A high, piercing scream shattered the graveyard quiet. The doves in the treetops took wing, their shadows dark against the moon.

"Shut it off," Young screamed. "I'll kill you." He aimed his gun and stepped forward. But I rolled to the right and as I did he tripped over another of the raised headstones.

In a flash I'd struggled to my feet and was off running, terror making me forget my injured ankle. I dashed behind the mausoleum, wormed my hands painfully to the left side until I could extract the key ring from my pocket. I dropped the Skreem-Alert to the ground, kicking it under some leaves.

Then I took off running like I never had before. I zigzagged across the plots to a huge magnolia, then ran a couple of hundred yards and ducked behind a huge marble-carved recumbent lion monument. The Lion of Atlanta. I waited. I could hear Young's shoes crunching on the pecan shells that littered the walkway.

The Skreem-Alert kept wailing away. I longed to step out from behind the lion and make a run for it. But where to go? The roads wound in and around the cemetery, and in the dark I knew I'd never find my way out. Besides, if I came out of hiding, Young could take a shot at me.

I searched the ground around the lion for a weapon,

a tree limb, anything I could use to defend myself. All I came up with was a handful of wet acorns. Kneeling, I peered into the dark at the area around me. Directly off to one side was an open field. Two-foot-high marble slabs stretched out in long curving rows. Confederate grave markers. There were holes in the rows where some of the markers had toppled over, leaving the row gap-toothed.

"Come on out, Julia," Young called softly. "You can run, but you can't hide." He stepped off the roadway and onto a large family plot. While he tried the door of a mausoleum I took the opportunity to dart over to the Confederate section. I crawled over to a toppled marker in the shade of a sprawling magnolia tree. My fingers gripped the cold wet marble. I pulled mightily. I could move it, even lift it, but it was too heavy to be of any use.

In desperation, I crawled toward the edge of the row where another large marble angel stood watch over the South's brave dead soldiers.

The white of the angel's wings gleamed in the moonlight, and I could see where she'd held something in her hands, something that had been rudely lopped off, probably by vandals.

"Let it be there," I prayed as I crawled. "Let it be there."

I groped in the dark at the base of the statue, repeating my prayer. Finally I found something smooth and cool. With effort, I picked it up. It was an open marble Bible. The good book. And it must have weighed twenty pounds.

I heard the crunching of pecan shells again, and Young's voice calling softly. I got to my feet and peeked from behind the base of the angel. He was maybe ten yards away, walking slowly toward me, gun drawn.

I shrank behind the base, hoping he hadn't seen me. It seemed like hours. He walked slowly, deliberately scuffling his feet. From the sound of it, he was closer, maybe only a few feet away.

I bit my lip and forced myself to stay still, hoisting

the stone Bible to shoulder level. My arms ached from the weight.

The shuffling came closer, and closer still. I could smell his aftershave. I wondered if he could smell the perspiration pouring down my back. When he came even with the angel, I darted out, the Bible raised high above my head.

"What the . . . " he started. I heard him cock the trigger, and then I brought the Bible down as hard as I could. It glanced off the side of his head, striking his right shoulder and arm.

"Mother fuck," he howled, dropping the pistol and falling to his knees, cradling his wounded arm with his left hand.

I dropped the Bible to the brick walkway, and the sound of shattering marble seemed to echo in the darkness. It was dark and it took forever to find Young's gun, but I finally found it five feet from where he writhed on the ground, crying and cursing.

Despite all the noise we'd made, the watchman I'd seen near the visitors' center was nowhere in sight. I pointed the pistol in the air and fired twice. Aiming directly at Young's crotch, I bent down and pulled my own gun out of his waistband.

"Bitch," he spat. Blood ran down the side of his face from where I'd scraped it with the broken hunk of marble. "You broke my arm, bitch."

"Not me," I said grimly. "It was the Bible did you in. Yes, Jesus. Gimme that old time religion."

EPILOGUE

I PULLED THE PILLOW over my head, but it didn't drown the ringing of the phone. "Get that, will you?" Mac said groggily. I kicked him with my good foot. "Edna can get it," I said, turning over.

"She went to stay with your aunt Jean last night," he reminded me.

"Damn. That's right." I reached blindly for the phone, dropped it off the nightstand, leaned over and nearly fell out of bed trying to retrieve it.

Mac leaned over, grabbed my arm and hauled me back onto the mattress.

"Collect call from Neva Jean McComb for Callahan Garrity," a muffled voice said. "Will you accept charges?"

"No," I said emphatically.

"Callahan, cut it out," a familiar voice cried.

"Okay, put it through," I said.

"Callahan?"

"This is coming out of your paycheck, Neva Jean," I said. I propped myself up on one elbow and looked at the clock on the bedside table. It was eleven A.M.

"Where are you?" I asked.

"Where are we again, hon?" I heard her ask.

"Swannelle says we're between Bogalusa and

Waxahatchie," she said, then, playfully, "Quit that, you scamp. I'm talkin' long distance."

"Isn't Bogalusa in Alabama?" I asked.

"Alabama or Mississippi," she said airily. "I lost track after we passed Villa Rica. Hey, Callahan, Swannelle's doctor said he's good as new, so we're going on a kinda honeymoon. Swannelle's gonna teach me to pitch crickets and deep-dive crankbaits. Rooney Deebs, remember, he's Swannelle's cousin? He bought the bass boat off Swannelle, then turned around and loaned it to us for the trip."

"That's nice," I said sleepily. Then I was jarred back awake. "Wait a minute, Neva Jean," I said. "Today's Sunday. How are you planning to be back here by tomorrow?"

"That's why I'm callin', Callahan honey. Don't I have some vacation coming?"

"You took a week when you and Swannelle went to that Bass-O-Rama show back in October," I said. "You're not due vacation 'til July."

"Okay, well, I'll owe you," she said cheerily. "See you next week."

I dropped the receiver back onto the floor and tried to ignore the persistent beeping noise. Mac yawned loudly, got out of bed, walked around and hung it up. He leaned down and kissed me, then touched my bruised cheek lightly. "This is looking real nice. Sort of a sick asparagus color."

"It's only been a week," I said. I lifted my sore ankle a couple of inches off the bed, then dropped it again. "Now if this thing would just start healing. Neva Jean's not coming to work this week. Looks like I'm back in the saddle again whether I'm ready or not."

"Can't Edna help out?" He sat on the edge of the bed and began pulling on the jeans he'd dropped on the floor the night before.

"Not really," I said. "Aunt Jean's been staying over at the McNairs' a lot lately. With Bruce locked up at the federal pen and DeeDee skipping town in disgrace, somebody's got to look after those kids."

It was the first time in a week that we'd had time to discuss what had happened. I'd fractured my left ankle when I'd tripped over the stump in the kudzu field, and then torn the ligaments when I was running away from Young at the cemetery. That meant surgery and painkillers and a lumpy looking walking cast that left my toes sticking out in the cold.

"Do you really believe your cousin didn't know Bruce was behind Patti's murder?" he asked.

"Yeah, I'm afraid I do," I said. "DeeDee was never terribly perceptive. One french fry short of a Happy Meal is how Caitlin described her to me. And I think she was so involved in this little clandestine love affair of hers that it never occurred to her that Bruce was capable of something like that."

"Well, your aunt's in her seventies," he pointed out. "She can't handle those kids with her heart condition, can she?"

"No," I said. "I don't know what's going to happen. Beverly Updegraff called yesterday after I got home from the hospital and said she heard the scuttlebutt around town is that the Cobb district attorney has Jerome Young agreeing to change his plea to guilty. He'll roll over on Bruce and Xavier Draper and they'll agree not to ask for the death penalty."

"Draper?" Mac said. "What can they charge him with? I thought Bruce and Young were the ones trying to frame him."

"For starters, the feds are taking a long, hard look at racketeering charges for those nightclubs and the money laundering that was going on there. Plus, when Young led the cops to that abandoned well on Draper's property up near the Tennessee state line, they found a surprise: the remains of Draper's first business partner, with a nice, neat thirty-eight-caliber bullethole in the skull."

"Not the same gun," Mac said incredulously.

"Yep," I said. "Apparently Draper kept the gun out of sentiment. He'd bragged to Bruce about dumping the body there when he was threatening to do the same thing to him if he didn't hand over the money he'd skimmed. That's apparently when Bruce got the bright idea to set up Draper for Patti's murder and later, Stovall's."

"Bruce still hasn't confessed?"

"He says he's innocent," I said. "But the feds are going to charge him with kidnapping, murder for hire, and racketeering and drug laundering. Cobb County will charge him with murder. Beverly said his lawyer had a press conference yesterday charging the feds and the state with giving Young a sweetheart deal in exhange for Young's lies."

Mac pulled his shirt on and started buttoning it. "What do you think really went down when Patti was killed?"

"With a pair of lying scumbags like Jerome Young and Bruce McNair, I doubt we'll ever know the truth," I said. "But Charlie Fouts called yesterday, too, to fill me in on some of the gaps. He says Young told the cops he met Bruce through Stovall while he was trying to convince him to let him perform at Laffactory. Young told Fouts he and Bruce got high together a couple of times, and after one of those times Bruce asked him if he'd like to make some real money. Young says it was Bruce's idea to send Patti out to Bankhead Highway, with Young trailing behind in his truck. Bruce gave Young a beeper, and after he'd talked to Patti on the car phone, he beeped Young to tell him to take her out. When she realized how lost she was, she pulled into that Popeye's to ask for directions and when she pulled out on the other side onto that side street, he was parked at the stop sign with his hood popped to make it look like he had engine trouble. When Patti pulled up behind him, he walked back, shot her, and grabbed her purse."

"And that's when Dylan woke up," Mac said. "Poor kid. How's he doing?"

"Not so bad," I said. "He's still in therapy. And you know, Michael took a leave of absence from his job in Charlotte and he's been staying at Aunt Jean's and spending a lot of time with Dylan and the girls. Edna says he's amazingly good with them."

"Any chance he could take over the kids?"

"I think the kids would like it and he would too," I said. "But his lover is back in North Carolina and I'm sure they want to be together. The problem is, Michael still hasn't told his mother that he's gay. And Bruce's father and sister are making noises about fighting for custody of the kids. Aunt Jean says they're just interested in getting their mitts on Patti's insurance money, which will probably go in a trust for the kids now."

Mac bent over to tie his shoes, then stood up to help me out of bed. I eased myself up slowly, stood up unsteadily, stretched and yawned. Mac wrapped his arms around me and held me tight, then whispered tenderly in my ear: "Were you still awake when they called the final score on that UNC-Duke game?" I pushed him backwards onto the bed and stumped awkwardly to the kitchen to beat him to the newspaper and the crossword.

CALLAHAN GARRITY RETURNS!

The VelveTeens, Callahan Garrity's absolutely favorite girl group from the sixties, are all set to join a reunion tour when their one-time producer Stuart Hightower orders them to stop using the VelveTeen name and to stop singing the songs he claims he owns. When Stuart is discovered shot dead in his swimming pool and VelveTeen Rita Fontaine is found unconscious holding a pistol, Callahan swings into action to prove her innocence. But can she solve the case before the real murderer comes after her?

The sixties and the nineties collide in this fourth installment of Kathy Hogan Trocheck's acclaimed series about Atlanta's most inquisitive cleaning lady.

Coming in May 1995 in hardcover from

▲ HarperCollins*Publishers*

0-06-017637-7 • $20.00